THE STEPFATHER

THEO BAXTER

INKUBATOR
BOOKS

Published by Inkubator Books
www.inkubatorbooks.com

ISBN (eBook): 978-1-83756-140-7
ISBN (Paperback): 978-1-83756-141-4
ISBN (Hardback): 978-1-83756-142-1

1

DAMON

The sun was shining too brightly, entering the car through the windshield at an almost blinding angle. Damon tried to reach for his glove compartment with his right hand while maintaining the course with his left. As he turned onto Oak Street, he managed to fish out his sunglasses. He felt much better with his shades on.

It was a bit strange, but he hated the sun. The brightness, the heat, it was all too overwhelming for him, especially after his last tour in Afghanistan. It didn't matter that Chicago looked nothing like the places he had been stationed while overseas. The scorching gold ball of gas was the same, taking him back to that hell in an instant. Every time he felt it on his skin, Damon started to feel odd.

You got out; you're not a soldier anymore, he tried to reason with himself while sweating and squeezing the wheel as though his life depended on it. The pep talks sometimes helped, sometimes not. It was a constant gamble.

As his heart raced as though he were in the middle of a fight, pumping his system with adrenaline, he glanced toward the dashboard where he'd taped a photo of his daughter,

Connie. She was the sole reason for his existence. *You came back for her.* That did the trick, and he managed to reach his destination without completely freaking out. He hated this shit. Although he wasn't the first or the last soldier to have to deal with this, it still didn't make him feel any better.

Parking in front of his doctor's office, he tried to banish all thoughts of war from his head. He knew Dr. Weldon would find some other painful, traumatic event from his life to talk about. Therapy was fun in that way.

Dr. Nathaniel Weldon, a brilliant man in his sixties, was the therapist Damon had started seeing in secret after the divorce from his wife, Madelyne. The divorce wasn't his idea, and it deeply affected him. While being overseas, fighting and surviving for a living, the only thing that had kept him going was the thought of home and his family. Once he lost that, Damon completely fell apart.

A part of him couldn't fully believe that he'd actually done something like this—sought help. It was so not him. He was the one who helped, not the other way around. At the same time, he was more than aware of what the alternative would look like. He'd lost a lot of friends, good people, to this disease. A bullet through his head wasn't an option. He needed to stay alive. *For Connie.*

Reluctantly, he left the comfort of his car and crossed a small street to reach the residential building where his thera-pist had his private practice. Thankfully, he was all alone in the waiting room. There was nothing worse than meeting someone at your therapist's office and wondering what his brand of madness was, as he did the same to you.

The waiting room, much like his office, was decorated in neutral colors. Damon was certain that was done on purpose, to project calm emotions and tranquility to its visitors. It didn't help. He was anything but calm. On top of that, Damon felt slightly nauseous. That happened every time. He would much rather be on some sandy road, trying to defuse a mine, than be here.

That was a lie, of course.

Since he was the first patient of the day, Damon walked right in and greeted the doctor.

Dr. Weldon looked pristine, like always, clean-shaven, with perfectly trimmed, cottony hair. He was small and chubby with age. He was always dressed in pressed pants with matching shirts that were topped with vests. That always made Damon feel slightly underdressed, coming in his faded jeans and black T-shirts. At the same time, it wasn't like he owned anything else. He had one suit that he'd worn on the day of his wedding, and that was all.

"Have you spoken with Madelyne recently?" the therapist asked almost right away, as though sensing that was something he struggled with the most. Dr. Weldon was good like that. Also, he didn't believe in small talk, so they always dove right in as soon as Damon settled on the couch.

Damon shook his head. "No. I saw her last weekend when I went to pick Connie up. I waved, but she returned to the house without acknowledging my presence in any way."

Being no idiot, Damon knew it was due to the fact that they'd had a loud screaming match over the phone the day before. It still felt wrong, hard, to see her act in such a way. Shouldn't they at least try to be civil, for Connie?

"How did that make you feel?"

Like shit. "I don't know. Angry. We've been married for twenty years, and now she doesn't even want to say hello to me."

And it wasn't like he'd cheated on her, although there were times he'd thought about it. He'd never mistreated her in any way. She basically gave up on him, on them, filed for divorce, and walked away like he meant nothing to her, like he was nothing.

Sure, they'd had problems like any other married couple had, especially once he returned from his last tour. Damon struggled with a lot, and instead of showing an ounce of understanding, Madelyne just packed up and left, taking Connie with her.

"Do you continue to feel betrayed by what she did?" Dr. Weldon asked, as though reading his mind.

It was hard not to feel like that after so many years together, after sharing everything and forming a family. "I guess," he admitted reluctantly.

What made matters even worse was the fact that she'd immediately married someone else. A wealthier-than-him restaurateur who probably didn't have a care in the world. Damon really hated that guy.

"It's hard not to feel resentment, but I'm trying to push that behind me." Damon shook his head. This sharing crap was the most challenging thing he'd had to do in his entire life.

"Go on," his therapist encouraged.

"I'm just afraid that all this"—he gestured toward his head—"is going to ruin my relationship with Connie." That was what he feared the most. He'd already lost the love of his life. It would be the death of him if he lost his daughter as well.

"How so?"

"Well, I'm so angry at Madelyne, and I'm sure Connie sees that. I don't want her to feel like she has to choose between us." Despite everything, Madelyne was a good mother.

Dr. Weldon readjusted his glasses before replying, "From what you've told me about Connie, it can be deduced that she is a bright young girl, and I'm sure she knows how much you love her. I'm confident that she knows that your relationship with her has nothing to do with your relationship with her mother."

Damon really hoped so. At the same time, there was one more factor to take into consideration. "I'm sure George talks shit about me."

George Elway was Madelyne's new husband. He was a bear of a man who looked more like a criminal than a business owner. Understandably, the two men rarely spoke, but Damon detested him on an almost cellular level. It didn't help that George always had this self-satisfied smirk on his face. As though not so subtly telling him how he had everything that was once his and he enjoyed it immensely. It went without saying that Damon would like nothing more than to wipe that look off his face with a fist.

"Has she mentioned something like that to you?"

"No, but she's a good kid. I'm sure she doesn't want to hurt my feelings."

"Try not to read too much into things," his therapist advised. "You should be focused on your daughter, your relationship with her, and nothing else."

"I know. I just want her to be happy." Even if he wasn't.

"And I'm sure she is. As long as you focus on her and not on George, you'll be fine," he encouraged.

Easier said than done. There was something about that guy that rubbed him the wrong way. *Something?* The guy was with the woman Damon had loved his entire adult life. Of course they wouldn't be best friends. George was the man who took his place, and Damon didn't trust him one bit. And it went well past simple hate for the new man in his ex's life. Or so he believed. Damon had a gut feeling that something was off with that man, although George never did anything to confirm his suspicions. He appeared completely normal.

And that irked him further. Here Damon was, in therapy, while that other man appeared to be put together and perfect in every way. Madelyne really knew how to hurt him.

"I don't know how to shut everything off and simply be with my daughter."

"You don't need to shut anything off. Acknowledge that there were circumstances you can't change, and focus on what you can, like strengthening your relationship with your daughter."

"Thanks, Doc." That was actually helpful, but would he be able to let go of the past and find peace in the present? *I guess I have no choice*. If he wanted to get better, this was what he had to do. He was no quitter.

Each time, Dr. Weldon gave him homework to complete until their next appointment. It was ridiculous that Dr. Weldon assigned him homework like he was a little kid. Today, he was supposed to write about his feelings, do breathing exercises, and whatnot, which made him feel like he was back in school. He was a forty-three-year-old war veteran, for crying out loud. He didn't do homework.

Exiting, he knew he would do everything that needed to be done though, because there was nothing he wouldn't do to fix his screwed-up head. Damon desperately needed to be a good father to his daughter, since he'd already failed as a husband. He banished that last thought. Dr. Weldon said there was no point dwelling in the past, and that he should focus on the future instead.

Then what's with all the speaking of the past? That was a mystery yet to be solved.

After such a productive morning at therapy, sharing his feelings, crying—okay, he didn't cry—there was only one place he wanted to go. Checking the time, he was disappointed with how early it was. However, he shot a text to his best friend anyway, then went to work. He desperately needed a drink.

They met in their favorite bar for lunch. Damon could use a beer... or ten. Something Dr. Weldon had said to him kind of stuck. Was his obsession with George merely a product of jealousy?

You think?

Since Madelyne and her new husband had been the focus of today's therapy, Damon couldn't stop thinking of them long after he had his first, second, and third beer.

"That bastard stole her away from me," he admitted to Jason while ordering another round.

Jason Leonov was his best friend from high school. They'd even served together. Like him, Jason had left the Army and was now working for the fire department. He'd traded one inferno for another. Sadly, they both had issues, but dealt with them the best way they could.

Jason looked at him, quite unimpressed. "That is a load of shit, D. You can't blame that guy for your failed marriage," he told him.

Damon loved Jason like a brother. The other guy had only one flaw. He was always brutally honest, and at times, it could seriously hurt.

"She changed once she met him," Damon insisted, holding his ground.

"That's probably true. And you have to accept the fact that she is even happier now."

Happier than with you was implied.

"But that's no reason for you to get all obsessed with her new man."

Dr. Weldon said the same thing, Damon realized glumly.

"Remember Carlos, Nick, Patrick?" Jason started citing men they knew, and Damon could assume where this was going. "They all went ballistic, pathologically jealous of their exes' new men, and what good did that bring them? Nothing. They all ruined their relationships with their kids."

Damon's heart squeezed a little bit harder inside his rib cage. That was his biggest fear, that he would lose Connie too.

He would be a good father to his daughter, no matter what. She was the only good thing he had left in this world.

"You're right," Damon replied eventually.

Jason took a sip of his new beer. "Of course I'm right."

"Don't be an ass."

"Can't do. That is a gift, like my Dr. Phil skills," he deadpanned.

Damon laughed.

Despite his friend's words, Damon couldn't completely shake the feeling that there was something strange with Madelyne's new man, and that wasn't so easily ignored, since his gut feeling had saved his ass many times in the past. Quite literally. Damon had to be one hundred percent sure George was decent, because he had custody of his daughter five days a week. And he couldn't let anything, or anyone, hurt his daughter.

"I'm starving; let's order something," Damon said, still brooding about everything.

Jason went with it. Without any kind of embarrassment, as they waited for the burgers to arrive, his friend took his shirt off in the middle of the bar. "Check out my new tat," he said, proudly showing his back.

The black ink on dark skin looked incredible. Having a few tattoos of his own, Damon appreciated nice artwork. "Where did you get it?"

"Pete did it."

"Really?"

Devoting his attention to something else for a change, other than his screwed-up life, Damon relaxed, if only for a little bit.

2

MADELYNE

Madelyne was sitting at her vanity table, preparing for her day. Although she worked from home, she liked to make herself presentable before going to the drawing board. She never understood people walking about in their PJs. She could never do something like that.

George loomed over her, buttoning up his shirt. She could see his expression in the mirror. Something was bothering him. And she had an inkling of what. Connie. Her daughter was a constant topic as of late.

She was right. George shared his concerns about her daughter. She tried her best to placate her husband, but it wasn't working.

"I'm telling you, she doesn't like me."

"She's a teenager, George. She doesn't like anyone," she defended her daughter, keeping her voice down. The last thing she needed was for Connie to hear their conversation. Her room was right next door.

"Can't you see how she treats me? I always feel like a guest, and in my own home," he pointed out.

"Give it time," she advised. "She needs an opportunity to get to know you."

He smiled humorlessly. "Connie doesn't want to spend any time with me." He sounded genuinely hurt.

Madelyne sympathized. She wished for her husband and daughter to get along, but that proved easier said than done. Connie was never openly rude to him, but she was detached. And it was true that she didn't want to spend any time with George. Yet that wasn't exclusive to him. Connie avoided all family outings and dinners, preferring to spend time with friends or her father. Madelyne tried not to take that to heart, understanding that this was a phase, but it was difficult, not to mention tiring.

"She's that way with me, as well." And that was God's honest truth. A part of Madelyne believed her daughter resented her for leaving her father, and she hoped that would change with time. Her daughter had many ways to show how disappointed she was with her mother. Madelyne chose to ignore that.

Connie had to see how good George was to her, to them, and would come around. Sadly, George was frustrated and losing patience. That was why Madelyne had already tried to speak with her daughter about her relationship with her stepfather. Unfortunately, she'd encountered a wall of resistance.

"George would like to spend some time with you," Madelyne offered while making breakfast. "How about you go to his restaurant after school?" When she was younger, Connie liked to help out in the kitchen, so Madelyne hoped meeting a real chef would be interesting to her.

Connie looked at her like she'd just offered for her to go dumpster diving. Her next words confirmed as much. "To spend time with that creep? No thanks." And before Madelyne could object, she added, "Besides, I already have plans with some friends."

After that delightful exchange, Madelyne didn't insist or restart the conversation. She didn't want to push too hard. Connie was already angry at her for leaving Damon. She didn't want to completely alienate her daughter and make her hate Madelyne further.

For George's sake, she would now have to have another talk with her. She couldn't understand why her daughter was acting so stubbornly about this. George was a part of the family now. It would be natural for them to become closer.

In a perfect world, maybe.

"I don't know what I did wrong," George said in exasperation.

"You're taking this too personally. She's a teenage girl who is exploring the limits of her independence, rebelling against authority."

"She doesn't have issues spending time with Damon."

That was sadly true.

"Connie feels sorry for him," Madelyne said before she could stop herself. That was what she believed, but it was still too harsh to say out loud.

George shook his head even before she stopped speaking. "I'm convinced that Damon coaches her to hate me. He blames me for the divorce, after all," he said, deeply troubled.

Madelyne felt bad for causing him such discomfort when he had been nothing but good and kind toward her right from the moment they met. That didn't mean his assumption was false.

Damon and Madelyne had had a rather contentious divorce, and Damon truly seemed like he hated George at times. All the same, she was sure it was a wave of passing anger and hurt. Despite everything, she wished him all the best in life and was saddened for her part in his pain.

Damon had changed a great deal throughout their marriage. That wasn't so strange considering his previous work in the military. But Madelyne knew there were some lines he would never cross, and intentionally poisoning his daughter against George was exactly such a line.

"He would never do that. No matter what he thinks of you, or me, for that matter. He loves Connie with all his heart."

Damon was angry at the moment, but he was a decent human being. *More to the point, he has every right to feel like that,* she reminded herself. Madelyne had gotten engaged to George only three months after the finalization of their divorce and had been dating him the whole time. She'd never cheated on Damon with George. She'd met him after they separated.

Having all this in mind, Madelyne knew Damon had nothing to do with Connie's behavior toward George. It wasn't in him to do such a thing, which was troubling on a whole different level. The question remained, why did Connie behave the way she did? Was it from a misguided loyalty toward her father?

Madelyne continued to hold some residual guilt for hurting Damon, leaving him the way she did. She hated the idea of hurting him. He was her first love, after all, the father of her only child. That was something that would always bind them together. At the same time, she'd sacrificed a great deal for him, and he hadn't been there for her, wasn't her partner, and she needed him to be. So she had to leave him, for her sake, for the sake of her happiness.

"I'm sure he does love her," George snapped her from her reverie. "That doesn't mean he's not manipulating her," he insisted.

It was funny, but not in a classical sense, how Connie had said the very same thing, only about George. Right before

Madelyne married him, Connie had had a fit, and they'd had a pretty heated argument.

"Mom, can't you see he's manipulating you?" she'd pleaded then. "He's not a good guy."

"Oh, stop exaggerating." Madelyne had dismissed her words, fed up with all the drama. "I understand you don't like him, feeling loyal to your dad, but don't ruin this for me. I deserve to be happy."

Connie had stormed out and spent the night at her father's house. She was always a daddy's girl. Damon could do no wrong in her eyes. Which made Madelyne the bad guy, always.

Although Connie's words had hurt at the time, she was convinced her daughter would come around if given the chance. That was why it was imperative for her to spend some quality time with George and get to know him. Madelyne deserved a happy, loving family after everything Damon had put her through.

Snapping back to the here and now, Madelyne turned to look at her husband, and standing up, she reached for his hands. "I know this affects you, because you're a good man. I'm asking you to just be a little more patient with Connie. She'll come around and see what I see." She delivered the words with an encouraging smile.

"And if she doesn't?" George asked, still doubtful. "I don't want to live like this. I can't."

Madelyne felt conflicted. On one side, she needed her daughter to be happy, but on the other, the same could be said for her husband. *Being in the middle sucks.*

"Connie will change her mind, you'll see," she said, trying to reason with him. At times, it felt like she was living with two teenagers.

"Your daughter doesn't respect me, and I'm the head of the family now."

Madelyne sighed. "So what do you suggest?" Honestly, she was running out of ideas, and if he had something to share, she was prepared to listen.

He hesitated before replying, "I think boarding school would do her some good."

"What?" Madelyne exclaimed. She didn't see that coming. A camping trip, a family vacation to some nice all-inclusive resort, maybe, but not a boarding school. "I don't want to ship my daughter away." She was aghast that he would even suggest something like that.

"And I don't want us to send her either. I just believe that is the best option for her," George defended.

"How so?"

"It appears to me that no matter what we do, no matter what we say, she is under a bad influence, and spending some time apart could bring her clarity."

Well, when he said it like that, it did make sense. Nevertheless, she didn't want to part from her baby girl.

"I'll think about it," she hedged. "And in the meantime, I'll speak with her," Madelyne promised, hoping like hell that her daughter would have a change of heart. Because George was right. None of them could continue living like this.

"Thank you. I'll send you the email about the best places in the area." George kissed her before leaving for work.

Once left alone, Madelyne returned to her previous spot and absentmindedly started to braid her hair. George's words shook her to the core. It hurt that he believed the best option for all of them was to send Connie away.

What if she really is under Damon's influence? she questioned. *Impossible.* Although she started to doubt.

Madelyne needed Connie home. She was already sixteen, which meant she would leave for good in a few years. Madelyne didn't want to lose that precious time with her daughter before she left for college.

What if boarding school was the only way for George to be happy? She had to consider his feelings as well, since he was a part of the family now.

There was no way she could send Connie to boarding school. She would make her see reason some other way that didn't involve her living someplace else.

Then it hit her. If she was so adamant about this subject, then why did she lie to George, telling him she would think about it? Why did she remain silent? Why didn't she argue with George, stop him from such an insane idea in the first place? By his words, she could only assume that he believed that sending Connie away was a done deal. She couldn't allow that. Yet she didn't move from her place.

Madelyne realized she was doing this, avoiding arguments with George at any cost all the time. She let him have his way. Usually, she didn't mind, merely brushed it off, attributed it to marital compromises. Those discussions were of no real importance, like where they would get married, go on their honeymoon, or live after the wedding. The question that arose was simple. Why did she censor herself around her husband if their relationship was so perfect? She didn't dare answer that. Besides, she had more pressing issues at the moment.

This time around, the argument was different. This time, the topic was her daughter. She understood that George struggled with the responsibilities of raising a teenage daughter. The answer to that wasn't boarding school, but rather only understanding and patience. On the other hand, Connie had to stop with all the attitude and give poor George a chance.

Finally leaving her room, she discovered she was all alone. Her daughter had gone to school and her husband to work, so Madelyne had to postpone the talk for later. She headed to her office to try to do some work, although she didn't feel like it.

The day's responsibilities and tasks managed to take her mind elsewhere, and the day passed in haste, like always. Illustrating a children's book helped a great deal in calming her.

Going to the kitchen hours later to have some water, she found Connie eating cereal. Madelyne made a face. "There's dinner in the oven."

"I know."

Arguing about her eating cereal over roasted chicken with vegetables felt like a lost cause. "At least put some milk on it."

"It tastes better like this."

Damon used to say the same thing to her.

"I want to speak with you about something," Madelyne started carefully.

Connie groaned, putting the half-eaten bowl of cereal on the counter. "Let me guess, it's about George."

"Yes, and before you attack me or say anything, please listen to me."

"Why don't you listen to me? I respected your wish to marry that guy. Why can't you respect mine that I don't want to have anything to do with him?"

"Because that's not fair toward George or me."

Connie shook her head. "Typical, you only think of yourself and no one else."

That hurt. "That's not true, and you know it. I think about you all the time."

"If that were true, then you wouldn't be doing this at the moment." She started to leave the kitchen.

"Where do you think you're going?" Madelyne snapped. "We will have this conversation whether you like it or not." She was sick and tired of her daughter's attitude.

"Well, I don't want to talk with you about your stupid

husband. I hate him," she replied in the same manner before running out of the kitchen and out through the front door.

"Connie!" Madelyne ran after her, but she was already gone.

Damn it.

3

DAMON

"You have to move faster if you don't want to end up knocked down by your opponent," Damon advised Tommy.

"I'm not worried, Coach," the boy said after taking out his mouthpiece. "Mike hits like my grandmother."

The other boy pounded his gloved hands. "Grandmother? I'll show you the stars for that," he replied as the rest of the boys cheered. That started an avalanche of teasing.

Damon smiled at their good-natured teasing. He liked having the boys around. For him, there was nothing more rewarding than seeing younger generations taking an interest in boxing and wanting to come train in a real gym.

At one moment, they did get a bit loud, disrupting the rest of the people in the gym working out, so Damon had to call it quits.

"Okay, okay, knock it off. The class is over; go, get out of here," he said to them, still wearing a big smile on his face.

"Thanks, Coach."

"Bye, Coach."

In high spirits, laughing, the kids complied as they

continued to jibe one another on their way to the locker room. Damon could only look after them. He loved that rowdy bunch. They were all mouthy, and each of them had enormous potential.

Still smiling, Damon prepared for his next class. From the moment he'd decided to open a boxing gym instead of becoming a firefighter like Jason, he knew he wanted to teach, not just wrestling or boxing, but also self-defense classes to women. He thought it was important and something every woman should know, how to defend against any danger. This was not just because he was the father of a teenage girl.

While a soldier, he had witnessed a lot of injustices toward women. It pained him that he'd had to turn a blind eye to some of it because it was required of him to respect other cultures. Damon personally believed wrong was wrong no matter how you looked at it or what language you spoke.

When his fellow soldier Nancy Burrows had had some issues with a commanding officer, Damon couldn't look away anymore. There were no words to describe the rage he was capable of upon learning someone was trying to use his position to force women into compliance. He broke the guy's hand back then and had been sure he would be discharged for it. That didn't happen. His whole squad had testified that the commanding officer merely tripped and fell, and the matter had been closed. Sadly, that wasn't an isolated case.

So now, Alisa Cantwell, a friend from his Army days, came three times a week to teach a class with him here at his gym. Unfortunately, tonight, he was flying solo, since Alisa had gone out of town for a few days to her sister's wedding.

She'd asked him to come with her, as a friend, of course, and he would have, but he didn't have anyone to leave in charge of the gym. The place couldn't operate without him, which reminded him that he needed help. So far, he'd had no luck finding the right person for the job. Damon needed someone who would care about the work and the people coming into the gym.

About a dozen women of all ages came to these classes. Damon couldn't decide if he was happy about that or not. On one hand, having that many women come each week to learn how to protect themselves was amazing. It was admirable that they all wanted to take charge of their lives.

On the other hand, listening to their stories, it also showed him an ugly truth. There were a lot of bastards out there who thought they could do whatever they pleased just because they'd been born male. To Damon, they weren't real men but weak cowards, and it was his job to even the field. And he was good at it. It wasn't his plan to teach these women to be killing machines, only to teach them how they had the power as well.

Before each class, Damon gave a little introduction of what they were going to be doing. Learning the *why* behind something was equally as important as knowing *how*.

"I want you to be aware of one thing," he started explaining, standing in front of a semicircle of his students. "There is a natural tendency to freeze or hesitate when faced with violence. And that's not gender exclusive. We all act that way."

Damon could see on their faces how some were surprised to hear that, but that reaction didn't surprise him. It was a devastating fact that this was something rarely spoken about. He continued. "When I was in the Army, that was the first thing they taught us, how to push past that moment and act quickly despite the predicament or our feelings. It's natural to be afraid. That is what has kept us alive through centuries, but you shouldn't allow it to paralyze you. This is the most important thing and something you need to work on," he stressed, knowing how this first step was probably the hardest.

Nobody liked to get hit. Nobody liked to experience pain. The point was to move past it, to be able to hit back.

"So that is precisely what we will be focusing on, for the time being, to get you out of that mindset," he concluded.

He looked about the class. "Okay. Pair up," he commanded.

He started showing them some basic exercises, moves that were designed to help them break out of that vicious cycle of doing nothing.

Damon really enjoyed teaching this class. Not because he had such a high opinion of himself as tough, or that he was doing an amazing altruistic thing by teaching this class, but because he was fortunate enough to meet all these remarkable people who proved to be excellent students.

Having been an instructor for a while now, Damon discovered that women possessed an additional drive, which was a useful tool for him to use while trying to teach them self-defense. He could relate to that, since he too felt deeply passionate about doing this, not just teaching this class, but owning a boxing gym in general. There were a lot of people who would feel completely lost, himself included, if there weren't this safe haven for them.

It was a bonus that he had a lot of punching bags hanging around when he needed to blow off some steam. He was full of anger, especially once Madelyne had married that jackass. The bags helped relieve some of that anger.

Banishing that, he refocused on what was going on around him.

"No, Mary, your right hand should move like this." He showed her the correct way, and she mimicked it. "Good. It's Karen's turn to try it, then."

Damon continued to walk through them, offering small corrections, pieces of advice as they did their routines. "Great job, Dawn."

An hour and a half passed in a flash. At times like this, he felt like he was making a difference, and it felt good.

"See you the same time next week." Damon dismissed the class.

Like always, he remained behind to clean up. This was the last class of the day, and it was time to go home and crash. He felt spent, but in a good way. That was the benefit of doing something he loved.

He could hear the front door opening and was about to yell that he was closing up, when he saw his daughter approaching. He could see on her face that something was wrong, but he was still very happy to see her. Weekends weren't enough, as far as he was concerned.

"Connie, what a pleasant surprise," he greeted, opening his arms to receive his hug.

It was getting late, and he wondered what she was doing here in the first place, not that he minded.

"Hi, Dad," she replied, squeezing him tightly.

"You missed the class," he said.

Connie attended his classes whenever she could, and he was grateful for that. It provided him with peace of mind, as did the pepper spray he made her carry around all the time.

"That's not why I came," she replied, and once again, he could sense that something was off with her. There was something in the sound of her voice he didn't particularly like. His protective instincts sparked to life, but he reined them in. He knew better than to start interrogating his teenage daughter on the spot.

"Were you in the area with friends?"

Her best friend, Tamara, had gotten her driver's license recently, which was a big deal. To be honest, Damon dreaded teaching his daughter how to drive. Emotions tended to run hot in her these days. Being hormonal meant she frequently fought with her peers, and Damon hoped that was the case this time around as well. It wouldn't be the first time she'd argued with Tamara, then came to hang out with him instead of going home.

Connie shook her head. "I fought with Mom." She made a face. "I just had to get out of there."

That would have been his next guess. Madelyne and Connie, unfortunately, couldn't see eye to eye as of late. He knew Connie was angry at her mother for remarrying, and he didn't know how to fix that. Although he felt the same way, he wanted his daughter to have a good relationship with her mother and not take off every time they argued.

Damon realized she'd had to change quite a few buses to reach him. *Maybe teaching her how to drive and getting her a car isn't such a bad idea,* he realized.

"What happened?" he asked softly.

She sighed before replying. "The usual. She is so blinded that she can't see what's in front of her," she said, with the utmost frustration, the kind that only those at the age of sixteen could master. "Can I stay with you?" she pleaded.

Damon sat down on the mat and patted a space next to him. "How about you calm down and tell me what happened first?"

She complied, plopping down beside him. "Dad, she won't stop pestering me about George," she complained.

"How so?" he asked, working hard to stay calm and expressionless. This kind of thing affected him greatly, but he couldn't show it, not to his daughter, knowing how something like that would only make matters worse.

"She doesn't like how I behave around him, how I speak with him, or don't, how I *breathe* around him," she ranted.

From what Damon gathered, Connie treated George like he was a stranger. Damon was glad that she liked him better than that other man, but he knew that had to be frustrating to Madelyne and George.

Damon was about to reply, to try to calm his daughter in some way or offer a compromise, although it pained him to facilitate creating a relationship between his daughter and that man, when his phone started ringing.

Taking the thing out of his pocket, he was mildly surprised to see Madelyne's name on the screen. Madelyne hated calling him. She must be feeling desperate if she'd decided to reach out to him. Since they argued every time they spoke, she'd stopped calling him altogether. If she had a message for him, she would send it by Connie.

Damon showed the screen to his daughter, and in return, she rolled her eyes.

"I turned my phone off," she admitted, looking anything but remorseful.

So Madelyne's freak-out was well founded. He groaned inwardly before answering. Damon was sure his ex would find some way to blame him for what was happening.

This is going to be fun, he thought sarcastically.

4

MADELYNE

Madelyne was beyond upset, nearing outright anger. She'd tried to talk with her stubborn daughter, but Connie refused to even listen to her, storming out and leaving her to stew. At first, Madelyne believed she would return immediately after calming, but when Connie failed to do so, she started to worry. Naturally, Madelyne did the most logical thing, tried to reach her on her cell, but Connie didn't answer. *Where is that girl?*

It was getting late, and she couldn't be sure if her daughter was intentionally ghosting her or if her battery had died. That infuriated her further. *That girl will be the death of me.*

Trying to avoid creating all kinds of scenarios in her head about Connie being hurt, lost, or kidnapped, she poured herself a glass of wine and continued to wait. Connie was doing this on purpose. She was punishing her mother for remarrying, plain and simple. Finishing her drink, she felt even worse. Since that didn't help her calm, she changed tactics.

Madelyne tried to calm herself while pacing around the

house with thoughts about how Connie wasn't usually an unreasonable kid. She knew how to take care of herself. She was smart. The only problem was that she was known to act out when things didn't go her way. Like today. She'd taken off even before Madelyne had managed to say anything to her regarding George. That was something she'd recently started doing.

Seeing no other way, she called Tamara and some of Connie's other friends to find out if anyone had seen her or was with her. They all replied in the same way, that they hadn't heard from her. Which could only mean one thing.

I should have known, she thought with additional annoyance. Gritting her teeth, she called her ex. Sometimes, she thought Connie did this only to spite her, hurt her, and nothing else.

"Hello, Madelyne," he answered instantly.

"Is she with you?" Madelyne countered, not feeling like indulging in any kind of small talk. She was worried about her daughter, among other things. She needed to make sure she was safe before grounding her.

"Yes, she just got here," Damon reassured her.

Madelyne felt instant relief. It was good that she was safe, because that meant Madelyne could solely focus on being upset all over again. Her daughter displayed an immense lack of respect, as George had observed, and that was something she couldn't let slide.

"Great," she said, through gritted teeth. "Please inform her that she's grounded."

Considering Madelyne's state of mind, it would last a long time, maybe even until she became legal.

"For what?" Damon asked.

Madelyne made a face. She was certain Connie had already told him everything, painting a picture that completely villainized her. Although he spoke very calmly with her, it irked her to no end.

"She knows why," she answered vaguely, not wanting to get into it with Damon, since this was between her and her daughter.

Madelyne could hear Connie saying something, probably complaining.

"The longer she keeps this charade up, the longer she will be grounded," Madelyne added. *She can forget about that concert she talked about.* She started making a list of restrictions. *She will go to school and immediately return home until she learns to behave.*

Damon sighed. "I think both of you need to calm down and start listening to one another."

Look who decided to act like a parent, she thought snidely. For years, it was only Madelyne and Connie, alone, functioning without him. It was true that he was absent a lot, and sadly, even when he was at home, he chose to stay away, always leaning on her to do all the hard stuff. She resented Damon for pushing her into such a role.

"Madelyne, you can't force a relationship with George onto her," he added with utmost conviction.

That snapped her from her thoughts. "Excuse me?" she demanded.

"Connie told me what happened."

Madelyne could only imagine what *that* had entailed.

"And you need to back off. You're making things worse," Damon concluded.

Madelyne saw red. How dare he tell her what she could or couldn't do regarding her daughter! This was her family and her matter. He was the one who needed to back off.

Madelyne scoffed in return. "Of course you would say that. You don't want Connie to have any kind of relationship with George because it makes you feel threatened."

"Why would you say that?" he challenged.

Because it's true. "Because it's obvious. You're jealous," she added simply, shrugging although he couldn't see her.

"You're wrong. This is about Connie."

By the sound of his voice, Madelyne knew she was dead right.

"And I understand that, I truly do," she continued, as though he hadn't said a thing. "However, that isn't fair to George."

"What's not fair is you trying to force our daughter to do something she clearly doesn't want to do," he replied, raising his voice ever so slightly.

"Sorry to inform you, but being a parent sometimes means pushing children into doing something they don't want to. It's called being a good, responsible parent," she threw at him.

"Oh, come on, Madelyne. This isn't potty training we're talking about. Connie is sixteen. She needs to start making her own decisions regarding her opinions."

Unfortunately, Madelyne had a sinking feeling that Connie was not acting out of her own persuasions, but Damon's. She was doing this for him while punishing her, and she just couldn't understand how Damon failed to see something like that. *He doesn't want to see.*

"I would very much appreciate it if you would keep your opinions to yourself," she snapped.

"This is my daughter we're talking about."

It was funny how he chose to remember that only when it was convenient for him.

"True, but at the same time, this has nothing to do with you, so stop undermining my authority." It was getting harder by the minute to remain calm.

"You're exaggerating, Madelyne, and you have no right to

tell me not to get involved when my daughter's happiness is in question."

She couldn't believe him. And she absolutely hated when he spoke like that to her, like she was the unreasonable one, when in reality, he loved nothing more than to make a bad guy out of her. Because that would mean Connie could always run to him and seek his protection. She was always the bad guy considering their daughter, she was the bad guy in their marriage, and honestly, she was sick and tired of it. It was time for him to share some, if not all, of the blame. However, that was an issue for some other time. She needed to stay on topic.

"Fine, Damon, whatever, just please stop trying to ruin Connie's relationship with George." Madelyne needed her husband and daughter to get along. Was that so much to ask?

"That home-wrecker does an excellent job on his own without my help," Damon replied instantly, sounding annoyed.

Madelyne jerked, startled. She couldn't believe he'd said something like that to her and, clearly, in front of their daughter. It was no wonder Connie thought she could behave how she pleased, with that kind of attitude as a role model.

"Oh, I don't know, I would say he had plenty of help from you," she replied, in the same manner. "If memory serves, you stopped being a part of our family, our marriage, long before I met George. Or did you forget about all the drinking, your angry outbursts, vanishing without a word?" Sometimes, he would be gone for days, leaving her wondering if he was alive or dead.

Madelyne wasn't trying to be unnecessarily cruel. It was just that he needed to be reminded of the facts. George had had nothing to do with the ruination of their marriage. Damon had done that long before George came along.

At one point, it had gotten so stressful, difficult, that

Madelyne was constantly scared, not of him but for him. Damon was never violent toward her or Connie. He would snap and be in a bad mood, but the depression was the worst. It was obvious that he was on the path of complete self-destruction, while refusing any kind of help from her, from anybody.

Maybe it had appeared selfish and cruel of her, but she'd had to leave him. She'd hoped that would snap him from that state. And besides, she didn't want Connie to be constantly surrounded by that. It wasn't healthy for her to live and grow up in that kind of environment.

"I didn't forget," Damon replied grudgingly.

"And don't get me started on your behavior at my wedding with George."

He'd made quite a scene while drunk, of course.

It was quite a shock to all the guests to see him there in the first place. Madelyne included. George was the one who'd invited him, but he'd done that out of the kindness of his heart. He'd hoped that would symbolize how they could all co-exist together. Damon would always be a part of their lives as Connie's father. Unfortunately, Damon took advantage of that to try to ruin her big day.

"Well, maybe you should have considered how sadistic that invitation was for me, forcing me to watch you marry another man," he suggested.

Made him? What was wrong with that man? Madelyne hadn't made him do anything. She had been surprised he was there. At first, she'd hoped that meant he was coming to terms with the fact that she was moving on. Boy, was she wrong. George's friend had had to escort him out.

Long after the wedding, Madelyne continued to wonder why he'd gone in the first place. If not to accept them, then why? What did he hope to accomplish, apart from the obvious? Did he really hate her that much? She dismissed that thought immediately, dreading the answer.

At the same time, there was no dismissing what he'd said to her now. *Made him. How dare he,* she fumed.

"Then why did you come? Nobody really wanted you there. It was a courtesy invitation."

Madelyne regretted saying that last part. It was obvious the argument became pretty heated up to that point, and emotions were running wild. Sadly, this was nothing new. Nothing they hadn't done before. All their talks ended up pretty much in the same way, with them blaming each other for all the past mistakes. And this specific topic was nothing new either, nothing she hadn't heard before.

That was one of the reasons she didn't like speaking with him anymore in the first place. It brought her too much anguish. No matter what, they always ended up at this precise place, and that was counterproductive. Madelyne was trying to get on with her life and hoped Damon would do the same.

Madelyne desperately needed to finally start living in the present with George, not dwell on the ruined past with Damon. Sadly, it looked like Damon was only interested in living in the past. No matter how cruel it sounded, that was his problem and not hers. She deserved to be happy, and wasn't about to let him ruin yet another marriage for her.

Apparently, Damon realized this, at least in part, that they'd gone too far, because he said, "I'm sorry, Madelyne. I'll drive Connie home after we grab a bite to eat."

"Fine," she replied somewhat calmly.

5

DAMON

Damon felt like shit after that conversation with Madelyne, and the sad truth was that wasn't the first time it had happened. It was obvious they both harbored a lot of negative feelings toward one another, and that was far too depressing. To make matters even worse, Damon had had such an argument in front of Connie. If she was angry before with her mother, Damon had managed to make matters worse.

"Why can't I stay with you?" she whined.

"You know why."

The court gave him weekends, and that was that. Considering the state he was in during the divorce and custody battle, it was a miracle they hadn't taken her permanently away from him. He was sure that was due to the fact that Madelyne wanted Connie to spend some time with her father, and for that, no matter all the rest, he would be eternally grateful.

"That is so not fair."

"Come on, help me lock up." He needed to distract them both, at least for a little while, from the reality they lived in.

It took some coaxing, but Damon successfully managed to convince his daughter to return home. Every time she told him how she wanted to stay with him, it broke his heart. He knew that Madelyne would never agree to that. The weekends were the best he could hope for, and Connie knew that as well.

He didn't want to rush her. He took her to dinner first, but he kept in mind how late it was on a school night. Madelyne was angry enough as it was. He didn't need to escalate this further. And afterward, Damon had to have a serious conversation with himself. He couldn't believe he'd let himself lose his temper in front of his daughter in such a way.

It was like he'd wasted all those hours and hours in therapy. He'd let his pain and anger out in front of Connie. He felt shitty that she'd witnessed that side of him and that side of his relationship with her mother. No matter what, he'd always tried to shield her from it. They both had.

Great work, asshole.

Unfortunately, Madelyne had managed to push all his buttons in a split second, and he'd completely forgotten that his daughter was beside him. He cringed, repeating the whole exchange to himself, trying to understand how that looked from a sixteen-year-old's point of view. *Not good.*

Damon really didn't want Connie to end up like him: broken, angry, going to therapy. He vowed to do better, be better from now on.

"How's school?" Damon asked a typical parent question, trying to start a conversation on their ride back.

Connie shrugged, looking through the side window. She was still sulking hard, which was understandable, considering everything.

Damon's heart went out to her. It must be difficult for her to live with her mom and George. Damon hated how powerless he felt, since he didn't know how to help her or change her circumstances. Reassuring her that she would soon be off to college, leaving all this drama behind, felt like the wrong move. It was like telling an innocent man in jail that he only had another two years to serve.

"Look, Con-Con." He used her baby nickname. "I know this is a shitty situation, and I promise you it will get better," he said, praying like hell that he wasn't full of shit. "It's just that we're all pretty new at this. We'll get there, learn how to live like one big, happy family." He was proud of himself that he'd said all that without throwing up.

To his relief, his words somewhat helped her relax, but that quickly changed once they reached the house. Connie became tense, visibly upset anew, and Damon didn't like that one bit. He was sure another fight between mother and daughter was on the horizon.

He gritted his teeth, feeling like he should march inside the house and have a long talk with Madelyne and George about leaving his daughter the fuck alone. It was her prerogative to choose with whom she wanted to spend time.

Sadly, he knew he couldn't do that, which drove him insane. He was certain his raising his voice like he'd tried tonight would only make matters worse. He knew Madelyne. She would consider that an attack, and the already dire situation would become a shit storm. His ex could be stubborn like that. A trait their daughter inherited.

He only hoped Connie would understand. He was afraid of losing custody. He couldn't lose Connie, not after fighting so long and hard to keep her. Primarily, that was a fight with himself, which Madelyne understood, and that would disappear if he fucked up. Of course, he couldn't directly say all that to Connie because she was already mad enough at her mother. Damon desperately sought some way to fix this, but he didn't know how.

As he stopped the vehicle in their driveway, Damon could

see Madelyne looking at them through the living room window.

"Better not make her wait longer," Damon said simply, knowing that look on his ex's face all too well.

Although Connie made a face in return, she didn't comment and said instead, "Thanks for dropping me off, Dad."

"And promise me, no more gallivanting all across town at night. If you want to reach me, call me. I'll pick you up."

"Okay."

After kissing him on the cheek, she reached for the door, and Damon stopped her. There was something else on his mind he had to share.

She looked at him questioningly.

"Hey, Con, if that creep ever does anything to make you feel unsafe, come to me immediately," he stressed.

Because then Damon would definitely have a serious conversation with that man.

"I will," his daughter promised. "And thanks for dinner."

That helped him center, helped his sanity as well, allowing him to avoid making a scene, as he wanted to.

Damon could understand she wanted her new husband —oh, how he hated even thinking in such terms—and daughter to form a relationship, but nothing could be done by force. Especially not with a teenager. A part of him started to wonder if this was all George's doing, since Madelyne had never been this unreasonable while being with him. Sensing how ridiculous those thoughts were, he dismissed them.

"No need to thank me, kid. Love you."

"Love you, too."

It was hard watching her leave. It always was. He stayed put until she went inside. Damon watched as Madelyne opened the door for their daughter. As he'd noticed before, her expression promised a storm was about to hit. Luckily,

Connie was his daughter and knew how to handle her mother, even on her worst day.

Knowing he couldn't intervene, since this was something the two of them needed to settle for themselves, Damon started the car, waving to his daughter. She repeated the gesture as Madelyne closed the door with unnecessary force.

Driving off, he couldn't help feeling restless. This had started as a normal, regular day, but had turned out to be a pretty shitty one. It was funny how one event could change a man's perspective in an instant. It was hard when things like this occurred because Damon felt depressed and lonely on a good day.

When days like this hit him in the gut, when he had to witness his daughter in distress and couldn't do jack shit about it, he felt even worse. One would think that wasn't humanly possible, that he'd already hit rock bottom, but life always found new ways to torment him further.

Going to therapy for a while, he knew all these thoughts that he was having weren't helping him. The point was that he didn't know how to turn all the different voices inside his head off. He wanted to rage, to break something; then he wanted to get drunk and try to forget everything. Just thinking about a nice cold beer made his throat dry.

When he passed a random bar, he wanted to pull over and have a couple of beers to try to decompress. Damon prepared to turn into the bar's parking lot, when Madelyne's words stopped him. *Did you forget about all the drinking, your angry outbursts, vanishing without a word?* He bypassed it. She'd accused him many times of being a drunk. It was true that he'd had moments when he wanted to loosen up, but did that make him a drunk?

His therapist would look at him like he was full of shit. If he wanted to get better, then the first thing he needed to do was be honest with himself. There were times, and recently, when he had been going to alcohol too much when upset and angry. And Madelyne was right: he had been in a really bad place after his last tour and had been drinking all the time.

He wasn't trying to justify his actions, but what he'd witnessed, experienced there, all the death and destruction, losing close friends... it all stayed with him, and unfortunately, he didn't handle it the right way. That would stop right now. He couldn't allow Madelyne to be right about him.

Besides, if he genuinely wanted to be a good role model to his daughter, he needed to lead by example, so all the unnecessary drinking had to stop. The same could be applied if he wanted to show his wife how he was capable of change. *Ex-wife*, he corrected himself somewhat grudgingly.

Having that moment of self-reflection allowed him to continue driving, and Damon managed to go home without making a stop. Although that wasn't so big an accomplishment, he still felt like patting himself on the back. *And having a beer to celebrate*, he thought.

Of course, he didn't do that, but fell on the couch, too exhausted to walk all the way to his bedroom. Besides, at times, he preferred to sleep in the living room on the couch. The king-sized bed in his bedroom mocked him with all that space. Although exhausted mentally and physically, Damon knew he wouldn't be able to fall asleep that easily, so he grabbed the remote and started browsing through the channels. It was weird how he had all these channels and nothing to watch. That was one of the curses of the modern age.

Eventually, he settled on some channel that always showed old movies. It was fortunate it was one of his favorite films. He knew it by heart and at times spoke alongside the actors. Sadly, not even that could hold his attention for long.

This whole issue with George trying to force a relationship on Connie was bugging him. And Damon had to look inside himself long and hard to determine precisely why. Was Jason right when saying Damon was jealous of the other man? Was he blowing this out of proportion, fearing Connie's relationship with George could somehow jeopardize his relationship with his daughter?

It was true that he was scared shitless that he would lose her like Madelyne, but was that the only drive behind his feelings toward that stranger who took his place? Was there a chance he was exaggerating? Connie felt the same way, but he couldn't take that into account until he learned the truth about his own feelings.

The bottom line was his gut feeling was telling him something was off with that creep. That same gut feeling had helped him many times in the past to survive, so he couldn't take it lightly. If he added Connie and how she felt the same way into the mix, then the matter turned pretty serious.

Unfortunately, since he had no additional information to go on, only time would tell if he was a selfish bastard who didn't want his ex to be happy with someone else, or if there was a secret Mr. George Elway tried to hide from all of them.

6

MADELYNE

Ever since she ended her heated conversation with Damon, Madelyne had sat in the living room, waiting for her rebellious daughter to get home. She should have known that Connie would use any excuse to go running to her father. That really went too far, and she needed some way to stop this madness. This constant struggle would accomplish nothing. Connie needed to understand this was their life now. George was Madelyne's husband, not Damon.

Connie couldn't just storm out of the house every time she heard or learned something she didn't like. Life didn't work like that. And Damon was to blame. He encouraged such behavior.

Madelyne was all alone in this, without allies. Damon obviously wanted things to stay the same, George wanted Connie to go to boarding school, and apparently, nobody cared what she wanted. What she needed. And what she wanted was for her daughter to stay home and accept George as family.

But first things first. Her daughter needed to be taught a

lesson. She was old enough to understand how each action had consequences. For turning her phone off, while running away for no reason, Connie would lose it.

Madelyne knew the instant Damon drove her daughter home, recognizing his car's engine. It had a distinct sound. He insisted on driving this restored muscle car even though it was a complete piece of junk on wheels, as far as she was concerned.

You didn't mind it while you were fooling around with Damon in his backseat. She shook off that thought. The machine required constant repairs, and at times, Madelyne was worried about Connie's safety. She'd tried speaking with Damon about it, but he'd brushed it off, accusing her of exaggerating, like always. Either way, Madelyne knew that death trap was a battle for some other day.

Tonight, she had more pressing issues. Standing up, she crossed a small distance to open the front door as Connie approached. Without greeting her or acknowledging her presence in any way, Connie walked inside with her chin raised ever so slightly.

She ignored Damon's stare at her while she glared at Connie. It was hard to snub the urge to slam the door behind her. She was the adult, after all. However, she still used some force to close it, and it could be heard.

Connie went straight for her room, climbing the stairs. Madelyne was used to receiving the silent treatment, but her daughter couldn't just go to her room without learning what her latest behavior and lack of respect had brought her.

"Don't know if your father told you, but you are grounded."

That froze her in her tracks, and Connie turned to glare at her. "For what?" she demanded.

Are you kidding me? Madelyne's expression said in return.

Still, since she was the adult in this story, a parent, or at least tried to be, she decided to illuminate her only daughter.

"Oh, where to start? For disrespecting me, for taking off while I tried to speak with you, for ignoring my calls," she counted.

"Well, if you would stop pestering me about George, I wouldn't have to run away from my own house in the first place," Connie said, with an attitude known to every parent of a teenage child.

At times, it was hard not to lash out, but Connie wasn't her equal, not an adult yet, and Madelyne always had to have that in mind when dealing with her. No matter what, she was a child, her child, and teenagers were known to act out, with or without reason.

Madelyne only wished Connie would rebel in some other way and stop hating her stepfather for no reason. She could pierce her nose, date a bad guy for a while, get drunk from one bottle of beer... anything would be better than constantly fighting to give George a chance. Considering the list she'd just made, Madelyne decided she wouldn't like any of those things, either. She didn't want her baby girl to date anyone, let alone some loser. Besides, Connie found other ways to show her disobedience.

Madelyne decided to try again, reining in her temper. "I really don't understand this animosity you have toward George. Do you feel like you would be betraying your father if you let George in?"

"This has nothing to do with Dad," Connie snapped in annoyance.

Madelyne begged to differ. "This has everything to do with him, and the fact that you ran off tonight to see him proves it." She was sure of that.

"So now I'm not allowed to see Dad?" she argued.

"I didn't say that. However, you broke our agreement."

"I was upset."

"Over nothing."

"You don't understand anything," Connie said in exasperation while shaking her head.

"You can have a relationship with George and still love your father, spend time with him as well." Madelyne tried to reason with her.

Connie grabbed the railing as she leaned forward ever so slightly. "I don't want any kind of relationship with George," she stressed. "He's your husband, I get it, but leave me out of it."

Anger that Madelyne had felt before started to rise all over again. She couldn't understand this level of stubbornness. Connie behaved unreasonably because she felt like she could, and Madelyne didn't know how to respond in return.

"Like it or not, George is a part of our lives now," she insisted. "It's completely unacceptable for you to treat him in such a way. You're disrespecting me, and you're disrespecting him."

"So send me to live with Dad, and problem solved."

"No," Madelyne replied instantly. "This is your home, so the sooner you accept that there will be changes around here, the better."

"And the sooner you accept that I'm safer taking a few buses across town to see Dad than staying home alone with a creep like George, the better."

Madelyne gritted her teeth. "Why do you keep calling him a creep?"

Something like that was well past hurtful, and Connie knew that. She was smart enough, old enough to know how words could hurt more than actual wounds. George was nothing but kind and supportive toward her daughter, and Madelyne was certain he would be heartbroken if he ever heard Connie say something like that in his presence. He didn't have children of his own and considered Connie his daughter. For her to speak of him that way was a complete travesty.

Madelyne waited patiently, but Connie remained silent, clearly having nothing to say in her defense.

"Right," Madelyne commented eventually.

Connie rolled her eyes. "You wouldn't understand anyway."

Madelyne felt like rolling her eyes in return and suppressed the urge. "Try me."

"It's just a gut feeling. I don't trust him."

And just like that, Madelyne understood everything. This was all Damon's influence, of course. He'd instilled in her this ridiculous notion of how she should always listen to this nonexistent inner force inside her. Damon trusted his gut feeling immensely and had passed that along. As far as Madelyne was concerned, that was an excuse that people used to justify certain actions and nothing else.

Madelyne would prefer if her daughter learned how to think with her own head rather than let emotions govern her way, masking them with gut feelings. Using such ridiculous notions could do her a lot of harm.

A lot could be said of such foolishness. A man lost all the money he had on gambling, having a gut feeling he would win. One kissed someone else's wife while having a gut feeling that she would reciprocate. And then when reality hit, they could only scratch their heads in wonder, unable to understand what had happened, what had gone wrong.

Well, reality happened. No, no, Madelyne couldn't allow this. It was ridiculous that Damon had done this to their daughter.

Connie scowled. "I knew you wouldn't understand," she added, seeing Madelyne's expression.

And she was one hundred percent right. Madelyne

couldn't understand because her daughter was using some made-up feeling to justify her unreasonable disdain toward George. And honestly, Madelyne was fed up with it. If Connie demanded to be treated like an adult, then she needed to start acting like one. At the moment, she resembled a spoiled brat. Not that she said that out loud.

"There's something I do understand, Connie," Madelyne started, but the sound of the front door opening stopped her from finishing.

George entered the house wearing a big smile on his face upon seeing the two of them. They were both so immersed in the argument that neither one of them had heard his car in the driveway.

Out of the corner of her eye, Madelyne noticed how Connie straightened up, letting go of the balustrade. Madelyne returned the smile. Apparently, they'd both decided to behave as if nothing were amiss.

"Good evening, honey." He gave her a quick kiss on the mouth before refocusing on her daughter. "Good evening, Connie."

"Good evening, Mr. Elway," she replied somewhat awkwardly while looking at Madelyne. Connie refused to call him by his first name.

"Did you have a pleasant day?" He tried to chat with her for a minute.

"Exceptional," Connie replied. "May I be excused?" she asked politely.

Madelyne felt the need to pinch herself, since this wasn't her daughter standing in front of them. *This must be a case of body snatching.* That almost made her smile. At the same time, Connie always acted like this in front of George, as though needing to be on her best behavior, which was something Madelyne couldn't understand. Why was she feeling so awkward? Seeing how her daughter waited for a reply, Madelyne started to nod and then remembered this couldn't just end like this. Connie had run away from her today, and there had to be some repercussions.

"Yes, but you forgot to give me your phone," Madelyne said, opening her palm.

After heavily sighing, Connie reached into her pocket, and taking her phone out, she leaned forward to place it into Madelyne's hand.

George watched the exchange with interest.

"Can I go now?" she asked again.

There she is. Madelyne had worried for a moment that her daughter had lost all the attitude, but it was back. "Of course."

"Is everything okay?" George wanted to know once there were just the two of them.

"Now it is."

"What was that about?" he pressed, gesturing with his head toward Connie's room.

Madelyne really didn't want this drama to continue, or speak about it further, for that matter, yet she saw no way to prevent it. More to the point, for some reason, Madelyne didn't want George to know what Connie had done today.

"I spoke with her," she replied simply, hoping that would be enough for her husband.

"Good." He sounded pleased, and Madelyne was relieved. "I'm starving," he announced in the next instant, going to the kitchen to investigate what she'd made for dinner.

Although George spent all his day at the restaurant he owned, he still preferred to eat the meals she prepared for him. Madelyne found that to be quite endearing.

As she followed him to the kitchen so they could share a meal, she couldn't help wondering about something that had happened right after George walked inside the house. It was hard to miss the fact that the atmosphere had completely changed in an instant.

Both mother and daughter had pretended like everything was all right, and Madelyne wondered why. She more or less understood Connie's stance: she didn't like George and did everything in her power to make him feel like an outsider. But what was *her* problem?

Why can't I fully be myself in front of my husband?

She'd never had such problems while being married to Damon. He knew the real her, with all the good sides, bad sides, and all the fun sides in between. Since that was a truly troubling thought, she instantly shoved it away.

7

DAMON

After that fight Connie had had with Madelyne, and the one he'd had with Madelyne, things settled a bit, or so he hoped. He took it as a good sign that Connie didn't come crying to him late at night again. They spoke on the phone almost every day, but she never mentioned something else like that happening.

That didn't have to mean a thing, but all the same, he was really looking forward to the weekend when he would be able to hang out with his daughter as much as he pleased, drama-free. This wasn't a direct critique of Madelyne or her parental skills, although she would definitely have seen it that way.

Damon was looking forward to having Connie all to himself. He trusted Madelyne immensely regarding Connie's well-being. It would be impossible to live if he didn't. She was the mother of his child, and that would always mean something to him. *Everything* to him. It was just that he had zero trust in George.

He couldn't understand all that tension that had accumulated between Madelyne and Connie regarding George. How did that happen, and why? George wasn't a good guy. There was just something about him that made Damon wary of him, and he wouldn't rest until he got to the bottom of things and learned who this guy really was.

No matter what his best friend had said, Damon wasn't jealous. At least not entirely. He still felt grief for what he'd lost, but that was something else entirely. His therapist had also tried to explain to him how he was getting too obsessed with his ex-wife's new husband, if not in those exact words.

Dr. Weldon would never say something like that. He had all those fancy words, medical terms to throw his way when he was trying to make a point. Despite those voices of reason in his life, Damon was on Connie's side on this. There was something off about George.

All their troubles had started when he appeared, and that couldn't be a coincidence. Connie and Madelyne had never fought like this before, so George had to be the reason. Damon was sure the man couldn't be trusted, which made him more alert when he was nearby or when his name was brought up. He watched his phone, waiting for Connie to call him in alarm, so he could declare DEFCON 1.

Was he paranoid? *Perhaps a bit.*

If the guy so much as looked at Connie oddly, made her feel uncomfortable in any way, Damon was going to take him down, no matter the consequences or what his ex would think about it. Some things had to take precedence.

With those delightful thoughts on his mind, he went to pick Connie up. Usually, Damon picked her up on Friday after school. That way, he didn't have to look at the happy couple. Even if she had plans with friends, he was more than happy to play chauffeur for her, but since she had some school project due Monday, she asked if he could drop by the house on Saturday morning instead.

Naturally, Damon agreed to that, although he was a bit

saddened that he would have less time to spend with her. Sometimes, he couldn't sleep at night worrying that she would soon vanish from his life, going to college not knowing how much he loved her. Those were irrational fears, of course, but they were very much real to him.

He'd prepared a whole weekend of entertainment—a movie night, which he'd gotten tickets for beforehand, for a show she wanted to see. And if she felt like it, they could go to Lake Michigan for a day in nature. Was he trying too hard? Most definitely.

He was aware there was a big chance that Connie would spend the entire weekend with her friends, but he didn't mind. It was good to have something to offer her if she decided to stay and hang out with him. It was true that Madelyne had grounded her, but some rules were meant to be broken.

It was obvious his daughter was stressed with all this bullshit regarding Madelyne's new husband. He couldn't help cringing every time he thought of that fact. Damon felt like he should try to get her mind off everything, cheer her up a bit. She always loved to go with him on all kinds of adventures, and luckily, that hadn't changed once she became a teenager, although they had less time for their father-daughter moments. At first, he blamed Madelyne for that, but now, thanks to Dr. Weldon, he knew better.

Reaching the house, he honked once before turning the engine off, knowing his daughter would need some time to gather all her things. He hated this house. It wasn't the one that he'd bought with Madelyne when they'd first married. They had practically buried themselves in debt to get their dream house back then.

During the divorce, Madelyne had insisted that they sell it and pay off the mortgage, then split the rest. Of course, Damon had been against it. He'd loved that house. Unfortunately, he didn't have the money to buy her out, because all his savings went to the gym. He'd had to agree. Madelyne had broken his heart in a lot of small ways. Losing that house had hurt like hell, especially when he'd encountered this ostentatious piece of crap that George had moved them into. The house screamed money, and Damon was dead sure that was by design. *Pompous ass.*

At the same time, it would have been pure torture having that impostor living in his former home. Feeling a bit restless, Damon exited the car, which was something he never did, always choosing to sit behind the wheel, waiting in silence for Connie to come out. Today, he couldn't do that. It was simply too hot.

Could have cracked the window. Not even he believed in that excuse. He leaned on his favorite vehicle, mentally urging the front door to open. Instead, Connie appeared at the window. She was still in her room, in her pajamas. Damon mentally groaned. This would take a while. He smiled at her, waving. "Good morning, honey."

"Hi, Dad, I'll be down in two minutes," she promised.

He seriously doubted that. "Take your time," he reassured her in return.

And there was a reason behind it. Although this was something never spoken of, they all knew she was the biggest klutz on planet Earth, without any exaggerations. At times, walking was an extreme sport for his daughter.

Connie would get embarrassed, even hurt, if someone pointed that out to her, so both Damon and Madelyne ignored her lack of balance. For the love of him, he couldn't understand her attitude, since he found it extremely funny, even endearing. Naturally, he respected her wishes. So, at the moment, it was imperative for her to take her time because he didn't want to be forced to rush her to the emergency room on their weekend together. After all, she could trip over her own feet.

Although she was seriously challenged, blessed with two left feet, they'd had only a few minor incidents that required medical attention over the years. All the rest of her acrobatics were hilarious as hell.

Connie disappeared from the window, and Damon had to smile. He really was blessed with an amazing daughter. It improved his mood that she was so openly excited to spend the weekend with him. To his surprise, when the front door opened, it wasn't Connie who came out. It was Madelyne. Damon instinctively braced himself for whatever would come next.

"Could you please bring her back on Sunday night so she can prepare for school?"

"Of course," Damon said, refusing to whine that his father-daughter weekend was being shortened yet again.

To his chagrin, George decided to join the party. And to think his day had started pretty well. He woke up, came here... He wondered what brand of hell this little gathering would bring him, since he enjoyed the small talk immensely. On the other hand, he would be personally responsible for creating said hell if they mentioned Connie or her behavior in any way.

Calm down; nobody has said a word to you.

"What an interesting ride," George said, gesturing with his chin toward Damon's car, completely taking him by surprise. It wasn't like George was seeing his baby for the first time.

"It's a classic," Damon replied simply.

George chuckled before replying, "I guess working in a gym doesn't pay that much."

There was that smirk again, and Damon couldn't decide

what irked him the most, his words or his face. *His face*, he decided.

And he didn't just work in the gym, he owned it, and George knew that very well. So was it only his imagination, or was good old George trying to provoke him? From that irritating expression on his face, Damon was inclined to believe that was the case.

Asshole.

Damon stretched his mouth in an attempt at a smile before replying, "Probably not as much as owning a restaurant." There, that would show him Damon wasn't so easily provoked.

George didn't lose a beat to say, "Oh, it's a hard business, but definitely not without perks. I have the privilege of affording better cars, better women..." he added, patting Madelyne on the cheek. Only a neon sign above his head saying, *I stole your wife because I'm better than you in every way*, would be slightly more obvious than what he was doing at the moment.

Damon was certain the bastard was trying to bait him for some reason, not that he would take the bait. At least not in front of his ex-wife.

If they were alone, they would be having a different kind of conversation. The thought of running Madelyne's hubby over with his 'interesting ride' almost made him smile. Not that he would ever do such a thing. Violence was an answer only in special circumstances, but it was still good to daydream.

Instead of lashing out and calling him on his bullshit, Damon said, "I bet."

There was a small twitch of George's left eye, as though not pleased that this wasn't going as he planned, but he masked it well. That cheered Damon up to no end. He realized that irritating George was better than therapy, although

Dr. Weldon would probably disagree on how therapeutic something like this really was.

His daughter chose that moment to appear, rushing out of the house carrying a backpack and a small bag. Why on Earth would she need so much stuff? To Damon's surprise, she rushed into his arms.

The bag hit him straight in the kidney, but he took it like a man. He squeezed her tightly.

"Two hugs in the last two times we saw each other. I must be dying," he teased.

"Ha-ha, very funny," she commented, rolling her eyes at him. As she settled inside his car, Damon packed the bags in the trunk. Seriously, what did she pack in those, her rock collection?

Closing the trunk's lid, he looked at the happy newly-weds. "It was great catching up."

Madelyne smiled, if in a somewhat forced way, while waving at her daughter.

Unfortunately, George looked like he wasn't finished. "Are you sure that thing is even drivable? It looks like it'll leave parts on the road, like it's ready to explode," he mocked.

That was it. Nobody was allowed to say crap about his car. Completely ignoring George, or the fact that he had an arm around Madelyne, Damon nonchalantly strolled to her, and looking her in the eyes, he said, "Are you sure that thing"—he made sure George could hear him loud and clear—"is your definition of trading up? Because he looks ready to explode." He delivered all that with a straight face before walking away and getting into his car.

Madelyne's baffled and slightly worried expression surprised him, but at the moment, he really didn't give a shit. That asshole needed to be taught a lesson, and he was the perfect man for the job.

8

MADELYNE

"This is madness," George snapped, returning inside the house.

Madelyne could only stare after Damon as he cheerfully drove off with their daughter after that delightful comment.

What had possessed him to say something like that, and in front of George? It was hurtful to both of them. At the same time, George had started it, which was a different matter altogether. Today, she'd seen something unexpected from her husband and was baffled by it.

She dreaded going after George, fully knowing that he would stay angry because of this for quite some time. Of course, Madelyne was sure that had been Damon's intention in the first place. She could sense something was brewing under the surface when George had started commenting on Damon's car.

Damon loved that car more than anyone in this world apart from Connie. She was perplexed as to why George had chosen to say something like that. Damon had certainly found a way to have the last word. And now he'd created tension between her and her husband.

Thanks, Damon, she thought, finally returning inside.

Following all the noises, she located George in the kitchen. As expected, he wasn't in the best of moods. And the day had started so well, with their speaking of a trip out of state. George had mentioned how they would be able to have spontaneous trips all over the country once Connie was in boarding school.

His jaw was clenched as he prepared himself a cup of coffee. Since the restaurant was open every day, George had to go to work, but on the weekends, he could allow himself a little leeway because they didn't serve breakfast or lunch.

Madelyne racked her brain for something to say to try to change the mood, but George beat her to the punch.

"I can't believe you were ever married to that brute." He paused just long enough with his task to glare at her. Apparently, he wanted them to stay on the subject of her ex. *Great.*

"It didn't help, your mentioning that his car was a piece of crap," she pointed out.

Madelyne avoided defending Damon to George, but in this case, it couldn't be helped. And she certainly didn't miss the fact that her husband had bragged about being with her, as though she were a piece of meat. George had never acted in such a manner before, so she was quite shocked. He'd acted as though he was jealous of Damon, which was ridiculous. They were already married, for Christ's sake.

It was on the tip of her tongue to ask him what had possessed him to act that way unprovoked, but she held her tongue. Sure, he had problems with Connie and was frustrated by it, but that wasn't Damon's problem. At least not entirely. So this passive-aggressive behavior was a novelty that Madelyne didn't like one bit. George had behaved maturely up to this point, so she decided to let this slide.

"It was meant as a joke," George defended, turning to look at her while waiting for the coffee to brew. "It's not my fault that he has no sense of humor."

Damon had a great sense of humor and had never had a problem taking a joke, especially if it was at his expense. The problem was George's tone. He'd intentionally tried to provoke her ex, although she couldn't say why.

Suffice to say, Madelyne wasn't buying this excuse, at least not entirely. There was a possibility that George had tried to make friends, but chose the wrong approach, she rationalized.

"Maybe next time, refrain from joking," she offered, "so we can avoid such unnecessary scenes."

"So now I have to change myself because of him?" Not pleased, he turned to pour himself a cup of coffee and went to sit in the living room.

Madelyne sighed, choosing some tea for herself before joining him. For a moment, she debated whether she should go and do some work, leave him be, but she decided against it. They spent too little time together as it was. He always came home late at night and went in first thing in the morning during the week, since they opened early for lunch service, and he had to prep the kitchen.

He was on the phone when she entered, but finished once he saw her.

Madelyne sat beside him. "George, I don't understand you. What brought all of this on today?" she said in a calm manner, pleading with her eyes for him to talk with her.

"And I don't understand you," he snapped.

"Excuse me?" she said, taken aback.

"Why do you allow him to come here in the first place?"

That was such a random question she didn't see it coming.

"Because he has to pick Connie up." Madelyne felt ridiculous that she had to point something like that out since it was obvious. It wasn't like Damon liked to drop by. That wasn't a social visit. He came to take his daughter to his place, plain and simple.

"Why don't you file for full custody of Connie?" he continued in the same manner.

"Because it's important for Connie to have her father around and spend time with him."

"We know he's a bad influence. It would be good for everybody to just get rid of him for good."

Madelyne was starting to get testy. "No, absolutely not. I won't punish my daughter in such a way. I'm not going to take her father away from her because you don't like him," she insisted. "At times, I don't like him either, but it is what it is."

He grimaced. "At least now I know why she has zero respect for me. She learned it from him."

Madelyne couldn't fully agree with that assumption, but remained quiet.

At times, she felt like she was in the middle of a strange game of dodgeball. She stood in the middle of the court, and all the teams, represented by Damon, Connie, George, and her parents, always hit her. And she was getting tired of it. Why couldn't they all just get along? *Because we don't live in fantasy land, but in the real world.*

Sadly, this was no game that she could merely walk away from, and the teams constantly hitting her were her closest and dearest, so she couldn't just abandon them either.

"I think you need to calm down and stop overanalyzing everything," she said as delicately as possible while wondering when George became so sensitive. Damon had acted much worse in the past, and George had never reacted in the manner he did today. All of this was absolutely baffling.

"And you need to stop defending him and see that man

for what he really is, a loser and a troublemaker," he said, even more annoyed than before. "In case you've forgotten, I'm your husband, not him."

It really bothered her that he threw something like that in her face.

"No, I haven't forgotten, but apparently, you forgot you were an adult and not a child," she replied in the same manner, completely losing her temper, which was a bit ironic considering her words.

Either way, that made him pause.

"Fine, have it your way. I'm the problem," he said eventually. "However, if you don't put him in his place, know that I certainly will if that is what it takes to keep the peace and restore order in this household."

Madelyne didn't like that one bit and thought he wasn't being fair. More to the point, it made her aware of how he phrased things. Deal with Damon how? Also, while he was saying all that, his eyes flashed with some unidentifiable emotion that made Madelyne worried, even a bit frightened. She'd never seen this side of her husband before. It made her question whether she knew him at all.

Of course you do; don't you start exaggerating as well, she snapped at herself. He was frustrated like the rest of them. She couldn't really hold that against him.

She needed this conversation to end. They'd spent too much time talking about Damon, and as George had pointed out himself, he was her husband and not Connie's father.

She decided to try again to appease him from a different angle. "Please, George, calm down. You're getting upset over nothing."

"So my feelings are now nothing to you."

"Of course not," she said reassuringly. "I hate seeing you like this. I know you voiced these issues because you care."

"Of course I care. You and Connie are my family."

Madelyne's heart melted. "Of course we are, but please bear in mind, Damon is Connie's father and will always be a part of her life, like it or not."

He was prepared to say something in return, and Madelyne stopped him. With one swift move, she sat on his lap, wrapped her arms around his neck, and pulling him closer, kissed him with all her might. At first, he merely let her lead, probably startled by her actions, but he recovered quickly before starting to reciprocate with vigor.

"Besides," she continued once they parted, not moving from his lap—the way he held his arms wrapped around her waist, there was a chance that he wouldn't let her even if she tried—"having Damon around to take Connie away has its perks." Her voice was playful now.

"Like what?" he grumbled, evidently still in a bad mood, but Madelyne could feel his arousal, so she pressed on.

She leaned forward to speak against his lips. "We have the house all to ourselves."

Apparently, those were the magic words because he whisked her off to their bedroom. George was a real bear of a man, who liked to work out. When he picked her up and carried her to their room for the first time, Madelyne had been exhilarated. She liked how small she looked while in his arms.

That was what had attracted her to him in the first place. George was a good-looking man, tall, with a great smile, gray eyes, and salt-and-pepper hair. He had a bald spot at the back of his head that he was very self-conscious about, but she didn't care about it. He was hot as hell, period.

Once he laid her on the bed, they continued to kiss. Madelyne loved foreplay, but it always felt too short with George, as though he couldn't wait that long to have her. Which was okay. All women cared to be desired, especially by the men they loved. And George always wanted her.

If she were completely honest with herself, that wasn't the reason she'd initiated sex this morning. She needed to calm him down, and this was the quickest way she knew.

There was clearly something going on with him, and she presumed it was work related. That was the only reason he was acting like that with Damon and lashing out at her, and Madelyne needed that to stop. She'd had enough drama with an emotionally unstable man in her previous marriage. She didn't want to go through that again.

George is nothing like Damon, she reminded herself.

She was sure that George would reach out to her, share his problem in due time. In the meantime, she couldn't fix problems with Connie and Damon if he was making matters worse. She knew her daughter. She was a stubborn being, so Madelyne had to handle her delicately.

You did a fine job so far.

As though needing to get all that negative energy out in some way, George was slightly rougher than usual. Madelyne couldn't say she fully enjoyed it, although it wasn't terrible either. It all ended pretty quickly.

Afterward, he left for work, mumbling something about a delivery he needed to personally oversee, and she continued lying in their marital bed, troubled and completely unsatisfied.

9

DAMON

Connie couldn't stop laughing as they drove away. Of course, she'd heard the entire exchange. "That was epic, Dad!"

He groaned inwardly. *Damon, you are so screwed.* Despite his best efforts, he couldn't keep his mouth shut.

"I shouldn't have done that," he said, believing he had to maintain the appearance of an adult. In reality, he was as happy as a boy who'd performed his first prank. That felt beyond good, and the expression on George's face—priceless. *That'll show him that he messed with the wrong person.*

On one hand, Damon had been surprised that George had acted like that. On the other, he was thrilled that it finally happened.

George presented himself as this sophisticated, wealthy man who always said the right thing, did the right thing. Basically, a saint who always tried to help. However, as it turned out, George could be petty and jealous like the rest of them.

Damon was glad the other man had finally shown them his ugly side, dropping that Mr. Perfect façade. As it turned out, George was an asshole, and that was something Damon could understand.

"Oh, come on, you definitely should have," Connie countered. "And don't try to deny it, you liked telling him to back off."

She had him there. There was no way he could deny it without lying to her, and that was something he didn't like doing. He looked at his daughter without commenting, and she started laughing even harder.

Although Damon was glad this little show amused his daughter, because she rarely laughed with such intensity anymore, it didn't amuse him. It bothered him to no end. George apparently had an agenda. He couldn't explain why the man had felt the need to provoke him that morning, but it was apparent that he had. What was he trying to accomplish?

If it was a bloody nose, he didn't have to work that hard. Damon would happily oblige, if only the man had asked. He shelved that question and many more for later, not wanting all that to ruin his time with Connie. "What do you want to do first?"

Connie smiled, and he regretted asking. "Shopping."

They had a blast. For a while, they drove around, then went to a mall, and when Connie got hungry, he took her to the best fish restaurant in the city. His friend Don worked there as a chef. He had been a cook in the Army as well, while Damon's expertise had been explosives. Connie was like her dad and could eat fish every day, so he knew she would like it. And he was right. After that, they went to the latest Marvel movie she'd been dying to see. Later, when they returned home, they had an *Avengers* marathon, for the tenth time, eating pizza right from the box for dinner, as it was meant to be eaten.

Connie fell asleep on his shoulder during an epic scene, but he didn't wake her up. He lowered the volume and continued watching until the end. Connie didn't like the last film, declaring it was too sad to watch, so they always watched just the first three. Damon didn't mind.

After the movie ended, he debated whether he should carry her to her room like he had done when she was a little girl, but ruled against it. Extracting himself proved to be easier than he thought. His daughter was a sound sleeper. Throwing a blanket over her and letting her be, he retired to his bedroom, where he did absolutely nothing.

He couldn't settle down for some reason. The bed felt alien. Probably because he rarely slept there—only when Connie was visiting, he realized. Damon tossed and turned like an idiot.

Why don't I have a TV installed in here as well? he fumed at himself in those moments of 'peace'. Part of him wanted to go to the gym and work out for a bit, not knowing what else to do with himself, but at the same time, he didn't want to leave Connie alone.

She's sixteen, not six, a part of him pointed out. He stayed put, struggling to fall asleep. The problem was that his brain refused to turn off. George was on his mind, which was kind of creepy since it was the middle of the night, and he was in his own bed.

Giving up, Damon stood. He opened the window and climbed through to the emergency stairs, breathing some fresh air. Although his apartment wasn't anywhere near the center of the city or downtown, it tended to be lively, even at night. There was always something going on, since a lot of people didn't sleep, like him.

He sat on the chair he'd installed there months ago, taking in the city around him. He couldn't see the stars at night, which bothered him. Damon liked nothing more than to lie down on his back, gazing above and wondering, what did it all mean? Most of the time, he would share his problems with the big unknown. It made him feel better in a way, not so alone.

Back in his hometown, the stars were bright and beautiful. If he didn't feel so lonely after his parents passed, he would never have left that place. Instead, Damon had moved to the big city, then joined the Army just to be surrounded by people.

His beginnings in this world weren't what was plaguing his mind right then. There was something strange about George, Damon was sure of that, and he needed to find out what. Despite Jason's warning, Connie was right. His daughter had an amazing sense regarding other people. George was a creep and an asshole. His behavior that morning had confirmed as much.

Of course, Damon didn't have any information regarding why he would suddenly act in such a way, but that small exchange between them showed him plenty. George was a bad guy, just like his daughter had tried to convince him and Madelyne from the start.

Realizing this didn't make him feel better. Quite the contrary. Despite everything, he would much rather suffer in silence, knowing George was a good man and kind toward Connie and Madelyne, than have to go through this. If George wasn't the man he pretended to be, then who the hell was he? The unknown was bugging Damon to no end, because that man, like it or not, was in charge of his family now.

As though this wasn't enough worrying on his plate, something else came to mind that really alarmed him. Connie was the first one to express any kind of concern about the man. She was the first one who said anything negative. Of course, Damon had hated the guy from the first second they met, but as everybody pointed out, he was a jealous ex, a bastard who didn't want his ex to be happy.

But Connie was different. She was pure, though a hormonal teenager. It made him super worried, on the verge of paranoid, how she knew George wasn't all that perfect. How did she come to that conclusion? More importantly, what did George do that made her see what no one else could? That made his heart beat a little faster, thinking of all the possibilities, since Connie wasn't normally so distrustful of other people.

If something bad had happened, Connie would have definitely told him. *Wouldn't she?* Considering she knew her father very well, knew what he was capable of, there was a chance that she would omit things. That made him pause.

It was true that Connie and Damon had a decent relationship and were close. In the past, she'd always come to him when she had a problem. And that hadn't changed over the years. Even now, when she'd had that fight with her mother, she'd chosen to seek him out rather than go to her best friend.

All the same, there was a big chance that she would keep quiet about something if she believed she was protecting him. That realization made him see how this might be the first time he couldn't be one hundred percent sure that she'd told him everything she knew about Madelyne's new man. He wondered if his daughter had failed to tell him something for fear of his reaction. Damon gritted his teeth, not liking where his thoughts were going.

She would never keep secrets from me about something this important, he tried to rationalize. *I did have a fit of anger when she told us a boy was bullying her in school.* But she was in fourth grade, and the boy in question liked her.

This time around, Damon hoped that his daughter knew that the situation was completely different. Just in case, Damon planned on speaking with her quite openly about George first thing in the morning. *It's going to be a great break-*

fast topic. He cringed. Sadly, not even that decision eased his mind or helped him relax.

Sighing, Damon returned inside and crashed back to bed. Since he had nothing better to do, *Because sleeping is for losers,* he continued to stress about George. Damon could count on both hands how many encounters he'd had with the man where they'd exchanged a few words. And that was completely by design. Damon didn't want to get friendly with the guy. It felt unnatural to him, especially since he had a gut feeling that the other man was kind of off.

Damon tried to recollect each of those delightful moments spent in his presence, and tried to see if there was something he missed. Maybe George had revealed something he shouldn't have, had a slip of the tongue that Damon missed because he'd been too focused on the fact that the guy was Madelyne's new man, the new love of her life.

To his surprise, a pattern quickly emerged. Damon started to remember how George had always subtly coaxed Madelyne into doing things she didn't want to do. At the time, Damon had thought nothing of it.

Now, looking at the bigger picture, he realized that George had done that a lot. It showed how the man always had to have things his way. His was the last word. That was troubling because it showed a person prone to manipulations.

It was safe to assume that if he liked to always be in control, he did it in all things in his life, big and small. That was problematic because Connie was now part of his life as well, no matter how much Damon hated that fact. And Damon couldn't allow his daughter to live in that manner, since that wasn't a life at all. Not if she couldn't make her own mind up about anything.

Damon couldn't believe it had taken him this long to see it. It was so apparent. His daughter knew something was wrong, had told them he was manipulative, and nobody believed her. Not even him, not completely, since he'd struggled with his own demons at the time. Despite everything, Damon was impressed with his daughter.

Something else came to mind. The way Madelyne spoke of George, the words she used, it was obvious, now, that her new husband played with her emotions to get what he wanted. Damon was dead sure that all these issues with Connie had started because George had said something. Madelyne wouldn't insist on her own. It wasn't in her nature.

Something else was in her nature, though—to make sure everyone around her was happy. If someone had an issue, she took it upon herself to fix it. That wasn't a bad attribute, but it was easily exploitable. And if George was like that with her, Damon was sure he treated other people in the same manner as well.

That made him angry. On one hand, he knew that kind of entitled behavior wasn't so uncommon among wealthy men, who felt it was their prerogative to get all they wanted, the way they wanted it. On the other hand, this was Damon's family George was mistreating, and that was something he couldn't allow. That shit wouldn't slide with Damon. He would defend those he loved.

Luckily, Damon had his daughter on his side, a true ally in combat, so he was certain of his victory. They would destroy that asshole long before he tried to destroy them.

10

MADELYNE

Madelyne tried to put what had happened that morning behind her, but she failed miserably. Not even George's returning home early, bringing her flowers, prevented her from worrying.

Once they retired for the night and George fell asleep, softly snoring, Madelyne rose from their bed and went downstairs to prepare herself some calming tea.

Usually, Connie would send her a message while visiting Damon, wishing her goodnight before going to bed, but she didn't do that now. *You took her phone, remember?* She knew the situation was much more complicated than that.

Of course she couldn't sleep. This whole issue with Connie and George and Damon was seriously taking its toll on her. She was mentally exhausted from all the drama. It drove her insane that they couldn't all get along and leave the past in the past. She couldn't concentrate on her new marriage because her daughter and her ex had teamed up against her.

Why couldn't her daughter and Damon just let her be, let her be happy? Didn't she deserve that right, after all the years she'd spent with Damon, tolerating all of his crap, how he had to go away to some distant foreign country to defend their freedom, his family's safety? Madelyne was sure he didn't have to travel that far and risk his life to do just that. All the same, that wasn't the real problem anymore. She'd left all that behind in search of something better, something that would completely satisfy her on a deeper level.

Are you satisfied? a small voice inside her questioned. *Are you happy?*

Seeing how this was going to be a long night, Madelyne took her cup of steaming herbal tea and went to sit in the living room, curling up in her favorite chair.

Am I happy? she repeated. Madelyne tried to be. She really tried, but it was proving easier said than done, especially since she had something, someone, thwarting her. *Damon.*

Despite her own promise to herself that she would live only in the present moment, she couldn't, especially not after the couple of crazy days she'd had. All the interactions with Connie and Damon were forcing her to look back at the past. She was aware that some of the mess that unfolded was her own doing, consequences of her actions.

She was still racked with guilt and full of regrets about ending her previous marriage. In silent moments like this one, she believed there were things she could have handled better. Sadly, she was only human and couldn't change the past, only learn from her mistakes and try to implement that knowledge in the future.

All the same, she continued to believe it had been in her best interests, Connie's too, to leave Damon. She felt bad that he was this hurt because of it. It was never her intention for their marriage to end the way it had. Looking back, she'd been convinced their marriage would last forever. Of course, she had been too young, too idealistic at the time.

In reality, marital life with a soldier had showed her a different side of that coin. Although she'd hoped she would spend the rest of her life with Damon, she'd had to leave, because at that moment, it was the best thing that she could do, for Connie and herself.

Seeing Damon struggle to get back on his feet, to move on, still in obvious pain, made her question herself, her convictions, and she didn't want to do that. It made her resent him for making her feel bad, when all she was trying to do was make her life better.

She didn't want to feel like this anymore, like she was the bad guy. Madelyne had done that plenty while married to him, and finding the courage to divorce him was the hardest decision she'd made in her entire life. No matter what he thought or if he believed she'd merely given up on him, Madelyne really struggled to come to terms with the fact that she felt that she had to rip her family apart. However, there was no dwelling in the past. Nothing good could come from that. Now was the time for another chapter in her life, a happy future with George.

Madelyne had to find a way to create a bridge between past and present, between Connie and George, and Damon and George. And she didn't have the faintest idea about how to achieve something like that. The trouble with all this was that Damon resisted any kind of chance. He was always like that. Unfortunately, their daughter was proving to be equally stubborn and challenging. No wonder George was angry and frustrated when presented with such resistance.

Naming the problems was just the first step in trying to fix them. Madelyne focused on Connie. She'd made all kinds of complaints regarding George, especially right before the marriage.

She called George a creep a lot, but she had no proof for such an argument, only her *gut feeling*, which in Madelyne's book didn't count for much. Connie was using that to hurt Madelyne, she was sure of that.

Next, Connie complained about how much Madelyne had changed. She really hoped that was the case. Damon, although a good man, had caused her many grievances, and George was trying to make her happy. Although Madelyne did wonder what Connie had meant by it being something else, how she was too blinded to see.

How was Madelyne blinded? She saw her husband for what he was, a hardworking, respectable member of society who tried his best to care for his new family. Connie insisted that George manipulated her, which Madelyne found extremely ridiculous. He would never do such a thing.

It was true that George had a strong personality. He was the owner of his own business, after all, and at times, he liked things to be his way, but that was something else entirely. It wasn't like he was bullying her into agreeing to something she didn't want. When he had better arguments than her, she was inclined to change her opinion. That made her an adult.

Lastly, Connie resented her for giving up their previous house, selling it, and splitting the money with Damon. She didn't see any problem with that. Of course they'd decided to move into George's house after the wedding. That was only logical.

Besides, she was sure Damon could use some extra cash because all of his savings had gone into buying that gym. When George pointed that out, Madelyne was inclined to agree. Of course, Madelyne couldn't say that to Connie, not wanting her opinion of her father to change.

The move was the most logical thing in the world, but she did start to see things from Connie's perspective. All her memories, her childhood, were linked to that house. Of course she felt the loss of it. Madelyne felt it too. Connie's first steps and her first words had been made inside those walls.

She'd laughed and she'd stumbled quite a bit while being chased around while playing with Mom and Dad.

Madelyne understood it was a big deal to lose that connection. She was on the precipice as well. George didn't have that kind of connection with his home, since he'd bought it as a present for her, for their engagement. That had been a sweet and romantic gesture that showed her he was serious about spending the rest of his life with her.

If memory served, she'd only said yes to the move after George presented her with the alternative, telling her she —*they,* she corrected—deserved a fresh start, without all the reminders of Damon. She understood Connie was bothered that Madelyne had given up their home that easily, and at times, especially now, she wondered if she'd made the right decision.

It wouldn't have been the end of the world if George had come to live with them. Perhaps then Connie would have been more agreeable toward the wedding. Eventually, Madelyne had realized it would be better to leave all that behind, not wanting George to feel uncomfortable in any way. Of course she was worried about her husband's needs, but did she at times think more of his needs than of her own? Connie would say yes.

Madelyne and George had had different ideas for their wedding, and in the end, she had been the one who relented. There was a logical explanation for something like that.

George had wanted the ceremony to be held at his restaurant, and Madelyne had wanted an outdoor wedding next to a river or a lake. In other words, someplace romantic. George agreed at first, but then pointed out how they couldn't control the weather if they held it outside, and how they would be spending an unnecessary amount of money on renting a venue, when they already had one for free and could use the extra cash for the honeymoon.

After some thought, she'd decided he had a good point and had gone with his idea, although she'd been saddened that she wouldn't get her dream wedding. George had made it up to her by taking her on two honeymoons.

Having all this in mind, was Connie right? Did Madelyne go with his decisions without considering alternatives? She did act differently while in his presence. She had realized that a couple of days ago and was troubled by it. Why was she doing that? It was like she had no will of her own around him.

Madelyne was captivated by him, but there was more to it. She trusted his judgment more than her own. She'd made a ton of mistakes in her life, and he was so put together. That was evidence enough that he sometimes saw something she failed to see.

Madelyne had never met a man like him before. George was very charming, sophisticated, successful. It was intoxicating to be in his presence. In the past, she'd believed that letting things be his way was for the best, but now she questioned whether she was doing herself a disservice.

Maybe I should speak to him, she thought.

And tell him what, exactly? she thought, with increased uneasiness. Could she tell him how she wanted a wedding do-over? Because she really didn't. Despite Damon's best efforts, it had been a very happy day in her life.

Move someplace else? That would stress her to no end, since she'd barely gotten used to this house. Madelyne really didn't see the point in rocking the boat for such silliness. How about telling him it was for the best to leave her daughter be and not send her to the boarding school?

That last one made her pause. She could picture that conversation in her mind. It made her way too nervous. That fact worried her. What if what her daughter had said had merit? At least in part.

Sure, believe your teenage daughter over your own spouse, she snapped at herself, starting to feel quite exhausted, mentally and physically. If George was highly opinionated and passionate, that was because he cared. He cared for her and Connie, and of course, it troubled him that her daughter acted in such a way toward him, when all he wanted was to tend to and provide for her, love her like a true parent.

This whole mental workout was a waste of time caused by a comment her ex made to make her husband feel bad, make her question everything. *Well, mission accomplished.* She should have known better than to fall for it.

George was her husband now, her rock, and of course, she would lean on him and seek help. That would always be the case, no matter where they lived or where they'd wed in the first place. She was stuck with him, but from now on, she would try to make her opinions known, just so her daughter wouldn't have any objections about it.

With her mind settled, Madelyne was able to return to bed, to her loving husband, and fall asleep.

11

DAMON

I *must be out of my mind,* Damon thought to himself, wiping the steamed mirror so that he could look at himself. After showering, he shaved, which was something he hated doing.

This is crazy. He continued to have only fun thoughts as he tried to make himself presentable. Damon wished he had been drunk when he was agreeing to this. It could explain this madness and make him feel better.

Don't be such a coward.

Unfortunately, Damon had been stone sober as he'd nodded his head like an idiot, which made matters even worse. He was exaggerating, of course, feeling nervous. And Damon didn't do nervous.

While in his regularly scheduled therapy session, Dr. Weldon had spoken about moving on, about the importance of identifying all the stumbling stones in his past so that he could work on them while living in the present. He'd used a lot of technical terms to explain the most basic things, not that Damon minded. It was merely that, at times, it sounded like he was in deep shit.

Basically, what Dr. Weldon had meant was that Damon needed to get on with his life since he'd been kind of stuck since the divorce. Sure, he spent time with his daughter and worked at the boxing gym, but mentally, he was all over the place, torn between his time in the military and the divorce with Madelyne. According to his therapist, to fully move on, Damon couldn't simply sit on his ass feeling sorry for himself. He actually had to do something concrete.

"If you're busy in your current life, and I'm not merely speaking of your work, but filling your time with new experiences, then you won't be able to stress about the past or Madelyne and her new husband," Dr. Weldon had explained, and that made sense to Damon.

Although he wasn't giving up solving the mystery of George Elway, he still felt like the doctor had made a good point. He needed to come to terms with the fact that his marriage had ended.

Damon had looked dubiously at his therapist. Even though he'd agreed with his words, there was something that he found slightly problematic. *"Doc, I don't have time for hobbies. I spend all day at work, and the weekends are reserved for Connie."* He didn't want that to change.

Dr. Weldon had looked at him over his glasses. *"You can always make time for important things. And your mental health should be the most important thing."*

Point well taken, Damon had thought at the time.

"Besides, I wasn't talking about your starting to knit or going to a pottery class."

"Then what?" Damon had asked.

"I believe it is time for you to go on a date with another woman."

Damon had stared at his therapist for a few moments. *What did he just say to me?* His brain had stopped working.

He'd heard what the doctor had said, but failed to understand what he was saying.

"On a what?" he'd asked like an idiot once his brain rebooted.

"On a date," Dr. Weldon had repeated patiently.

Damon had shaken his head. He wasn't easily scared, but the prospect of going out with some random woman, having to spend time with her and talk about nothing important, completely terrified him. *"I can't do that,"* he'd confessed.

Despite the fact that he was currently getting ready for said date, he couldn't even picture himself with another woman, let alone go out with her.

"I wasn't suggesting a romantic involvement or marriage, merely a single date," his therapist had hedged.

Somehow, that hadn't made him feel any better. *"I don't think I'm ready, Doctor,"* Damon had insisted.

"You'll never be ready if you wait around. You need to act," Dr. Weldon had insisted, in return.

Honestly, Damon had expected better advice than that for the money he paid the man. That advice had reminded him of an old saying, *fake it 'til you make it.*

"Where am I going to meet a woman, anyway?" he'd blurted out before he could stop himself.

Damon hadn't been on a date in ages, decades, with someone other than Madelyne, so he hadn't been sure if the rules had changed. The only women he met these days were his former colleagues or clients, and he couldn't date any of them. Not because something was wrong with them, but because he didn't look at them that way. To be perfectly honest, there wasn't a woman he could imagine being interested in. He was still too hung up on Madelyne.

Maybe that's why you need to do this, he'd thought at the time.

As expected, while Damon had been having his internal

monologue, Dr. Weldon had looked at him like he'd asked the most ridiculous question. *"You had to have done this before. I'm sure it will all come back to you."*

"Thanks for your vote of confidence, Doc," Damon had grumbled in return.

"Cheer up, Damon. This just means you're ready for the next stage in life."

He hadn't felt ready then, and he still didn't feel ready to go on this date, despite having made it.

"Thanks, Doc, not helpful."

Damon had thought long and hard about the assignment Dr. Weldon had given him. He probably could have refused to do it, except what would that have accomplished? He wanted to move on from Madelyne. He wanted to put his time in the military behind him. He wanted to be a better man and a better father to Connie.

Damon had wanted to do this right, to take that step that his therapist was pushing him toward. The problem was that he didn't know any women he'd be interested in getting to know better. If Jason had been there, he would probably have advised Damon to ask out the first woman he saw at the boxing gym. But Damon really hadn't wanted to do that. He'd worked hard to create a safe space for women at his gym, and the last thing they needed was him or anyone else to hit on them.

Damon had started to dial Jason, thinking maybe they could go to some bar together to meet women that way. A bar was a neutral place, and he was sure women there would be interested in striking up a conversation with him. But the thought of meeting a woman who hung out in bars was a real turnoff for him, and he'd squashed that idea before he'd even finished dialing.

He'd dialed Alisa instead. Alisa was a good friend, and in the past, she'd tried to set him up with some of her friends, but he'd always found excuses to turn down her offer. But with this assignment, he'd realized Alisa could help him find a woman who might be interested in going out with him. Someone he might find interesting too. So he'd waited nervously for her to answer.

"*Hey, Damon, what's up?*" she'd said.

"*Hey. How was the wedding?*" he'd asked, making small talk like a nervous idiot.

"*It was beautiful. Carrie looked amazing. I think you made a mistake not coming with me. The place was packed with single ladies.*"

Damon had groaned inwardly, looking at the skies. It had felt like even the universe was sending him a message that he needed to man the fuck up and go on a date.

He'd taken a deep breath and said, "*Funny you should say that.*"

"*Oh? Why?*" Alisa had sounded intrigued.

"*Remember when you offered to set me up with a lady friend? Does that offer still stand?*"

"*Lady friend?*" She'd giggled into the phone, clearly amused by his turn of phrase. "What, are we in our seventies now?"

"*Please don't bust my balls. I'm nervous enough asking as it is,*" Damon had pleaded.

"*Okay, okay. Tell me, why the sudden change of heart?*"

He hadn't been sure how to respond to that. *My therapist made me* seemed wrong on so many levels.

"*It's time,*" he'd replied simply.

"*I hear you. Luckily for you, I know the perfect woman.*"

"*Great. Who is she?*"

"*Her name is Johanna, and I'll give her your number so she can call you, and you can set up a date.*"

"*Thanks, Alisa. I really appreciate your doing this for me.*"

"No problem, and since it's you, I don't have to mention that if you're not a perfect gentleman with her, I will kick your ass."

"Lucky me."

They had chatted for a bit longer before disconnecting.

The next day, Johanna had called him, just as Alisa had promised, and they'd set up a date for tonight. Damon was sweating bullets about meeting her. He had no idea what he should talk about or if he should buy her flowers. To him, it was a complete nightmare.

They had agreed to meet at the restaurant, but first, Damon had to make reservations before they could set a time. Johanna had mentioned how she'd heard good things about Nightingale. There was no way in hell he would take her there. That was George's restaurant, and he wasn't about to go on a first date there. Damon had really hoped Johanna liked fish, since the Drunk Trout was the only restaurant he knew of where he could get a reservation on such short notice. Luckily, when he'd called her with the time and place, she'd been agreeable.

Damon cut himself twice during shaving while he'd been recalling everything that had led up to this date. He cursed like a sailor. After shaving, he stood looking in his closet and found nothing to wear. In the end, he settled on a deep blue T-shirt that had no print on it. He made a mental note to go shopping since, apparently, most of his shirts displayed logos of his gym. The Drunk Trout was a casual place, so a nice T-shirt and jeans would be okay.

He stared in the mirror and made sure he looked okay, that there weren't any stains on the shirt or jeans. He didn't want to be embarrassed by something like that. He was nervous enough as it was.

Damon arrived a bit early, not wanting Johanna to wait on him. The hostess had seated him after he gave his name and explained that his date would be arriving soon. As he sat, he played with his napkin and waited for her to arrive.

"Damon?" A woman's voice snapped him from his reverie.

He jumped to his feet immediately. "Johanna?"

"Yes." She smiled.

"It's so nice to meet you," he murmured as they shook hands. He pulled out her chair for her before settling in his own across from her.

Johanna wore a lovely green dress. She was middle height, younger than him, and had lush, all-natural red hair and light blue eyes. She had a dusting of freckles across her nose and cheeks, and her smile was sweet as she looked around the restaurant.

"Interesting place," she commented, looking around at the decor, if one could even call it that—fishing nets and oars were hanging from the walls.

"Despite the name, the food is great."

"So you've been here before?"

"I come here a lot with my daughter."

"Great. I love fish, seafood in general. From the name, I assumed it was a seafood place. Glad to see I was correct."

Damon felt relieved to hear that. "I'm glad you agreed to it. I promise the food really is delicious."

Their waiter appeared, and they stopped speaking for a bit to look at the menus.

After ordering, Damon asked, "How do you know Alisa?" Since that was their connection, it was logical to start there.

"From high school," Johanna provided. "And just so you know, she speaks about you a lot."

No pressure, then. "All lies," he replied with a small smile, taking a sip from his drink. He felt parched.

She made a face as though recollecting something. "It was mostly good."

"Forget what I said. Alisa always speaks the truth."

Johanna laughed at that. "How about you?"

"We served in the Army together."

"Oh, yes, she told me that as well. We were all very worried about her," Johanna replied, looking serious.

It was always hard speaking with civilians about things like this. People could be sympathetic, but they could never fully understand what it meant to survive the hell of war until you did it yourself. That was something Damon didn't wish on anybody.

Once their food arrived, they continued to chat while they ate. Although Johanna was a perfectly nice lady and worked as a veterinarian in a small private clinic, Damon soon discovered there was no real spark between them.

He'd known he wanted to be with Madelyne, to marry her, from the moment he'd met her. He didn't feel like that now with Johanna.

After dinner, they went to see a movie. Damon felt like he was a teenager again. Did people even go to the movies on dates anymore?

"I haven't been to see a movie in ages," Johanna said.

I guess I got my answer. "I went with my daughter, Connie, to the Marvel movie last week, but other than that, it's been a while. I saw the preview for this one and thought I would suggest it."

"I'm glad you did. I looked at the reviews, and it looks like it will be a good one."

Damon understood why Alisa thought they could be a good match. Johanna was fun, smart, and beautiful, but unfortunately there was zero chemistry between them.

The film was a mystery drama that required his full attention to understand what was happening. Still, his mind drifted away. Everything about this reminded him of Madelyne. In the movie, the lead female protagonist trusted the wrong guy and landed herself in a world of problems.

Madelyne was like that as well, gullible. She always saw only the best in people. That was probably one of the reasons she'd stayed married to him for so long despite being unhappy. Considering how Madelyne acted around her new husband, was it possible that George was pulling some kind of con on her?

That was a bit of a reach, since his biggest crimes were wanting to spend time with Connie and talking trash about Damon's car.

Right, the guy is a true evil mastermind.

He guessed Jason was right all along. He was well past jealous and was getting paranoid over nothing.

"I had a good time," he said to Johanna. He hadn't paid that much attention to the movie, but from what he gathered by the ending, it had been a good one.

"Me too," she replied with a small smile. "Want to do this again sometime?"

Damon didn't want to end up like some of his friends, consumed with jealousy. So, although he wasn't that interested in her, he said, "Yes, I'd like that."

12

MADELYNE

Believing how honesty was particularly important in any relationship, and especially in marriage, Madelyne told George how she'd fought with Connie the other day, which resulted in her daughter running away to see Damon. Madelyne felt guilty for keeping something like that from her husband. Unfortunately, it completely backfired on her.

George looked at her with great annoyance. "She did what?" he snapped.

"I spoke with Damon immediately and knew where she was," she reassured him.

"That's not the point," he seethed. "I told you he's a bad influence," he pointed out victoriously.

Madelyne kept quiet, only because she didn't want to agree with him. "I took care of it. I grounded her. It's over," Madelyne replied dismissively, doubting her assessment that she should have been honest with him. This kind of scene was what she had been trying to avoid in the first place.

"I can't believe you kept this from me." He sounded equally as hurt as he was upset.

"I didn't want to worry you."

"Or you didn't want to hear me say 'I told you so'."

"George, please."

He shook his head in a way that suggested he was still stunned and processing things.

"Can we please sit to eat?" she added, needing them to move on from this.

"From now on, I will take care of things, since, clearly, you are not up to the task," he asserted, taking the bowl of mashed potatoes and leaving the kitchen to sit at the dining room table.

Madelyne jerked, startled that he'd said something like that to her. It was hurtful and completely uncalled for. She'd done the right thing by telling him, but now she was regretting it. Madelyne had taken care of her daughter's rebellion and told the truth. How did that make her incompetent?

Apparently, he was still in a bad mood, for whatever reason. To be fair, he wasn't constantly in a bad mood. He continued to take her out for dates. They'd had a lovely time at the movies the other night, but he was prone to snapping at her at times. She hoped he was close to solving whatever was bothering him, so they could fully be happy.

"Madelyne," he called, somewhat impatiently.

"Yes?"

"Could you bring that bottle of wine in here, or do I have to do everything around here by myself?"

"I'll get it."

I guess the honeymoon phase is over.

As she sat down, Connie came and joined them for family dinner as well. Per their agreement, and as a part of her punishment, she had to take part in all family dinners for the duration of her grounding. She wasn't too happy about it, but Damon had convinced her not to make a scene.

That somewhat irked Madelyne, that Damon had to

intervene, but on the other hand, she got what she wanted, so there was no reason to complain. Madelyne only in part felt like a bad parent for forcing her daughter to do something she clearly didn't want to do. All the same, that was the only way she could get her husband and daughter to be in the same place at the same time.

Madelyne hoped that some pleasant chatting and finding common ground would melt her daughter's heart toward her husband. Unfortunately, George had other plans.

"So, Connie, I heard you went on a trip last week, and on a school night, no less. Did you have fun?" George asked conversationally. His smile was just a little bit off while he spoke.

Madelyne groaned inwardly, fully knowing where this was going. *Please, George, don't do this.* Unfortunately, he couldn't hear her thoughts.

"What trip?" Connie replied, clearly confused.

"A trip across town to Shoeshine."

That was the name of Damon's boxing gym.

Connie looked at her as though wanting her to intervene, but Madelyne remained quiet. Her daughter refocused on George.

"I did," she confessed.

"Any particular reason for such an unexpected excursion?"

Connie failed to answer. By now, she realized George already knew everything and was merely playing with her.

"Tell me something else, Connie. Are we to expect you to run away every time you don't agree with something that your mother said to you?"

Madelyne hoped Connie would remain calm and not make a scene. That was the last thing they needed. Madelyne was fed up with drama as it was.

Connie put her silverware down, and Madelyne became

flustered. She couldn't let her daughter explode. That would make matters worse, and George was already in a bad mood.

"Connie knows she made a mistake and accepted being grounded. And she won't do anything like this in the future," Madelyne interjected, trying to calm the tension that arose.

"Really?" George replied, looking between the two of them and raising an eyebrow. "Is that true, Connie?" he insisted.

"Yes, Mr. Elway," Connie forced herself to say.

He sighed, settling. "Good. Though, I have to say, I'm quite disappointed in you. That kind of behavior is unacceptable."

George behaved like a disapproving father, and Madelyne couldn't understand what got into him. Before, he looked like a cool stepfather, but this was over the top and unnecessary.

"I don't know how your parents raised you so far, but in my house, we have strict rules," he announced, snapping Madelyne from her thoughts.

Luckily, her daughter didn't have a smart remark to that.

"Do you have anything to say in your defense?" George demanded, raising his voice.

Madelyne started to question whether he was drunk. "George," Madelyne snapped.

"Yes, Madelyne?" he asked, as though nothing were amiss.

"Can we please just eat? I've had enough of this topic."

"No," he replied, taking her completely by surprise. "This kind of shit happened because you have been too lenient with her."

"But, George—"

He spoke over her: "I need to set some ground rules here so this little act of rebellion does not happen in the future."

"Connie is a smart girl. She knows she can't pull the same stunt again," Madelyne argued.

He looked at her before turning toward Connie. "Connie can speak for herself. She is old enough, right?"

Madelyne could plainly see that Connie wasn't happy with this turn of events, and neither was Madelyne. All she wanted was a nice family dinner, and instead, she'd gotten this.

"Do you understand what you did, young lady? You disrespected me and your mother." George intently waited for Connie's reply.

"I understand, Mr. Elway," she said through her teeth, which only antagonized George further.

"This is my house, Connie, and if you want to continue living in it, you will do as I say."

Madelyne's head snapped to look at her husband. He'd gone too far. Speaking with her daughter about how she misbehaved was one thing. Openly threatening her was something else entirely. Something Madelyne would not tolerate.

"Excuse me?" Madelyne asked her husband. She really didn't feel like fighting, but he was being too harsh.

"You heard me," George said, unrepentant. "If Connie wants to live here, she needs to obey. I'm putting my foot down."

It flashed through her head how he'd thought of her as too incompetent to resolve this situation on her own. Although she realized he only wanted to help, this was taking it too far. He had to see that.

"Okay, and so you know, where my daughter goes, I go." That was Madelyne putting her foot down. It became clear that Madelyne would have to speak with George about his parental skills. "So bear that in mind when making such unnecessary threats."

He leaned toward her. "I am speaking now," he practically growled, giving her a cold, almost murderous look, clearly furious that she'd butted in, challenging him when he was evidently trying to establish some kind of authority.

Although she was certain that he hadn't meant it like that, it sent shivers down her spine. He could be formidable when he wanted to. It rendered her stupid. He'd never behaved in such a way before, and Madelyne couldn't understand what had happened for him to change.

George returned to his previous position, and to her utmost shock, he smiled, as though satisfied he'd accomplished the desired effect.

His next words confirmed as much. "Glad we're on the same page," he said, refocusing on her daughter. "Now, where was I?" George asked rhetorically before hitting the table with his open palm. "As I said before, this is my house, young lady, and you will have to live by my rules. That means no more acting out, no more running away, and especially no arguing or speaking back. I have zero tolerance for that. Understood?"

Connie nodded, glancing at Madelyne every once in a while with a look that was full of accusations.

"I can't hear you, Connie," George pressed.

"Yes, I understand, Mr. Elway."

"Good," he accepted. "By the way, what I said goes for the both of you." He looked at Madelyne sternly before continuing to eat.

I guess the lecture is over. Madelyne could only stare. *What just happened?* When did she land in an episode of *The Twilight Zone*? Because none of what happened made sense to her. She understood that he wanted to establish some kind of authority, show Connie she couldn't do whatever she pleased. Madelyne still thought he went too far.

Maybe I provoked him by meddling? Perhaps she should have let him have his moment. She looked at her daughter, realizing Connie had handled this well.

In return, her daughter's gaze conveyed, *I told you so.*

Madelyne ignored it. This was all for Connie's well-being anyway, she rationalized.

That was why she said, "Of course, George, whatever you say," feeling like she should make amends for before. "We're a family now, after all."

"Glad you think so, honey. Could you reheat this soup? It's tasteless this cold," he complained, pushing his plate away from him.

"Oh?" Madelyn hadn't noticed.

"Connie and I will happily wait until you reheat that for us."

"Certainly." Madelyne gathered the bowl of soup to take it back to the kitchen. "I'll be back in a flash." She tried to make a joke, but the other members of her family completely ignored her, staring at one another with intent.

She could understand that Connie was a bit mad, but that would pass. Soon, she would understand how George acted for her best interests. He cared about them very much.

Making sure the soup was just the right temperature this time around, Madelyne returned to the dining room wearing a big smile on her face. Her family was dining together at last. Her dream had come true.

13

DAMON

"You went on a date without telling me," Jason said incredulously. They were sitting in a bar after work, blowing off some steam.

Damon felt the need to point out how they were not thirteen-year-old girls who shared everything.

"Aw, you wounded me deeply now, my friend, my brother." Jason started to goof around.

Damon decided to roll with it. "Okay, I promise, next time I will take you with me, and you can hold my hand the entire time."

Jason grinned. "There will be a next time, then?"

He got him there. Damon shrugged, taking a sip of his beer. Damon promised himself he would lay off alcohol, but he figured one beer with his best friend wouldn't hurt him. If he stuck to one, it would be fine. *So far, so good.*

"So how was it, the date? I still can't believe you chose to ask Alisa to help you out over me," he added as an afterthought.

"Of course I asked her. You would simply give me the number of one of your ex-girlfriends," Damon deadpanned.

"True," he allowed unapologetically. "So what's she like?" Jason refused to give up.

His friend could at times be like that, act like a dog with a bone. Although to be perfectly fair, it was Damon's fault that they were speaking about this in the first place. He'd mentioned it first, opened his big mouth, and here they were, gossiping.

"It was nice." Damon paused, not really knowing what to say. Johanna was a great woman, easy to talk to. It was just that he felt like she wasn't right for him. There wasn't true chemistry.

Then why did you agree to a second date? he argued with himself. Because he was seriously messed up. And because Dr. Weldon was right, he needed to move on, no matter what. For the time being, his mantra was *fake it 'til you make it*. He did feel slightly guilty for using Johanna in such a way. Damon would do his best and make sure she had a wonderful time on their next date.

"That great, huh?" Jason commented, since Damon failed to finish his sentence.

"Johanna is great," Damon tried again. "She—" He was interrupted by the sound of his phone ringing.

"Saved by the bell," Jason joked as Damon grinned. His friend pointed a finger at him. "This is not over."

His smile grew once he saw his daughter was calling him. "Hey, Con-Con, what's up?"

"Dad," she replied, clearly distressed.

Damon was instantly on high alert. That small word, said in such a tone, made Damon leave the bar instantly. It was a bit noisy inside, and he needed to hear his daughter loud and clear. "What happened?" he demanded.

Jason was right beside him, clearly sensing something was off.

"George was completely weird tonight. It's freaked me out."

"Define weird, honey," he said, feeling angry that the man was causing his daughter stress. He tried to loosen up, so as not to alarm Connie further, but his jaw stayed locked. It took everything in him to rein in his temper.

Jason gestured with his eyebrows, clearly wanting to know what was happening. Damon wanted that as well.

"I don't know, Dad. It was just weird."

"What happened?"

"We were having dinner."

Oh, yeah, Madelyne must have been beside herself for having things her way. Since Connie had been grounded for that little stunt of running away, she was forced to eat with the happy couple. Damon thought that wasn't that big a punishment, but maybe he was wrong.

"And George totally freaked out. He started railing on me about fighting with Mom and coming to see you, and how that wasn't acceptable."

Jason waved, clearly wanting to know who they had to visit to kick some ass, but Damon ignored him, shaking his head. He needed to focus on his daughter. And maybe, just maybe, they would end up going to kick George's ass later.

"Go on," he encouraged.

"He was awful, Dad. He droned on and on about how I was misbehaving and how I needed to understand that I was living in his house and how from now on, I would need to follow his rules. He's a tyrant."

Damon didn't know what kind of macho crap George was pulling, but he didn't like it one bit.

"He said that if I don't start behaving and following his rules, he'll kick me out of the house."

"He said what?" Damon practically growled, not fully

believing what he just heard. *How dare he say something like that,* to threaten his daughter in that way? It was preposterous.

"Yeah, he yelled at Mom, too."

At the moment, Damon couldn't care less about that. Between his ex-wife and daughter, he chose his daughter. She was his priority. So he said, "And what did she do?"

Knowing Madelyne, she gave him hell in return.

"Nothing," Connie surprised him by saying.

"What do you mean nothing?" That didn't sound right. She let that man berate their daughter without saying anything?

"She did nothing, Dad. She just sat there as though nothing was wrong."

Damon frowned. That didn't sound like Madelyne one bit.

"I'm telling you, Dad, it was so weird."

He believed her.

"It was like George scared her into being quiet and accepting his wrath, without her seeming to notice it."

That was a lot of insight from a sixteen-year-old, but that was his Connie. She saw things no one else could.

"Are you okay?" Damon had enough presence of mind to ask. "He didn't hurt you?"

If he did, that would be the end of him. After Damon was done with him, no one would even find his body. And by the expression Jason was throwing his way, he was on board.

"No," Connie reassured him. "But I'm scared, Dad. He's completely changed."

Or he finally started to show his true face.

"I don't want to stay in this house anymore," she confessed, which was completely understandable.

Damon didn't give a shit why George had started to

behave all domineering all of a sudden. He had zero tolerance for that shit, and he would make sure the other man
received that message from him loud and clear.

"Calm down, honey, and try not to think about it
anymore," Damon advised. "I'll take care of it." He was so
going to take care of this. That asshole would think twice
before yelling at his daughter again, let alone threatening
her.

"What are you going to do?" she asked, somewhat
alarmed.

Damon realized she was scared, and that he would make
matters worse by going to the house she lived in and busting
George's face.

That was his first thought. *Guilty.* At the same time, she
acted as though he would kill the guy. Damon wouldn't do
that. *Yet.* Although that crossed his mind too.

"First, I'll speak to your mother." *Then I'll think about
breaking that asshole's jaw for speaking to you in such a manner.*

"Mom won't do a thing," Connie argued. "No matter what
happens, she acts as though everything is all right."

"Let me handle her, all right?"

"Okay." Connie trusted him, and he took pride in that.

"That woman has completely lost her goddamn mind,"
Damon snapped, to no one in particular, already dialing her
number.

"Shit, man," was Jason's only comment.

Damon looked at his friend. "You still think I'm a jealous
asshole?"

He knew something was off, and this was his proof.
However, that wasn't the most alarming part of this story.
Madelyne was. *What is wrong with that woman?* he asked
himself, and not for the first time.

"I wondered when I would be hearing from you," Madelyne said instead of a proper greeting, and that irked him to no end. That tone of voice, as though fully knowing he was about to overreact when nothing was amiss, was infuriating.

"Well, of course I called. When our daughter is upset, I take notice."

"Oh, please, she is just seeking attention." She tried to brush it off.

Damon reminded himself that he needed to stay calm, not go ballistic. This needed to be resolved in a mature, calm manner.

"So what you're saying is that she made it up that George was aggressive toward her during dinner," he said all in one breath, seething.

"Aggressive?" she asked, surprised. "Not at all."

"What happened, then?" Damon demanded, curious to hear her take on events. "Why did Connie decide to call me if it was a normal dinner?" he pressed for good measure.

"Because she overreacted, like always, and now you're doing the same. Honestly, Damon, I expect this kind of behavior from our teenage daughter, not from you," she chastised.

Damon was holding the phone so tightly it was a wonder it didn't break. "You haven't answered my question." Damon refused to be derailed.

Madelyne sighed. "George felt the need to speak with her about her behavior, and I agreed. She can't go running around doing whatever she pleases, whenever she pleases. Children need boundaries."

Damon agreed, but the delivery was what interested him the most. "Okay, but did he threaten her?"

She laughed, although Damon could detect some nervousness underneath it.

"He didn't say he would kick her out if she didn't start living by his rules?"

"He didn't mean it like that," she instantly defended. "As I told you before, Connie is obviously overreacting like always, and you're enabling her."

Damon didn't fail to notice how she did her best not to answer his questions directly. That made him suspicious. Madelyne was trying to sweep something under the rug, and he would discover what.

"Connie tells a very different story, and between the two of you, I'm inclined to believe her."

"I'm not surprised that you have that attitude."

Damon ignored that, pressing on. "I won't tolerate that kind of abuse toward my daughter."

"Excuse me? Abuse? You're out of line, Damon," she snapped.

"I don't think so. I know my daughter, and when she gets this upset, I know she has every right to be."

"She has you wrapped around her finger."

"I'm not the one wrapped around someone's finger."

"What's that supposed to mean?" she demanded, although Damon thought it was pretty clear.

"It means that you're defending that asshole, too blind to see what is really going on. But I'm warning you, Madelyne, if your poor choice in men results in exposing my daughter to any kind of danger, I will make sure you lose custody."

To his utmost surprise, Madelyne didn't say anything to that, just hung up, which in return spoke volumes.

"Fuck." He was decidedly frustrated. He couldn't understand his ex-wife one bit. It was true that she was always a bit stubborn, but this was far past that. It was like she was completely brainwashed. That made him exceedingly worried, since it wouldn't be the first time.

"Man, what happened?" Jason demanded.

In all this madness, Damon forgot his best friend was still

beside him. "I have no fucking idea, Jason, but I think I just started another war."

"Well, shit, let's gear up, then."

Damon's sentiment exactly.

14

MADELYNE

Madelyne fumed, wondering when all this madness surrounding her would end. Naturally, she'd expected that Connie would go and complain to Damon as soon as they finished dinner. However, what she didn't expect was her ex threatening her in such a manner.

She barely slept that night, thinking of his words. The next day was no better.

How dare he! she fumed, trying to finish one of her illustrations. So far, she hadn't made significant progress, since her mind kept drifting away. Damon had really crossed the line this time.

He'd accused her of abuse. *Abuse?* Her? That was well past cruel, especially from him.

Connie was a teenager. It was expected that she would make a scene. On the other hand, it was expected of Damon to behave like an adult, a parent, and explain to Connie how living and abiding by rules was a completely normal thing to do. They were human beings, after all, not animals.

Unfortunately, this proved how Damon had completely

lost his mind. He'd actually threatened to take Connie away from her. *I will make sure you lose custody* had been his precise words.

George was right; at times, not even she could understand how she'd stayed married to Damon for so long. First of all, how dare he suggest she would ever do anything that could potentially harm Connie? She was her mother, after all. All she wanted for her daughter was to be happy.

And it was ridiculous suggesting that George would ever do something to Connie that could harm her. He cared about her, worried about her future and what type of person she would turn into, like a true parent should.

Second of all, when Damon had been acting all fifty shades of crazy, drinking and having anger management issues, she hadn't been threatening to take Connie away from him. Madelyne had been full of understanding back then, even agreed on joint custody, although she had a bunch of reasons that she should be the sole guardian of her daughter.

The reason she hadn't done that was that she didn't want to take Connie's father away from her. Plus, she figured Damon would try to heal himself that much harder if he had reason to. Had she been a bad mother back then, as well?

She always gave him the benefit of the doubt, and he couldn't do the same for her, instantly imagining the worst. This was the thanks she got for agreeing to shared custody. He was now trying to steal Connie from her. *That bastard.*

Connie's place was beside her, not with him. Perhaps George was right; perhaps she should fight for full custody. She abandoned that thought immediately. Madelyne was done fighting. It was her time to be happy with her family, George and Connie.

Thinking of Connie, she glanced at the time and instantly jumped from her seat. Being so wrapped up inside her head, she completely forgot it was her turn to pick Connie up from school. She and Damon took turns, since he'd pleaded to be able to spend more time with her, not solely on the weekends. So she'd granted him chauffeur duty two times a week. And not even that was enough for him, apparently. Now he wanted it all.

Madelyne advised herself not to get carried away. Damon had probably said all that in anger. It was an empty threat and nothing else. Putting some shoes and a coat on, she ran out of the house and drove to Connie's school. Her daughter had hinted how she would like a car of her own, but at the moment, Madelyne wasn't sure if she could afford one, and she didn't want to ask George for money. On second thought, maybe she could talk with him about it. *We shall see.* Connie needed to prove herself mature enough before Madelyne decided anything.

Reaching the school's parking lot, Madelyne was relieved she'd managed to get there on time. Turning off the engine, she patiently waited for her daughter to arrive as her mind once again drifted away from the here and now, and she started stressing over Damon all over again.

Perhaps she'd never stopped. Which was a depressing thought.

To be perfectly fair, a part of her believed George did perhaps cross the line. However, it was completely unacceptable for Damon to try to get involved, as he had before. George should be an authority figure to Connie, like Damon was. George was no stranger, after all, but her stepfather.

Connie should have known better than to go running to Damon, figuratively speaking, this time around, telling on George for something he had every right to do.

All the same, Madelyne couldn't place all the blame on her rebellious daughter. She was still a child, after all, although she liked to think differently. The real problem around here was the grownups, specifically Damon and

George, who acted like two alpha males fighting for dominance. *Men,* she thought in exasperation. *Can't live with them; can't live without them.*

A slam of the door snapped her from her musings. While she was someplace else inside her head, Connie got in and shut the door with unnecessary force. She was still angry. Also, what Madelyne found irritating was the fact that her daughter chose to sit in the backseat.

"Hello, honey," she greeted, starting the car, and received nothing in return. Madelyne sighed, feeling troubled. She didn't have the faintest idea of how to resolve this issue. No matter what she did, no matter what she said, someone was always angry at her.

She felt like a chauffeur with her daughter all the way in the back, but she didn't comment on it. Madelyne had had enough of drama. *I want one peaceful day in my life,* she prayed.

"I was thinking I'd make a roast for dinner, what do you say?" Madelyne offered, hoping that would coax Connie to at least acknowledge her in some way. That had been her favorite meal since she was a little girl.

Connie shrugged in return. Madelyne took that as a good sign.

"Roast it is," Madelyne replied somewhat cheerfully. Was she trying too hard, perhaps? But she needed her daughter to start speaking to her again. "Do you mind if we drop by the store on our way home? I forgot to buy some things."

More accurately put, *all things,* since this roast was something that she'd just now thought of while trying to appease her daughter. Although George was right when saying that Connie needed firmer boundaries, Madelyne couldn't bear to see her daughter this unhappy. A favorite meal was the least she could do for her while she was grounded.

Connie shrugged again, and Madelyne smiled. Connie

would come around. She wasn't that unreasonable, not like her father was.

After such a lively conversation they shared in the car, Madelyne was quite surprised to see her daughter choose to come in the store with her instead of waiting in the car. For that, Madelyne put her favorite candy bar in the cart. Connie added another one, and Madelyne pretended not to see it. It was true that she remained quiet, but she was there, which was something, a step in the right direction.

To be frank, Madelyne wasn't even sure why her daughter was angry at her to begin with, but she knew better than to ask such questions. *Connie will calm down. She always does.*

Naturally, they ended up buying more stuff than they needed for dinner, or in general.

Returning home, Madelyne spotted an unfamiliar car parked in their driveway. "Do you know whose car that is?" she asked her daughter.

"No idea."

I guess we'll find out. Not giving that much thought, she added, "Could you please help me with the bags?"

Connie sighed heavily, but did as asked.

"Thank you, honey."

Entering, they could hear loud laughter coming from the living room.

"Remember that look on Mickey's face when you told him to fuck off?" an unfamiliar voice asked.

"He shat himself," George replied in the same manner, and another round of laughter erupted.

What the hell?

"I'm sure Dunwoody will act in the same manner," the man provided.

Madelyne, with Connie in tow, still carrying those bags, walked into the living room, wanting to see what was going on.

Madelyne encountered an unknown young man freely sprawled on her couch. By her assessment, he was probably in his twenties, very skinny, with curly brown hair and dressed in clothes that looked slept in. He nervously righted himself upon spotting her.

The two men instantly stopped talking and laughing once she entered the room, learning they were not alone anymore. They must have arrived while she was away, picking Connie up.

"Hello," Madelyne said politely with a small smile, eyeing the guest.

The kid waved at her in return.

She turned toward her husband. "George, you didn't tell me we would be having company." There was no reprimand in her voice, only pure curiosity. Who was this young man to her husband?

"This is my friend," George said in a strange tone while pointing at the young man.

Madelyne spotted a half-empty bottle of whiskey on the table. By their expression, it was safe to assume they'd started drinking someplace else pretty early in the day, then come here to continue partying. Madelyne disapproved.

"Does your friend have a name?" she asked good-naturedly, trying to make a joke, since her husband had failed to make introductions.

George frowned, looking at her with disapproval, as though she'd done something wrong, which surprised her, to say the least. *He's drunk*, she reminded herself.

"What's with all the questions?" he snapped at her. "Can't you see we have a special guest?"

That confounded her. What just happened?

"Stop embarrassing me in front of my friend, and instead of standing there interrogating us, go to the kitchen and prepare us something to eat," he demanded. "We're starving."

The other man cheered, since food had been mentioned.

Madelyne was about to excuse herself, not wanting to get into the middle of this, when Connie moved to stand in front of her.

"Don't you dare speak to my mother like that," she shouted, fully enraged. "She isn't your servant."

Madelyne could only stare as George rose from his seat. He wavered slightly, as though not completely stable on his feet. "You!" He pointed his finger at Connie, clearly losing it. "If you don't shut the fuck up right this instant, I will beat the living shit out of you, you spoiled brat," he threatened, shocking everyone present.

Madelyne dropped her bags full of groceries.

15

DAMON

"What happened then?" Damon prompted, trying hard to remain calm as he listened to his daughter's latest interaction with George. He'd complained about Dr. Weldon, yet that man was worth every cent. He was the sole reason Damon wasn't hunting George down, that bastard, and killing him on the spot.

"Mom sent me to my room," she replied.

Damon could hear in her voice how upset she was, which in turn made him even more upset. Up to that moment, he wouldn't have believed that was humanly possible.

Is she crying? Something inside him broke, and he saw red.

"And I don't know what happened afterward, or if Mom said something to them," she continued, unaware of the storm that was raging inside him. "All I know is that at some point, George and his friend left, drove off."

Drove off a cliff, I hope, Damon thought.

Damon knew it wasn't very Christian of him, but he hoped they would wrap themselves around some tree or hit a wall, since they were driving drunk. George deserved nothing less after speaking to Connie in such a manner.

To say he was extremely furious would be the understatement of the century. This was what he was afraid of, that he wouldn't be there to protect his family. This was why he'd tried to reason with Madelyne when she'd tried to brush him off and pretend everything was all right the last time George did something inappropriate. The hell it was all right. George was completely unhinged.

Damon could feel his stomach cramping every time his daughter called him on the phone, because lately, she never called to share what was new, what she learned, experienced in school, for example. It was always to complain about how stressful it was living inside that house with George and Madelyne. Unfortunately, this latest scene wasn't just stressful, it was downright scary.

I will break both his hands, each bone in his palms, for threatening her. As he continued to speak with Connie, he left the gym and jogged toward his car.

He must have slammed the door upon entering because the car protested, and his daughter inquired, "Dad, where are you?"

"I'm coming over," he replied matter-of-factly. What else would he be doing in such a moment? He was getting his daughter out of that house, and so help anyone who tried to stand in his way.

"Dad, I don't think that's wise, and besides, George isn't here."

That confounded him. "What do you mean, Con-Con?"

"I don't want you to get hurt, Dad."

His heart shattered in a million pieces. His daughter was worried about him in a situation where *she* should let him be worried about *her*. He felt desperate, powerless.

"Connie, you're not safe there." And then he added,

seeing how pointless this was, "Look, I don't give a shit about George. I need to see you."

He didn't give her an opportunity to protest, and hung up. Damon drove like his life depended on it, then forced himself to calm down, drive a little bit slower, since he wanted to get there in one piece. Connie wasn't in immediate danger, he reasoned.

As he parked in the driveway of the Elway residence, Connie burst from the front door, running toward him, and Damon caught her midway.

"Dad." She buried her face into him as he held her tightly.

To his chagrin, Madelyne came out to see him as well. "I can't talk to you right now," he said harshly. He needed to take care of his daughter first.

"Are you okay, Con-Con?" He started scanning her just in case she'd failed to tell him some detail, not wanting to worry him. She appeared unharmed, at least physically.

"I'm fine, Dad. I'm glad you're here."

"Of course."

"Damon, can we talk?" Madelyne insisted.

Damon saw red, seeing his ex-wife so calm, so undisturbed.

"Oh, we'll talk all right," he snapped in return, holding his daughter tightly.

"Not here. Can we please go inside?"

"What? Have something to hide?" Damon wanted all the neighborhood to hear what was happening inside this house.

"Dad, let's go inside," Connie pleaded.

Grudgingly, he allowed her to usher him inside. They ended up in the kitchen.

"Connie, leave your father and me to have a conversation."

"No way. My daughter stays with me," Damon insisted.

Luckily, Madelyne didn't press, although she didn't look pleased. He didn't give a shit about that.

"Care to explain what the hell happened today?" Damon demanded without preamble.

"I understand you're upset. We all are. However, this is no time for overreacting," Madelyne said calmly.

"I disagree. This is the perfect time for calling things by their true name." He raised his voice ever so slightly. Damon felt like breaking something, preferably George's face. Luckily, that coward wasn't around at the moment. "Your husband is a cretin and a bully."

"Damon, please," Madelyne countered, looking at Connie, as though not liking that their daughter was hearing this.

Damon believed that she should, since this was all happening because of her. Besides, Damon was convinced that his daughter already knew that George was a cretin.

"That bastard threatened to beat the living shit out of her." He pointed at Connie. "And you act like all is fine. *Fine* is not even in the same zip code at the moment." He couldn't believe he had to say that out loud. Was he the only one seeing how serious this situation really was?

"He was drunk. He didn't mean it," Madelyne said, speaking in her usual manner, trying to brush everything off.

Damon had been drunk many times in the past, more than he would like to admit, but he'd never threatened to harm a member of his family. He said as much.

Madelyne pressed her lips together before replying, "You're blowing things out of proportion." She changed tactics, shifting the focus from her husband to him.

Damon wasn't that easily manipulated. "I don't care. I'm going to the CPS right now to file a complaint. I will demand a full investigation from them."

Let them deal with that asshole if he was too sensitive and

always overreacting. Even his daughter believed he shouldn't be physically involved, fearing he would do more harm than good, so this was a nice compromise.

He had to admit, if only to himself, that Connie was right. If Damon went and found that asshole right now, someone would end up dead. And it wouldn't be him. At the same time, he couldn't sit around and do nothing. He feared for his daughter's safety.

"CPS?" Madelyne exclaimed. "You wouldn't."

"I most definitely will, because this went too far, Madelyne," Damon replied instantly. "George is clearly a bully, if not something worse, and I won't tolerate it anymore." He couldn't. His daughter's life was at stake. If Damon remained quiet, then George would believe he could do whatever he pleased, say whatever he pleased, and that was far from the truth.

"Please don't do this, Damon," Madelyne pleaded somewhat desperately. "You know how they are. They'll take her away."

"Well, maybe they should."

Madelyne frowned. "So you would much rather have our daughter taken away from all of us than let me handle this?" she challenged.

Damon couldn't let her persuade him. Contacting Child Protective Services was the right call.

"This is your doing, Madelyne," he insisted. He couldn't let her place the blame on him when she was the one who'd created this mess in the first place. "How could you just stand by and do nothing, say nothing, while someone was threatening our daughter?"

That was the part that astounded him the most, not that George was an asshole, but that Madelyne allowed it. What happened to this woman? He had been married to her for twenty years, and he'd never seen her behave like this.

Are you sure? He had a moment of doubt. Damon had been away a lot, and when he had been home, he hadn't been in a good place. Maybe he'd missed things. Something else occurred to him that made him uneasy. Maybe she'd spoken with others about Damon in the same manner, defended him to the end when he was having hard times.

"This is all a misunderstanding," she insisted. "Please, Damon, please don't overreact. They'll take our daughter away if you go there and complain."

"So you think they have reason to do so?"

"No, of course not," she instantly objected. "They won't understand, but you do."

What was that supposed to mean? "Madelyne, this was not okay."

"I know, I know." She spoke with haste, as though fearing something might happen before she finished. "George was drunk, and you're right, it was not okay for him to say all that, but please give him a chance to do better. I know he'll feel awful after sobering up. He isn't the man you think he is. He's good and kind, and he made a mistake while drunk." She was pouring her heart out, but Damon was still on the fence.

He shook his head. "It's great that you have such a high opinion of your husband, but I have to think of Connie."

"I'm thinking of Connie as well," Madelyne tried to reassure him. "I promise you, this will never happen again."

Damon looked dubiously at her before looking at his daughter. Every once in a while, as he argued with Madelyne, he looked at his daughter to see what was on her mind.

"Can you really promise something like that?" Damon challenged.

"Yes, of course I can. Just please, Damon, don't overreact now and do something that you'll regret forever."

Was he overreacting, like she continued to claim? "What do you think, Con-Con?" Damon asked his daughter.

She hadn't participated in the argument, solemnly listening to her parents trying to come up with the best solution to this mess.

"I think you should listen to Mom," Connie replied eventually, taking him by surprise.

"Are you sure?"

She nodded.

Damon exhaled loudly. "Fine," he snapped, feeling like he was making the biggest mistake ever.

Madelyne visibly sagged with relief.

Damon continued speaking. He needed her to understand that this was far from a done deal. "I won't do anything now, but hear me loud and clear, Madelyne. This is the last time. This is his last chance to clean up his act," Damon stressed.

"Of course, and thank you, Damon."

Don't thank me yet, he thought. There was still a decent chance that he would change his mind, since all of this felt wrong.

Was his jealousy spiking up again? He couldn't rule that out. *You are so fucked, Damon.* "Whatever," he countered.

"I'll give you two some privacy," Madelyne said, leaving the kitchen.

He gestured for Connie, and she returned to his embrace. He managed to take his first deep breath with her safely nestled into his arms. *Maybe we should make a run for it?* He banished that thought.

"Are you really okay with this?" He needed to make sure. "Say the word, and I'll go right now to report that asshole."

"Yes, I'm okay." She tried to reassure him, but her tone was off.

He leaned back so he could look her in the face. "You don't have to protect your mother. You are the one I am concerned about."

"This is the right thing to do," she countered.

Damon was torn and eventually relented. Connie was a smart girl, and he needed to trust that.

"Call me if you change your mind," he stressed.

"Promise."

Leaving was hard on Damon. He felt like he was abandoning his family all over again.

"Love you, Dad."

There was a big lump in his throat, but he tried to talk anyway. "Love you too, kid."

Damon didn't see Madelyne again, and maybe that was for the best. He felt like bashing his head against the steering wheel. This was maddening. He couldn't be sure he'd made the right decision. More to the point, the instant he'd agreed to let this slide, he started worrying that he should have acted differently. Had he let Madelyne guilt him into agreeing to something he knew deep down was the wrong call?

Feeling restless, Damon started the car and without conscious thought drove to Nightingale, George's restaurant. He needed to speak with that asshole as well, and convey his displeasure. It would go something like this. *Ever threaten to beat the living shit out of my daughter again, and I will not just beat you up, I will kill you, asshole*, or something like that.

Unfortunately for Damon, and luckily for George, the bastard wasn't there, which he found surprising. According to Connie, he spent all his time there.

Seeing no other way, since Damon was still pretty electrified, he called Jason.

"What's up, bro?"

"Have time for one quick drink?" Maybe Jason could provide better insight.

"Always."

16

MADELYNE

M adelyne sat on Connie's bed, waiting for her daughter to finish saying goodbye to her father. This was a nightmare, and she hoped she'd managed to successfully persuade Damon not to do anything stupid.

She couldn't even imagine how George would react if he learned that Damon had come here, threatening to take Connie away. She knew the instant Damon left, hearing his car engine roaring to life, then vanishing into the distance. *He will calm down,* she tried to reassure herself.

A few moments later, Connie appeared at the door. She didn't look that surprised to see Madelyne waiting for her. They had to talk. She was a bit surprised that Connie had sided with her.

Madelyne wanted to point out how the chaos was created each time Connie complained to her father. That was bad, because Damon was proving that he wasn't capable of acting reasonable, making matters worse. However, at the same time, Madelyne couldn't forbid her daughter from speaking with her father.

"If you have something to say, then say it," Connie said after a small pause.

Madelyne ignored the attitude. "We need to deal with this internally, since this has nothing to do with your father," Madelyne started.

Connie looked at her incredulously. "Are you actually criticizing me for speaking with Dad?"

"It's none of his business what happens inside this house." Madelyne remained adamant. "Besides, can't you see how he reacts every time you tell him anything?"

He would use any excuse to make a scene. Connie needed to see that. Unfortunately, she hadn't. Her next words confirmed as much.

"Do you hear yourself?" she snapped. "How can you remain so calm? Blame me or Dad when George is the one who's causing problems."

"That's not fair."

"It's the truth," her daughter argued.

It was a simplification of things. "Well, I guess I don't see things black and white like you and your father do."

"Obviously," Connie countered, making a face.

That irked Madelyne. She was such a daddy's girl.

"Connie, George was drunk, and things like that happen. There's no need to overreact," Madelyne pointed out.

Connie shook her head. "Instead of berating me about this, about something that wasn't my fault, how about you go and try to reason with your husband? He was the one who was saying all that shit and was out of line. I was fucking defending you, if you recall!"

"Connie, language, please."

"Mom, how can't you see that you are choosing him over me?"

"You provoked him," Madelyne pointed out, which was

true. If she'd only gone to her room and let the men have their moment of indulgence, none of this would have happened.

"Excuse me? Were you even there?" Connie exclaimed in utter disbelief. "I was defending you! He treated you like trash."

"Hardly." Once again, her daughter proved that she was just a child.

Madelyne patted the bed beside her, and Connie reluctantly sat down. She tried again to make her daughter understand.

"As you could clearly see, George was obviously drunk and boasting. Some men act like that while intoxicated, especially around friends. That was all talk until you provoked him."

"Mom, you're not being fair. This wasn't my fault," she whined.

"And I'm not saying it is, but all the same, you don't have to worry about this anymore. He didn't mean it."

"Yeah, right," Connie blurted out.

Madelyne felt hurt that her daughter had such a poor opinion of her husband. And the only reason she was like that, not wanting to give George a chance and judging him too harshly, was because of Damon.

"What's that supposed to mean?"

Connie looked at her as though she had been clear, but replied, "He looked pretty sure to me."

Madelyne was scandalized. "George would never harm you," she insisted.

"Mom, he jumped from his seat and fisted his hands. He was dead serious," Connie insisted, getting upset all over again.

Like always, she was highly exaggerating. George had

barely stood up, and Madelyne had sent Connie to her room before things could escalate further. Madelyne had apologized to George and his friend for her daughter's behavior, and that was that. Shortly afterward, they'd left on some business. Or so Madelyne believed. She was extremely worried that they'd left the house in such a state and drove away.

"He was drunk. Don't put much stock into what he said or did," Madelyne insisted, getting tired of having to say the same thing over and over again because her daughter failed to see reason.

"Mom, I haven't felt safe around George from the beginning," Connie argued.

Madelyne was now sure her daughter was using this unfortunate incident to justify her previous behavior toward George. Madelyne couldn't allow that. "You're exaggerating and being unreasonably unfair toward George."

Connie scoffed in return. "And if you weren't so wrapped around his finger, you wouldn't think like that. You would see what was really going on."

Madelyne had heard this story before. Damon had said the very same thing, which was proof they were united in their hate toward George.

"Connie—" Madelyne wanted to reason with her calmly, yet her daughter wouldn't let her.

"You only care about yourself. Even now, you refuse to see the truth. You're selfish," her daughter accused.

That hurt a great deal. "You're not fair. The only thing I care about is creating a life for us."

"The only thing you care about is yourself. You desperately want to preserve this illusion of a happy marriage, and you ignore everything else."

"That's enough, Connie," Madelyne snapped. "I can understand you're upset, but you're crossing the line. I'm still your mother, and you cannot speak to me in such a manner."

Connie shook her head, refusing to back down. "If I'm wrong, then how come you did absolutely nothing to defend me? Wasn't I your daughter in those moments, too?"

"Connie, he was drunk. You're judging him too harshly."

If George had been stone sober when saying all that, Madelyne would without a doubt object.

Are you sure? She dismissed that niggling voice as unhelpful.

Connie raised her hand. "You know what, I'm tired, Mom. I want to sleep."

Madelyne wanted to stay and make her daughter see that this was being blown out of proportion, but Connie was done talking. Which meant she'd lain down, turning away from her and throwing a comforter over her head. She was like that. She shut everyone out when she felt like she'd had enough. Madelyne sighed.

"I love you, Connie, and will always think of your best interests," Madelyne said, needing for her daughter to know that.

"Turn off the lights on the way out," came the muffled reply from her daughter.

Madelyne stood up and slowly walked out of the room. This troubled her deeply. She felt cursed, since no matter what she did, what she said, she always ended up being the bad guy.

She blamed George for drinking. He didn't have to bring his friend here. On the other hand, he was only human and needed a moment to relax and loosen up. *He works so hard,* she reminded herself.

Returning downstairs, she went to the living room to clean up the mess she'd created when she'd dropped all those grocery bags. *Silly woman,* she chastised. She didn't want George to see any of it once he returned home. He wasn't pleased by the turn of events one bit.

Madelyne couldn't stop thinking of Connie's words. Her daughter's insight disturbed her more than the whole scene with George. He was drunk and would feel sorry about what he did once he sobered up, and for her, that was that.

On the other hand, her daughter's opinion was going to plague her for a long time. Did her daughter really see her in such a light? Like she'd lost herself in this marriage? Connie described her as pathetic, being too blinded by her own desires to see what was really going on.

And what was going on? A few fights here and there? Well, all families fought. That wasn't the end of the world.

Madelyne didn't like Connie seeing her like that. Her daughter had such a poor opinion of her, and it hurt. Madelyne didn't deserve it, when all she wanted was for all of them to be happy.

How to make Connie see this was all for her own good? *What are you going to do about it?* What could she do?

Madelyne and her daughter didn't see eye to eye regarding some things, and Damon certainly contributed to that in a big way.

While she pondered on everything, she cleaned the entire living room, vacuumed, and sprayed some air freshener to remove the smell of alcohol from the air. Afterward, she proceeded to the kitchen to finally start making dinner.

Checking the time, she stopped. *Should I even bother?* she asked herself, since it was already half-past eight. Connie certainly wouldn't eat, choosing to go to bed early, and she hadn't heard from George since he'd left that afternoon. *He knows how to fend for himself.*

Perhaps she should follow her daughter's example and call it a night. This day needed to end, and the sooner, the better. Tomorrow would be a fresh start, and all of them would be able to look at things much better with a fresh set of eyes.

Suddenly feeling quite tired, mentally and physically, Madelyne put all the ingredients for the roast back in the refrigerator. She would make it tomorrow, and maybe one of Connie's favorite desserts, too, to cheer her up a bit. Madelyne was blessed that her daughter wasn't dieting like many girls her age, so she could eat whatever she pleased.

Turning the lights off and moving toward the stairs, her phone started ringing. She had no idea where she'd put it in all the madness.

Madelyne started to turn around, trying to locate the sound. Her phone was in the living room under the table. *How the hell did it end up there?* Not that it mattered at the moment. Checking the screen, Madelyne had mixed feelings seeing her husband was calling her.

She answered in haste. She was sure he was calling to apologize for his behavior.

"Hello, Madelyne."

"Hi, George."

"Am I interrupting you?"

"No, of course not. Did you need something?"

"Please come to the restaurant to have dinner with me. It's been a while since we dined just the two of us."

Madelyne was glad he sounded much better, as though he wasn't drunk at all. He probably went to his restaurant to sober up. Madelyne knew that he had a fully functioning bathroom in his office, with a shower. Also, he kept spare clothes if he needed to clean up on the spot.

"I'd like that," she replied.

"Good, see you in half an hour."

Madelyne changed clothes in haste, making herself presentable before rushing off. She reasoned that this would be a perfect opportunity to smooth things over with him so they could put this unfortunate incident behind them.

Families fought, after all, and they needed to move past

this and finally start living like one big, happy family. This was obviously a step in the right direction.

17

DAMON

Damon went to meet Jason in a pretty foul mood. The urge to break something, the rage, didn't go away. He was convinced he'd made a terrible mistake in agreeing to the status quo.

This was a serious matter, and he'd given up too easily, basically caved in. And why, one might ask? *Because I'm an idiot.* Mainly because he'd been accused so many times in the past of being unreasonable, and he needed to avoid that epithet at all costs. With all the other issues he had to deal with, he honestly didn't need another one.

Although he'd threatened Madelyne with CPS, he was scared of what they would find if they came knocking on his door. He couldn't lose Connie. That would be the end of him.

His daughter believed that this was the right call, for him to do nothing. At the same time, she was only sixteen. It was his job to protect her, not the other way around.

What did I just do? he questioned. *Nothing, asshole.* If he were a real man, he would hunt that bastard down and beat him so soundly that he would need to eat through a straw for the rest of his life. There was a small catch with that plan.

After doing something like that, he wouldn't be allowed to see Connie. So he had to rein in his temper and find another way to deal with George.

Damon ordered a beer, sitting at the bar, and a few minutes later, Jason joined him. His best friend looked at him once and knew something had gone terribly wrong.

Jason's words confirmed as much. "What's wrong?"

"Everything," Damon grumbled in return, taking a deep pull from his beer bottle. Then he realized what he was doing. This whole mess had started because George was drunk. *I am nothing like George.* Regardless, he put his beer down. "Fuck."

"Tell me about it. I just finished my shift, and at times, I wonder why I even bother. But then, I have to come here and babysit your crazy ass."

Jason was the one who'd stopped him from doing something stupid the last time George had crossed the line. His brother had his back. He was the smarter one between the two of them. He advocated caution and thinking before acting, choosing the right move, as Damon just acted.

"Speaking of crazy, George crossed the line again." Damon jumped right to it without a preamble. "And I'm seriously thinking about hiring a private investigator."

"I know a couple of guys who served who now work as PIs. What for?"

"I need to know where this guy came from, if he has any priors, because even though he presents himself as a restaurant owner, he acts like a brute." Damon was convinced that Madelyne's husband had a criminal background. His gut feeling was telling him that.

Jason looked at him as though not really knowing how to say something, which was comical despite the gravity of the situation, since Jason didn't do subtle.

"Just say what's on your mind," Damon snapped.

"Look, man, I know you got upset when George laid down the law for Connie. Perhaps he made a mistake, but shit, man, we all have kids and understand how rules are especially important at that age. So don't go overboard. Connie is a teenager. It's her job to complain, but Madelyne is there, and she will monitor the situation."

Yeah, right. "I'm not overreacting, Jason. That bastard threatened Connie."

"What? When?"

"Today. Apparently, Connie intervened on behalf of Madelyne when George spoke too harshly, and he got all up in her face, threatening to beat the living shit out of her... and Madelyne did nothing." Unintentionally, Damon fisted his hands. He was still too riled up.

"You're joking," Jason replied, astounded.

"Yeah, I'm joking. This is my joking face," Damon replied dryly, taking another sip of his drink. "So now I reckon it's better to come here and speak with you, find some way to take him down other than hunting him down and ripping his throat out through his asshole."

Jason patted him on the back. "Shit, man, I'm sorry for doubting you. I really thought he was a stand-up guy."

"Wouldn't like that either. It would be a better option, though," Damon replied.

Jason nodded. "What a cocksucker. That is some serious shit, man. You were right all along."

Somehow, hearing Jason admit that didn't make him feel better.

"So what happened?"

Damon told him everything. How George had been drunk when Madelyne and Connie had gotten home from the store, and had been boasting in front of some asshole. He had been rude to Madelyne, and Connie had jumped to her defense. "He didn't like that, apparently."

"Then what happened?"

"There was an altercation, and Connie went to her room. After she called and told me what happened, I went over there."

"Of course you did."

"The bastard wasn't there. He took off."

"Lucky son of a bitch."

Damon's sentiment exactly.

"How's Connie?"

Damon shrugged. "I don't know. Fine, I guess."

"And Madelyne?"

Damon looked at his friend. "What do you think?" he asked rhetorically. "In complete denial."

Jason cursed. "What did you do?"

"After having a conversation with Madelyne, where she accused me of constantly overreacting, I managed to calm down. I mean, I wanted to strangle the guy with my bare hands, but Connie helped me calm down."

"Good girl."

Unfortunately, his daughter knew him well. As though he needed more things to feel guilty about. It was defeating that his daughter knew he was capable of completely losing his temper and harming someone to protect her. Although in this case, Damon would feel completely justifiable in breaking George's jaw, he still didn't want Connie to be subjected to something like that.

"I feel so powerless. I mean, the guy is a bastard. He threatened my daughter, but Madelyne made it seem as though I'm the bad guy. She messed with my head."

"Women can do that to you."

"I dropped by his restaurant, but he wasn't there." Which was a blessing in disguise. Although Damon rationalized that he would have had a friendly chat with the guy, there was no telling what he would actually have done after seeing the bastard.

"Who was the other guy?" Jason asked curiously.

Damon looked at his friend incredulously. "That is your follow-up question after everything I told you? Who was the kid with him?"

"Well, yeah."

"Who the fuck cares?"

Jason shrugged. "I feel like there's more to this story than meets the eye."

"What are you talking about?" Damon wasn't drunk, nor was his friend, but Jason wasn't making any sense to him.

"It seems to me that George got all defensive when Madelyne started inquiring about that kid," Jason pointed out.

Damon shrugged. "Maybe," he allowed. "All the same, that's not the real issue here."

"Of course not."

The issue was how George only pretended to be a good guy when in reality he was a bully and potentially abusive, which was something Damon couldn't allow. He wasn't going to stand by as that asshole did what he pleased to his wife and child. *Ex-wife.*

There was something else Damon couldn't fully understand. Considering Madelyne's past, how could she justify George's behavior without raising her voice? Of course, he didn't share that with his friend.

"I don't know what to do, Jason. Did I make a mistake by not acting?" he asked, deeply troubled.

Jason thought about it before replying, "If violence isn't the answer, then what can you do? I mean, he is Connie's stepfather. Doesn't he have some rights?"

Damon scoffed. "He doesn't have the right to threaten my daughter, no matter who he is."

"Point well taken," Jason agreed. "But is there something you can do other than taking them to court?"

Could Damon file for full custody? He probably could, although he would try to avoid doing something like that. Despite everything, he knew Madelyne was a good mother, and the custody battle had been no picnic the first time around. He didn't want Connie to have to go through that again. It went without saying that he would do it if he decided that was the only way to protect his daughter.

"I was thinking about complaining to CPS, but Madelyne begged me to give George another chance." *And like an idiot, I caved in.* He made a face while saying that name, as though he'd just eaten shit.

Damon really was an idiot for letting his ex change his mind. He shouldn't care about her marriage, only for his daughter. *Connie agreed with Madelyne,* he reminded himself.

Jason shook his head. "I don't know, man. To me, that sounds like a promising idea."

"Yeah?"

"Hell yeah. You have to think of your daughter."

"She and Madelyne asked me to wait," Damon explained.

Jason frowned. "I say why wait? It's obvious this George character is spiraling. Who says that in another day or two, or a week, he won't try something worse?" Jason pointed out. "God forbid, of course."

Despite his growing uneasiness, Damon said, "Madelyne promised this won't happen again, insisted it was all just a big misunderstanding."

His friend made a face. "And you believed her?"

That was a good question, and Damon hesitated to answer. For the first time in his life, he wasn't sure. Up until today, he'd trusted Madelyne immensely regarding the well-being of their daughter, but he couldn't help noticing that she was changing because of that man, and not for the better. At times, it looked like she cared more about herself and that marriage than she did about their daughter. This was troubling on a whole different level.

"I don't know, man, I'm trying to," he replied honestly.

"That right there says it all," Jason insisted.

Damon finished his beer, still on the fence. It was hard to decide what was right when his instincts were all screwed up thanks to that damned war. Having Jason around providing his two cents helped, though.

"So you think I should go and report this?"

The big problem that instantly presented itself was that Damon had no proof. He'd threatened Madelyne with it, and it had worked, but if she stopped to think, she would see how his plan was flawed. All he learned, he'd heard from Connie. Since he couldn't be sure Madelyne would back her up, there was a big chance that she would continue defending her husband, and then it would be Connie's word against Madelyne's. He didn't want to subject his daughter to that.

"I do," Jason replied, snapping him from his reverie, "but considering your situation, perhaps it would be prudent to call your lawyer first and hear his take on all of this," Jason advised, as though reading his mind.

Damon was worried that he would have zero legal grounds for reporting George to CPS. He was a jealous ex-husband, after all, and George was an upstanding member of society.

Yeah, right.

"That's sound advice. Thanks, man."

"No problem. And if that doesn't work, I keep a shovel in my truck." His meaning was clear.

"Good to know."

They didn't talk much after that.

After finishing another beer, Damon went home. Since it was late, Damon decided to wait for the morning to call his lawyer, Nick Atkinson. Nick was a twin brother of Damon's Army brother Dan. He was a good man who'd helped him with his divorce.

Unfortunately, Nick was swamped all morning with court duties and couldn't get back in touch with him. It looked like Damon would have to deal with this George menace on his own. It was strange, but he preferred it that way.

18

MADELYNE

George felt so bad for drinking the other day and making such a scene that he decided to take Madelyne out on a proper date. Not that he said anything. She still hadn't had a chance to speak with him about Connie and what had happened, but she knew what was in his heart. He was a good man.

For that reason, Madelyne decided to give him some time, wait for the dust to settle before broaching that subject. She didn't want to embarrass him. That was why she kept quiet when he'd called her for dinner the other night, after the incident. They'd shared a fine meal and returned home. And George had acted like nothing bad had happened, which she took as a clear sign that he was struggling with his previous behavior.

However, once he suggested for them to spend the entire day together without Connie, she knew that was a good opportunity to talk. Connie and George had stayed out of each other's hair for the last couple of days, so Madelyne decided it was time to make peace. They were a family, after all.

George really put in an effort. It reminded her of the time they first dated. He spared no expense to make her feel how cherished and appreciated she really was.

"Are you warm enough?" he asked as they exited the car to have a walk by the lake.

After a meal, they drove to the shore to enjoy some nice weather and sun. It was very romantic there at sunset. Definitely one of Madelyne's favorite spots.

"Yes, I am, thank you."

"I have an extra jacket packed in the car. Do you want me to take it with us?" he offered as he took a blanket from the trunk.

"No need," she reassured him.

They walked for a bit until George found a perfect spot to spread the blanket on the ground. Madelyne enjoyed the view as George offered her some strawberries that he'd packed for dessert.

It was a perfect day, and Madelyne thanked God for it.

"Did you like that place we went to for lunch today?" George asked, looking at her with interest, as though really wanting to hear her opinion.

"It was lovely, and the food was delicious."

He nodded. "A friend of mine suggested it to me."

"I'm glad we went there."

Usually, since George owned a restaurant, they shared their meals there. It was a special kind of treat when Madelyne got a chance to dine someplace else. And the French restaurant he'd taken her to today was amazing. It was breathtaking. Madelyne really liked it, but she didn't want to share her complete awe with her husband, not wanting to insult him or his place. Madelyne loved Nightingale, but this was something else entirely.

He was putting forth an effort to make up for the other day, and she didn't want to ruin the mood. *You aren't the one he needs to make up to,* a part of her pointed out, and she shoved that thought away. *He will make amends to Connie as well.* She was sure of that.

"I promise I'll take you there again as soon as I can," he said generously, and Madelyne smiled in return. "Another strawberry?"

"No, thank you." She was quite full.

Despite her best efforts to stay in the moment and enjoy this magical day with her husband, something kept nagging at her. Something was wrong, so she really started analyzing her husband—the way he spoke, acted, gesticulated, and reacted to things.

She couldn't help noticing that there was a pattern in his behavior. He really liked having things his way, and he was relentless in achieving just that.

And that wasn't all. After a fight, he always acted like this. He was more attentive, more gentle, more romantic, as though trying to draw her back in when she was pulling back.

Is he afraid of losing me?

"How about we fly to Vegas for the weekend?" he asked, snapping her from her thoughts.

"Hmm?" she asked, since she wasn't that closely paying attention. Her mind was preoccupied.

"Let's get away for the weekend, just the two of us," he repeated. "Would you like that?"

"That sounds fun," she replied vaguely.

George wrapped a shawl around her shoulders, making sure she didn't get a chill.

Madelyne had to admit he was very charming all day long, caring, tending to her every need, but all the same, her daughter's voice kept haunting her, disturbing her peace. *He has you wrapped around his finger.*

Was that true? Was Madelyne being manipulated? She

realized she couldn't be sure, and that troubled her, caused slight panic.

It didn't help when George said, "It's a shame we can't stay longer, because of Connie. She has school." He sighed. Why did he say that, and in such a tone of voice?

Suddenly, in all her paranoia and confusion, Madelyne started to see manipulation in everything he said and did. *Will he now suggest boarding school?* she wondered.

"The weekend is plenty," she reassured him.

He offered a seductive smile in return. "Wouldn't it be better if we could just fly away and stay at least ten days?"

"The holidays are around the corner," she pointed out.

"Why wait?" he insisted. "Can you picture us on some sandy beach, with fruity cocktails in our hands and salt in our hair?"

He did describe heaven to her. "We both have our jobs to think about. We can't pack our bags and leave."

It was great to daydream, but they both had responsibilities.

"True," he said, with a deep exhale. "By the way, have you gone through that list I sent you regarding boarding schools for Connie?"

For some reason, what he said irked her to no end. "No, I haven't. I've been busy," she replied honestly. Madelyne felt like she didn't have a moment to herself. Something was always happening that required her attention. When she wasn't working, she was putting out fires created by her daughter, husband, or ex-husband. It was exhausting.

I honestly need a vacation.

"Okay, no rush," he reassured her. "When you get a chance, check it out. I believe there are some fine schools out there."

Madelyne didn't have doubts about that. There was only

one problem with it. "I don't want to send my daughter to boarding school," she told him.

"Read about their amazing achievements and school programs, then make a decision," George insisted.

She nodded, not wanting to discuss that now. On the other hand, speaking of Connie, there was something she wanted to talk about, but didn't know how to begin.

Although she'd defended George in front of her daughter and Damon, Madelyne was aware that his behavior was far from perfect. Although her daughter had some doubts, Madelyne wasn't an idiot. She was very much aware of the situation. She had to speak with him about it so he wouldn't make the same mistake in the future. There was a need inside her to especially emphasize how something like threatening Connie, in any context, was unacceptable.

Madelyne understood that George was in a strange position. Connie didn't like him, didn't want to get to know him, and that frustrated him. In his desire to establish some kind of authority, he'd lost his way. That was understandable, considering he was not a parent. So it was Madelyne's job to show him the way.

Here we go. "George?"

"Yes, my love?"

Biting her lower lip, Madelyne said, "I want to speak with you about what happened the other day with Connie." She made a small pause before continuing, "You really scared her, threatening her, and that was not okay."

Madelyne tried her best to tread gently about such a delicate subject. She was aware that she needed to be clear when advising what he could and couldn't do regarding her daughter. That was the most important thing, since it was proven that Damon was prone to overreacting. She couldn't allow her ex to use something like this against them in the future. She knew he would.

Next time, Madelyne was certain Damon would call the CPS, and then all hell would break loose, and they would lose Connie. *Next time?* She caught herself, which made her uneasy. There couldn't be a next time, not when her ex was this unreasonable.

"What?" George asked, frowning.

"You cannot speak to Connie like that in the future. I hope you understand that."

George looked at her with such fury, such disdain, that Madelyne felt the urge to run away. She stayed put as chills went down her spine. He'd managed to frighten her to the core with a single glance.

Apparently, it was hard for him to hear that, she instantly rationalized. She was prepared to apologize, when he smiled, taking her by surprise anew.

"Please, my love, can we talk about that later? I don't want to ruin our special evening with family business."

"Okay," she instantly agreed.

Perhaps she'd made a mistake by wanting to speak with him now. This was no time for serious discussions.

"Care for another strawberry?" he offered gallantly.

"No, thank you."

Once the sun set, it started to get chilly, and they decided it was time to depart. George folded the blanket as Madelyne picked up all the rest of the stuff, and they slowly walked back toward the car.

The car ride home was a quiet one at first. Madelyne was preoccupied with her thoughts, and apparently, so was George. Neither one of them mentioned Connie again.

At some point, George started chatting about simple things, and Madelyne tried to pay attention and contribute, although it was a bit difficult. She realized she was glad they didn't have to talk about Connie. More to the point, she was relieved he didn't restart the subject, and that worried her the most.

Madelyne felt wary after that look. George had looked downright scary in those moments. And now she didn't want to antagonize him further. Had she been too harsh with him? She loved her husband deeply and never wanted him to feel like there was a difference between him and her daughter. But he hadn't looked insulted or troubled in those moments, she argued with herself.

George had looked disappointed in her when she'd said all that to him, and she couldn't understand why. Was it because she was ruining the mood with such a serious subject, or was there something else? She couldn't know for sure.

One question presented itself in the midst of all this. What did it say about her that she was cowering like this, always choosing the easy way out instead of opposing her husband? She didn't dare look for an answer, fearing she wouldn't like it one bit.

19

DAMON

How did that make him feel?

When Damon first started therapy, he deeply hated that question... and now? He really despised it even more. Not that he would ever share something like that with Dr. Weldon. His therapist already dealt with a lot regarding his client. Besides, at times, Damon believed the therapist already knew that.

"I felt torn," Damon replied eventually. "I don't know if I made the right decision."

After that scene with George, fighting the urge not to kill the guy, Damon had decided he needed an emergency session with his therapist because he was feeling like he was losing his mind. *More than usual* was implied. And talking with Jason about it wasn't enough. He needed professional help.

"That is only natural, considering the situation you found yourself in. Everyone would feel exactly the same," Dr. Weldon reassured him.

Damon leaned on the couch. "That doesn't make me feel any better."

"It's not supposed to make you feel better, but it is supposed to provide insight," he explained.

"Great."

"What would make you feel better?" Dr. Weldon asked next, taking him by surprise.

Damon really gave it some thought. There was a lot, actually. He focused on the issue at hand. "It would make me feel better if Madelyne realized she has a problem," he replied eventually. George was her weak spot.

"Interesting."

Damon didn't know how to take that. Was his reply interesting in a good or in a bad way? He didn't have time to stress about that further, since Dr. Weldon added, "Please explain."

Damon took a deep breath before speaking. He was buying time while gathering his thoughts. "It's obvious to me, and Connie, how George is only pretending to be a good guy, and she refuses to see the truth."

"Is it important to you that your daughter is siding with you?"

"Well, yes."

"Interesting."

"I mean, I would much rather be wrong about this, because then they would be happy. Unfortunately, I know I'm right."

Dr. Weldon wrote something down before proceeding. "Do you believe that Madelyne could benefit from going to therapy?"

"Absolutely," Damon replied, without a thought, "but she would never go for it."

That was the tragedy of it all. Damon couldn't imagine suggesting something like that to her, knowing how she would react. Madelyne would go ballistic. That was part of the reason he kept his going to therapy to himself, knowing that she would judge him for it.

"Why do you say that?" Dr. Weldon seemed intrigued.

"Let's just say she had an unpleasant experience that shaped, if not cemented, her opinion about this entire process."

"Really? I'm sorry to hear that. Do you mind my asking what happened?"

"A therapist betrayed her trust," Damon summarized.

That was the first time Damon had ever seen his therapist showing emotions. He was disturbed by this, maybe even angry. "That's a shame. I'm afraid our profession isn't different from others in that regard. We harbor some bad apples as well."

"Oh, Doc, you don't know the half of it." Damon believed this was worse than that.

Since he felt like he wouldn't be betraying Madelyne's trust since he was in therapy, he decided to share her story and tell Dr. Weldon everything about what had happened to his ex. If he knew the whole story, then he was more likely to understand and be able to help Damon solve this whole mess.

"We were married for a few years when Madelyne finally decided to share something big with me."

Damon always felt like something was pressing on Madelyne, but he never probed, believing she would tell him everything herself in due time when she felt ready, and she did. Quite unexpectedly, one day, Madelyne completely opened up to him, and while shedding a lot of tears, she managed to share her darkest secret with him. Her traumatic experience with the therapist was a part of it as well.

While Madelyne was a child, she had been abused emotionally, physically, and sexually by her own father. It was the unholy trifecta of abuse. Living with her father had always been hard, but it had gotten worse once her mother passed away. To this day, Madelyne didn't know if her mother committed suicide in desperation to escape that existence, or if she was killed by her husband. Damon knew that plagued her a great deal, even later in life.

Once that tragedy occurred, a loss of the only person who genuinely loved her and shielded her from harm, her mother, the monster of her father had expected that she would take onto herself all of her mother's responsibilities, including sharing his bed.

Madelyne had lived in that hell for years, and it was only understandable that her father, if you could even call something like that *a father*, had managed to completely break her, shape her into the perfect woman for himself. Madelyne had become docile and compliant like her father wanted her to be. To the outside world, she had been a normal, happy girl, if a bit shy or withdrawn.

The problems had really started in high school, where she had been constantly exposed to a different kind of living and diverse kinds of families, loving families. Her classmates had had fathers who didn't beat them when they messed dinner up. Her mental state had rapidly started to deteriorate, forced to live like that, and Madelyne had stopped eating, at times hadn't been able to get out of bed.

Collapsing in class, she had been rushed to the hospital, where she'd been diagnosed with depression. Her doctor, worried, had suggested to her father that Madelyne should start going to therapy. Of course, her father had been against it, but he'd had to relent, keeping the pretense of a loving father.

Of course, he'd beat the living shit out of her for humiliating him like that once she'd been discharged from the hospital. Before her first therapy session, he'd threatened her that he would kill her if she said the wrong thing to that 'quack'.

Madelyne had gone, and she'd pretended everything was

fine. She'd chosen her words carefully each time she'd seen her therapist. Living under her father's thumb and having to lie each week had only caused additional stress. It went without saying that she hadn't gotten any better.

Her psychiatrist, Dr. Mathew Papinski, had soon realized that she was hiding something from him.

"It's very important to say that the guy was a Freudian," Damon mentioned. "It took him months to help Madelyne speak with him more freely."

She had been afraid of her father, but her desire to tell someone her story eventually overpowered everything else, and with great shame and through tears, Madelyne had told Dr. Papinski everything, had opened up her soul to him, and had finally accused her father of abusing her.

Damon could only imagine what strength it took her to tell someone out loud how she'd lost her virginity to her father. She'd trusted Dr. Papinski immensely, since he had been there to help her. And he'd completely betrayed her trust. He'd chalked everything up to her having an Electra fantasy. Said she'd wanted to sleep with her father, and when he hadn't fulfilled that fantasy, she'd decided to take revenge, and made up this disgusting story. He'd told her she should feel ashamed for behaving like that.

As far as Damon was concerned, Dr. Papinski was also a monster like her father, only a different kind. That event had completely broken her, and also in a way, it had helped her as well. She'd feared her father's retribution, since she had been sure Dr. Papinski would tell him everything, so she'd run away and had never looked back.

She'd supported herself by drawing illustrations, portraits of people on the streets. That was how Damon had met her. She'd drawn him and hadn't charged him. He'd loved her from the first moment she smiled at him.

Eventually, her father had remarried and had had

another family, and he'd tried to reach out to her, but Madelyne had refused to have anything to do with him. In a way, that was what had brought Damon and Madelyne closer together. They had both basically been orphans, all alone in the world.

Suffice to say, when Madelyne had finally opened her heart to Damon completely and told him everything, he had been ready to go to her father and shove a granite fist down his throat. He'd thought that a bullet to his head would have been too easy. A grenade would have torn him apart, which might have been more appropriate, considering what he'd done to his daughter. He'd wanted that man obliterated.

Damon was a father as well and couldn't understand how that man could have done something like that to his own daughter. He was no father, but a monster. Even today, Damon got all worked up thinking about it. Damon had tried his best to be a good husband to Madelyne, keep her from harm, protect her. He couldn't help feeling like he'd failed miserably.

Considering her experience, it was no wonder Madelyne didn't trust therapists. That man who'd persuaded her to trust him had completely betrayed her, blamed her for everything. In a way, he'd acted no better than her father.

Did I do the same to her? Did I betray and hurt her? Damon came to a dreadful realization. Although he'd never meant to hurt her, it was quite possible that he had. *Not like those men before*, his whole being rebelled, *but close*. Damon was nothing like those men. Damon loved Madelyne with all his heart. In a way, there was a possibility he still did. *You hurt her all the same.* He would find a way to make it up to her, he vowed.

He wasn't the only one feeling rattled. Dr. Weldon was aghast at what Damon had shared with him. "Could you repeat the name of that psychiatrist?"

"Dr. Papinski, first name Mathew, I believe."

The doctor wrote it down. "Do you have any knowledge of whether Madelyne ever reported him for malpractice?"

"I know she didn't." After she'd run away, she'd buried everything that had happened deep inside and refused to look back.

He shook his head. "I'll make sure he loses his license. This is outrageous."

As far as Damon was concerned, both men needed to be punished, because both had sinned greatly toward Madelyne.

"Thank you, Doc. I really appreciate it."

"I consider it my duty."

Damon could understand that. He had followed that same principle his whole life. It was his duty to protect his family. *And you already failed.*

He couldn't turn back time, but he could make sure that bastard of a husband of hers didn't hurt her. More than he already had, of course. It was clear to him now how her previous life had managed to affect her judgment. Unfortunately, as it turned out, Madelyne was susceptible to certain patterns of behavior. Dr. Weldon tried to explain that to him at length. With his help, Damon figured everything out.

Her father had been abusive toward her, and now George was trying to do the same. Since that was something she was used to, she failed to rebel.

"I never laid a finger on her, let alone our daughter," Damon said, struggling to understand.

"I believe you," Dr. Weldon reassured him. "It is possible that ending a marriage with you, where she experienced different kinds of relationships, made her regress."

"Why?"

"Pain can do that to a person."

Damon frowned. It was his fault after all. "I think she needs therapy," he said, somewhat defeated.

"I agree."

"But, Doctor." Damon started to speak in a rush, as though feeling he was running out of time. This knowledge filled him with panic, urgency. He had to fix this now, or everything would be lost. "How can I make her see that she needs therapy?" *And badly.*

"How? Very delicately."

20

MADELYNE

Despite her reluctance and wariness, Madelyne knew she had to speak with George about Connie, about his behavior toward her. Although he was trying to establish some kind of relationship and show authority, he was going at it from the wrong angle.

Madelyne knew he was remorseful by the way he was acting as of late. Connie refused to leave her room other than to go to school, so George focused all his attention on Madelyne. He was very attentive toward her, so full of care. That didn't sway her. She knew she had to say something so that he would understand how much his little stunt and his lack of judgment had hurt their little family.

For the sake of the family, peace, and happiness, Madelyne finished her latest sketch and went in search of George. He had returned earlier today. Madelyne knew he would have to go in again tonight, so it was imperative to speak with him while he was at the house. She found him in the living room, reading the paper. He was probably the only one around here who still did that. Most of the people their age preferred to read news online. George said he liked the feel of paper in his hands.

She sat beside him on the couch. Noticing her, George put the paper away. He took her hand to kiss her knuckles. "Productive day, my dear?" he inquired.

Hardly. "Very," she replied with a smile, although that was far from the truth. All the while she worked, she couldn't stop stressing about the dynamics of their family.

Her smile was short-lived, knowing what she had to do. Madelyne dreaded his reaction, and George noticed.

"Is something the matter?" He looked genuinely concerned. That helped her center, find her voice.

"I feel like we should finally talk about what happened the other day."

He frowned ever so slightly. "The other day?"

His question took her by surprise. How could he not know what she was talking about?

"When you were drunk and threatened Connie." She really tried to extract the reprimand from her voice, but wasn't one hundred percent successful.

He looked surprised to hear something like that. His next words confirmed as much. "Me threatening..." And then he appeared as though he remembered.

To Madelyne's utmost surprise, he started laughing. Madelyne made a face. She couldn't see how this was a laughing matter. When Damon had heard what happened, he'd come here to shout at her, and now George was laughing in her face.

"George?" Madelyne said in disbelief.

Clearly sensing that they weren't on the same page, he stopped, but remained in high spirits. "Was this the reason you've looked so worried the last couple of days?" he asked.

What a detective, she thought and instantly felt guilty for it. "Yes," she replied simply, and then added, "How could I not? It was incredibly stressful for all of us."

"Oh, my Lord, I apologize for laughing just now, but it's rather funny from my perspective."

"It wasn't funny to me or to Connie." Madelyne stood her ground.

George nodded before replying, "I can see that now. For future reference, you really shouldn't take anything I say while drunk seriously. I tend to turn into this macho man who likes to argue." He looked away for a moment. "It's embarrassing, really."

Madelyne didn't expect this conversation to head in this direction. She didn't know what to expect, but his trying to laugh everything away was certainly not it.

"I'm sorry if my behavior alarmed you, but I assure you, you have zero reasons to be concerned. I got carried away the other day. I drank one too many."

"I could see that."

"I'll speak with Connie and apologize. The last thing I want is for her to be scared of me." It was obvious that possibility troubled him, and Madelyne felt relieved.

"Thank you," Madelyne replied.

As it turned out, she'd worried for no reason. George would take care of everything.

"Is that all?"

Madelyne nodded, and they kissed.

She felt as though a big load of worries was lifted from her chest. As it turned out, she had been right all along. They had all overreacted for nothing, and by *them*, she meant Damon and her daughter.

They were more than ready to point a finger at George and declare him a bad guy. Now, the air was cleared, and all would return to normal. With this settled, Damon couldn't threaten her with CPS anymore, which was what troubled her the most.

While she patted herself on the back for remaining cool and trusting her husband when all the people around her lost their heads, she remembered one small detail from yesterday. The way George had looked at her as they sat by the lake. The last time she'd tried to speak with him about this, he... *He looked like Father right before he would...* She stopped herself right there. It was always a bad idea to think about the past. The past needed to be buried. It needed to stay where it belonged, in the past, undisturbed. Nothing good could come from thinking about it, speaking of it. Madelyne knew that all too well.

It made her realize that a part of her remained uncertain. Despite George's explanation, his reassurance, she remained on guard. She couldn't explain how or why, but she felt like George was hiding something from her. First of all, he had that mysterious drinking buddy. Then he tended to end his phone calls each time she would enter the room, as though he didn't want her to hear his conversations. *Does he have a mistress?*

No, she instantly rebelled. *Don't be an idiot.* George loved her. He showed her that every day. It was just that Connie's paranoia was rubbing off on her.

"I'll leave you to your paper, then," she said, giving him another kiss before leaving the room. She knew how much he liked to read the news about stocks.

Feeling better, she went to share this good news with Connie. Connie chose to spend most of her time in her room since her altercation with George. Madelyne didn't want her daughter to feel like she needed to confine herself. This was her house as well, after all. At least she was speaking with Madelyne, although it appeared her daughter was constantly angry at her these days.

At times, she missed those days when Connie was five or six years old and loved to spend her days by Madelyne's side. She could spend hours with her in Madelyne's study, simply watching her draw. It had filled her heart with joy when Connie expressed the desire to draw as well. Over the years, growing older, Connie had lost interest even though she had quite a talent.

"Connie?" Madelyne knocked, and no one answered, so she slowly walked in. Connie had her headphones on, typing on her laptop. No wonder she didn't hear her. Figuring she was doing her homework, Madelyne was prepared to leave, and her daughter spotted her.

"Mom," she said, taking her headphones off.

"Homework?" Madelyne pointed at the screen.

Connie shook her head. "Not really," she replied vaguely.

"Can we talk?"

Connie was reluctant, but nodded.

So far, so good, Madelyne joked to herself. "Well, actually, I only wanted to let you know I spoke with George." Connie rolled her eyes, but Madelyne ignored that. "As I tried to tell you before, he feels bad for frightening you."

"I bet," Connie commented in return, clearly not believing her.

Madelyne sighed. "Connie, it's not like that. It was all a misunderstanding."

"What you're saying is that it meant something different to him when he said he would beat the shit out of me?" Connie argued in return.

"He explained everything to me," she reassured her. "And believe me, he is torn apart about speaking to you in such a manner. I'm sure he'll come to speak with you and apologize."

"I don't want to speak to him."

"Please, Connie, give him a chance to make it up to you," Madelyne pleaded.

"Fine, I'll hear what he has to say."

Despite her words, it was obvious that she had no interest in what he had to say one bit, and wouldn't believe him. That saddened Madelyne. At the same time, there was a chance that Connie would change her mind once she saw how sincere he was, how sorry.

"Could you please try not to give him a hard time?"

Connie looked at her incredulously. Her face was saying, *Are you kidding me*? Madelyne ignored that as well.

"Please," she stressed.

Connie shook her head. "Fine, Mom."

"But?" Madelyne inquired, knowing one was coming her way.

"I'm sure he meant what he said the other day and is now telling you what you want to hear."

Madelyne was pained that her daughter had such a poor opinion of him. Although she had to be fair, that opinion was partly formed thanks to Damon and partly thanks to George's poor judgment.

And sadly, it was on Madelyne to remedy all that. "You're not being fair. He isn't the villain you constantly try to paint him to be."

Connie jumped from the bed, clearly irked by this conversation. "You know what? I'll prove it to you."

"Prove to me what, exactly?" Madelyne wasn't following.

"I'll find real proof that will force you to see the truth."

Madelyne folded her hands. "And what truth might that be?"

"George is rotten to the core and is only playing with you."

She locked her jaw. Once again, her daughter was

crossing the line. "What are you talking about? What proof? Connie, you're being ridiculous."

And once again, she could thank Damon for these kinds of reactions. Here she was, trying to share some good news with her daughter, and instead of feeling relieved that all was water under the bridge, Connie was stubbornly holding on to something that wasn't true. It wasn't only ridiculous, it was maddening.

Connie scoffed, grabbing her backpack and her phone. "You know what, this conversation is ridiculous."

Madelyne honestly felt exasperated. She didn't even know how to speak with her daughter anymore without it turning into a fight.

Connie started to move toward the door, but Madelyne got in her way. "Where do you think you're going?"

Her daughter was technically still grounded, although Madelyne had returned the phone to her after her weekend at her dad's, realizing her daughter needed it for more than socializing. It was a curse of the modern age. Their whole lives were packed in that one small device.

"I would like to go for a little walk, or is fresh air also forbidden to me?"

There was so much attitude in that line that Madelyne felt like screaming while forbidding her to leave that room.

Madelyne didn't do that, of course. Taking a deep breath, she moved to the side. "Return before dinner."

Connie nodded while putting her backpack on and taking off.

Teenagers, Madelyne thought with exasperation. As she returned downstairs, she continued to feel baffled about how her sharing some good news had turned into another argument. Not finding an answer, she could only shake her head.

Teenagers, she thought again. Living with one was hard

work. Madelyne hoped that her daughter would soon outgrow this phase.

George wasn't in the living room anymore, so she called out for him, "George?"

There was no answer. Was it possible he'd left without letting her know?

"In the bathroom," came a muffled reply.

Madelyne returned upstairs only to find her husband in their bedroom, freshly showered and shaved.

"Leaving already?"

"My business meeting was moved up," he explained, buttoning a clean shirt.

Madelyne thought he looked dashing in the shirt she'd bought him. It matched his eyes.

"Will you be returning home for dinner?"

He thought about it. "I'll eat at the restaurant," he reassured her.

"All right."

He kissed her goodbye before departing, and just like that, Madelyne was left all alone. Having the whole house at her disposal with nothing to do but think about all the things swirling inside her head, she didn't like it one bit.

I should make lasagna. Connie would certainly be hungry after her walk.

21

DAMON

"Hey, Madelyne. What's up? How's life? Good, good. You know, I've been thinking. I realized, while speaking with a doctor I've been seeing, that you need therapy too." Damon stopped himself right there. Yeah, he couldn't say that.

After therapy and returning home from work, he was walking around his apartment like an idiot, trying to figure out a way to speak with Madelyne. Dr. Weldon had suggested that he should speak with his ex about himself first, share his positive experience with therapy, then build up from there.

Damon could see the logic in that. The problem was, he was impatient and felt like he was running out of time. He wanted her to move away from that jerk as soon as possible. *You can't force certain things*, he reminded himself. There was a time in the not-so-distant past when he'd refused help as well. So he tried again.

"Hi, Madelyne. I have to confess something to you. I've been going to therapy. It really changed me, the way I look at things, at life. You should try it too."

If he said it like that, there was no universe where she

wouldn't get mad at him and hang up on him. That was precisely why he needed to have this conversation in person. *Oh, joy.* Damon cringed thinking about it. He was no coward, but all the same, some things, like a spitting-mad Madelyne, were things he preferred to avoid.

It was strange that she had no problem having a screaming match with him, telling him exactly what was on her mind, yet she played mute around George. That was one of the many reasons she needed professional help. There was no shame in seeking help when a person realized that he or she cannot deal with certain things alone. Damon had come to that realization and was now a better man, a better father because of it. Or so he liked to believe.

Unfortunately, Madelyne's aversion was greater, her wounds deeper. *I need to make her see.* Damon felt like everything depended on it.

During his mental workout, his mobile phone started ringing. Connie was the first name that came to mind. As it turned out, it was not his daughter calling him. It was Madelyne.

Speak of the devil, he joked. His mood shifted instantly since his ex's calling him couldn't be good.

"Hello?" Damon answered with substantial uneasiness.

"Is she with you?" she demanded in return. There was no reason to clarify about whom she was speaking.

"No, she isn't," he replied. Now he was really starting to get alarmed. Where was his daughter? What happened? Did she run away again? A million thoughts passed through his head in a second.

"I'm not in the mood for games, Damon," Madelyne insisted.

Damon was prepared to reply in the same manner and stopped himself at the last moment. His ex was afraid and lashing out, he realized.

"I'm telling you the truth, Madelyne. Connie's not here."

There was a pause from the other side.

"What happened?" he demanded.

That snapped her from her stupor. "Oh, my God," she cried out.

"Madelyne, talk to me," he pleaded. He was still pacing about his apartment, feeling like a caged animal.

"I don't know where our daughter is, Damon. I can't reach her. I think she really disappeared this time," she said all in one breath, through tears.

"Okay, don't panic." He tried to calm her while he was panicking beyond measure. "Take a deep breath and tell me everything. When was the last time you saw her? How did she look?"

"We were home and had this silly argument."

"Let me guess, about George." Damon really detested that guy.

"Damon, please."

"And then what happened?"

"Connie wanted to go for a walk to clear her head, and now her phone is off."

Maybe she turned it off, like the last time.

"And George left as well, so I have no one to help me go and look for her."

"I'll help you, Madelyne. I'll go look for our daughter." Damon knew all her favorite places.

"Can you come pick me up? I don't think I'm capable of driving."

Damon hesitated. "I think it would be better for you to stay home in case she returns."

"You think she will?" Madelyne asked, in a strange voice.

"At the moment, we don't have reasons to think the worst. For all we know, her battery went dead. Teenagers share a symbiotic relationship with their phones. It happens." He tried to reassure Madelyne or himself... he wasn't sure.

"Okay, if you think that is best."

"I do. I'll stay in touch."

Damon really thought he'd managed to calm her and was about to end this conversation when she started again. "Oh, my God, Damon, where is our daughter?"

"Don't worry, Madelyne. I'll find her."

There was no doubt in his mind that he would.

"Promise me you'll find her and return her to me," Madelyne pleaded.

"I promise."

"Call me."

"I will," he replied, hanging up.

Damon rushed out of his apartment and started his search. Madelyne had had enough presence of mind to forward him the contact list and addresses of her friends. Although he had most of them, this was better.

He decided it would be wiser to go in person than speak over the phone with them. He knew how kids could get, especially when angry at their parents. Someone could be covering for Connie. Damon couldn't be lied to if he was staring them down.

To say some—read *all*—were surprised to see him would be an understatement.

"Sorry to bother you, but Madelyne and I can't reach Connie. Is she here, by any chance?" he asked one of her classmates.

"No, Mr. Blake," a girl replied, getting all big-eyed. As it turned out, he wasn't fooling anyone with his calm-as-a-cucumber act.

"Have you called the police?" the father of the girl asked.

"We still hope she's with one of her friends."

The father gave him a look that Damon didn't want to interpret.

"Hope you find her."

Damon nodded, rushing back to his car.

Eventually, he reached Connie's best friend, Tamara. Unfortunately, she too didn't know where Connie was.

"I sent her a text hours ago, and she didn't call or text me back."

"If she reaches out to you, give me a call."

"Of course, Mr. Blake. And I'll go check out the school. Sometimes, we like to hang out there."

"School?" Damon didn't know that. Considering what he'd done under the bleachers, he realized he really didn't want to know.

She shrugged.

"Thank you, Tamara."

He returned to his search, visited the rest of the kids on his list. Unfortunately, he had no luck in finding his daughter. *Connie, where are you?* He asked the heavens for help.

At one point, he started driving around, visiting her favorite places, stores, malls. She had to be somewhere.

Come on, baby, tell me where you are. He was beside himself with worry as he pleaded for a miracle.

He spoke with Madelyne two more times, and so far, there were no traces of his daughter anywhere.

"Something must have happened to her," Madelyne cried out. "She wouldn't do this to us. She's a good girl. I can feel she's in danger."

"Don't think like that," Damon replied instantly. "I'm on my way to that pastry shop she likes so much."

"That was when she was twelve," Madelyne replied, with noticeable hysteria in her voice. He couldn't allow her to lose hope.

"I have a hunch she's there."

"Please find her, Damon, and bring her home."

"I will."

Damon felt like screaming. *Please, Con-Con, tell me where you are.*

Tamara texted him how she hadn't found Connie at their hangout place at school.

"Fuck." He was running out of places, but refused to succumb to despair.

Tamara suggested a couple more places that he should definitely visit. She apologized that she couldn't go there herself. It was getting late, and her parents didn't like her driving around alone. He thanked her.

Damon recognized some of the places and learned about others for the first time. He guessed he didn't know his daughter as much as he believed. *Don't think like that.* He made a hard left, since he almost missed his turn to visit some cafe.

I will find her, I will find her, he repeated like a mantra as he continued to cruise around town. He would find her because he had to. The alternative was not an option.

As hours passed, Damon became more and more desperate despite forcing himself to soldier on. He hoped police patrols wouldn't stop him for suspiciously driving around town. To the outside world, he looked like he was on the prowl, not in search of his only daughter.

Maybe he should go to the police and report Connie's disappearance. He clearly needed help. Despite the common misconception, Damon didn't have to wait for twenty-four hours to report his daughter as missing.

Besides, he had a lot of cop friends, former Army buddies who would help with the search as well. He was sure of that. That was something he should have done from the start, he realized. Unfortunately, he'd hoped this was all just a mistake, that she would come to him like the last time. He didn't want to alarm everyone if she had only gone for a walk and lost track of time. But now, every second counted.

"Damn it to hell," he raged, remembering how he didn't have Connie's picture on his phone. Connie hated taking pictures as of late. He had one that he kept in his wallet, but she was four years old in it. It was completely unusable in this case.

What to do? What to do? He urged his brain to work faster, offer some idea, any idea. And then it came to him. Connie had given him a framed picture of the two of them for his birthday. She'd agreed to take a picture only because he'd pestered her for weeks. Back then, Connie had agreed with a roll of her eyes. It'd made his day.

Making a U-turn and breaking several traffic laws, Damon gunned for his house. He needed that picture to show the police. It was close to dawn, and Damon was petrified that he'd waited too long to alert the authorities. *No, don't think like that.*

As he pulled in front of his rental apartment building, he could see a small shape sitting on the steps. He frowned, trying to decipher what it was. It was still dark, after all.

Exiting the car, he started walking, then running, toward the shape. "Oh, my God," he exclaimed, coming into view. He practically teleported himself there. It was her.

Oh, thank God.

"Connie?" Something was terribly wrong. She wouldn't look at him or respond to him. Connie was sitting on the steps, all balled up, shaking.

"Connie? Connie?" Damon tried again. What was the matter with her? Was she hurt?

Damon crouched beside his daughter, gently putting a hand on her shoulder. Yet she remained completely unresponsive. He had been in combat for years, so it wasn't that hard for him to recognize when someone was in a state of shock.

Oh, my God, Connie, what happened to you? he asked himself with dread.

"Please talk to me, Con-Con."

Very slowly, gently, as though not to spook her further, he wrapped his arms around her, but she acted as though she didn't even notice. Every protective instinct in him came to life.

What the fuck had happened to his daughter?

22

DAMON

No matter what he said, no matter how much he pleaded for Connie to say something to him, anything, she remained unresponsive. She looked so small, so fragile all balled up, shaking like a leaf. If one of his Army brothers were here instead and acted like this, he would try to slap him back to the here and now.

There was no way in hell he would ever try something like that with his daughter. Especially not knowing what had happened to her in the first place. He really tried not to think about that because it would drive him mad. Connie had come back to him, and she was his number-one priority now. He racked his brain about how to help her.

How about taking her inside, jackass? he snapped at himself.

"Let's get you inside." He spoke softly.

Damon moved and gently, as though she were the most delicate thing in the world, since to him she was, gathered her in his arms. With some acrobatics, he unlocked and opened the apartment door and carried her inside. He gently placed her on the couch, wrapping a warm blanket around her. She appeared as though she didn't even notice the change of location. That worried him. *Should I call a doctor or the police?*

Damon sat beside his daughter. "Please, Connie, speak to me. It's me, your dad. You're safe. You came to me, as you promised," he continued, pleading for her to say anything at all, over and over.

Connie kept rocking with her eyes closed, refusing to deal with the outside world as though what had happened to her was too horrific, so she had to get away, withdraw into herself.

Stop, Damon, you are spiraling, he snapped at himself.

"Please speak to me. Tell me what happened."

She looked perfectly fine, unharmed on the outside. Her clothes looked clean, untorn. There were no marks on her or evidence of being mistreated in any way. That worried him even more.

Although he didn't want to move an inch from her or leave her alone, Damon realized he had to call Madelyne and let her know that Connie had been found.

Was she technically found if she came here on her own? He must be in shock as well if his thoughts were this crazy. *Crazier than usual* was more accurately put.

"Tell me you found her," Madelyne answered after the first ring.

She found me, waiting on the steps, shaking. "I got her," Damon reassured her.

"Oh, thank God. Let me talk to her."

Damon hesitated. He didn't know how to tell her that although their daughter had been found, she was far from well.

"Damon, give the phone to Connie. I need to speak with my daughter, hear her voice," Madelyne pleaded.

"Madelyne—"

"I promise I'm not going to yell at her. I just need to hear for myself that she is okay," she interrupted, misunderstanding his reluctance. And although Damon understood the urge, he couldn't comply.

"That's the thing, Madelyne, I can't."

"I don't understand, is she or is she not with you?" Madelyne demanded.

"Yes and no."

"Damon."

He cringed at that tone of voice. He was messing things up; he was aware of that. "Listen, I found our daughter in front of my apartment building. She was all balled up and shaking," he explained in haste.

"Oh, God, is she all right?"

Looking at his daughter, Damon decided he didn't want her to hear the next part of the conversation. He moved into the kitchen. He could still see her, but hopefully, she couldn't hear him. "I think something happened to her."

"What?" Madelyne exclaimed. "What do you mean?"

"I don't know." He shrugged although she couldn't see him. "As I said before, I found her on my steps, completely unresponsive. When I call out her name, she doesn't respond, doesn't even look at me. I believe she's in a state of shock."

"Oh, my God. She was all alone on the streets. Who knows what might have happened to her?"

"She looks perfectly fine, physically unharmed." He was quick to reassure her, not wanting Madelyne to get the wrong idea.

He could hear her catch her breath before speaking again. "I'm coming over there."

Damon made a face. He didn't want to play devil's advocate, but he really thought that to be a bad idea. It went without saying that he understood she was a worried mother. He would be the same way if roles were reversed, but at the same time, they had argued before all of this happened.

Damon wasn't trying to imply that Madelyne had had

anything to do with the state Connie was currently in, but considering it, there was no telling how their daughter would react to seeing her. Damon wasn't trying to be unnecessarily cruel, simply thinking of what was best for his daughter at the moment. He believed she should be left alone. She would reach out to him when she was ready. After all, she'd come here when she clearly needed help.

Of course, he couldn't say all that to Madelyne. At least not with those exact words. He didn't want to cause her additional pain.

"I think you should wait," he said, closing his eyes, waiting for the storm that was about to hit him.

"Excuse me? Something happened to my daughter, and I must be there with her, for her."

She had him there. At the same time, he believed he was right. "Maybe we should not overwhelm her."

There was a small pause. "Have you called the doctor?"

"Not yet. I called you first."

"Oh, my God, Damon, what do you think happened to our girl?"

Damon closed his eyes for a moment, shaking his head, trying to fight all the dark thoughts, the dreadful possibilities that swirled inside his head. "I don't know, Madelyne, but she looks traumatized."

He couldn't say if something had happened to her or if she'd seen something. Whatever it was, it was horrific enough for her to shut down like this.

Madelyne openly started to cry, and Damon decided to share his theory with her. "I think someone tried to take her against her will, and she managed to run away."

"Please stop, Damon. I can't bear it," Madelyne said through sobs.

"I'm sorry, Madelyne," he said, defeated. This was his personal defeat. Once again, he'd failed to protect his family.

"Do you think we should call the police?" she added, managing to calm herself. Madelyne was always a fighter. Despite her breakdown, she was great in a crisis.

Damon had been prepared to do just that before coming here and finding her. He said as much. "Considering everything, I think that would be for the best, but maybe we should wait until morning." Until Connie could tell them what had happened.

"I'm coming over as soon as I reach George."

George. Oh, how much Damon despised the mere mention of that man. Considering he was the root of all their problems, he didn't want that bully anywhere near his daughter.

"Fine," Damon agreed, "only don't bring him with you." Their daughter had been through enough.

"What?"

"Please, Madelyne, this one time. Come alone. Don't bring George with you," he insisted.

As he said that name, he could see his daughter jerking as though someone had slapped her. Their eyes locked, and she started crying.

"Connie?"

"What's happening?" Madelyne demanded.

Damon didn't know how to respond. "I believe she's snapping out of it," he said eventually.

"And?"

Damon felt torn. Realizing he couldn't stay on the phone and take care of his daughter, he said, "Look, I'll take care of everything and keep you posted." He didn't give her a chance to reply and hung up.

He rushed back to the living room, crouching next to his daughter. "Connie? Can you hear me? What happened? Why are you crying?" He bombarded her with questions, then shut up, realizing what he was doing.

He felt powerless, desperately looking at his daughter crying her eyes out and not knowing how to help her.

"Connie," he tried again, petting her hair. "Daddy is with you; you're safe."

Damon kept saying all the reassuring lines, trying to soothe her, and he couldn't be sure, but he felt like it was helping. He gathered her in his arms, rocking her back and forth like when she was a little girl. "I got you. I got you."

"Dad?" she said eventually. That was the loveliest sound in the world, the sound of his daughter talking, although her voice was a bit hoarse from all the crying.

"I'm here, baby," he replied softly, kissing the top of her head. She came back to him. She was fine. Unfortunately, his relief was short-lived.

Connie hugged him hard, burying her head into his shoulder, and started sobbing even worse than before.

"What is the matter, Con? Speak to me," he pleaded in exasperation.

She didn't reply, or so he believed. She was saying something over and over again, but it was muffled due to her position.

He shifted ever so slightly so he could understand her.

"Oh, my God, oh, my God, he killed him," Connie rambled through the sobs.

Damon's whole body went numb. "Connie, what are you talking about?" he inquired, but his daughter continued repeating the same thing.

What did his daughter get herself into? He couldn't help wondering. Although since she kept repeating that one line, it was safe to assume that she'd seen something she shouldn't have.

"Who got killed, honey? Who killed who?" Damon asked, changing tactics. Unfortunately, she kept crying.

This was one of those times he wished he could read his

daughter's thoughts. He desperately needed to know what had happened to her, how to help her, and he didn't know precisely how. Connie was the only one who could tell him how to help her.

"Everything is all right. You're safe. I got you. Please calm down," he pleaded. "I need you to tell me what happened to you. I'm going crazy over here. I'm scared." Only when he said all that did he realize he'd said it out loud. He felt like smacking himself in the head, except he didn't want to let Connie go.

Miraculously, something he said reached her, and slowly, Connie stopped crying. Damon thanked the heavens and all the angels for that small blessing.

His daughter calmed down, stopped shaking as well. He patiently waited for her to fully return to him, petting her hair. Eventually, she looked at him.

He smiled, or at least he tried to. "You got me worried for a minute there, kid."

Her face was smeared with tears, her nose runny and red, yet her eyes were haunted. Damon knew that look very well. He could see it each time he looked at himself in the mirror. Unfortunately, that wasn't all he saw in his daughter's eyes. Connie was frightened.

What did you see, Connie? was on the tip of his tongue, yet he forced himself to remain quiet. He didn't want her to return to that previous state, not when it had taken her so long to find a way back.

"Sorry," she mumbled.

"No need to apologize. Everything will be all right now."

To his surprise, Connie moved to sit on the couch. "Nothing will ever be all right, Dad."

"Why do you say that?"

Without hesitation or looking away, Connie said, "Because tonight, George killed someone."

23

MADELYNE

Madelyne looked at the phone in her hand. Damon had hung up on her. She didn't blame him for doing that. Their daughter had to come first. *Dear Lord, what happened to her?* Madelyne blamed herself for what had happened to Connie. It couldn't be helped. She was the reason her daughter had decided to go for a walk in the first place.

Don't think like that, she warned, realizing that was a road to madness. At the same time, how could she not? If only she'd stopped herself in time, stopped herself from arguing, then none of this would have happened. Connie wouldn't have stormed out of the house on some wild quest, but would be safe inside these walls. *This is all my fault.*

Why did Madelyne have to do this? Act like this? Was Connie right about her? Was Damon right? *Am I too stubborn defending my stand, my point of view, when I should be more open-minded to accept the truth?* Was this her stand or George's? Her mind was all over the place. What was the real truth?

It was true she always sided with George, but wasn't that

was she was supposed to do? He was her husband, after all, and she trusted him.

Should you trust him?

People who were involved, married, had to be there for one another.

Is your love making you blind?

That stopped her in her tracks. Her daughter certainly believed that was the case. Madelyne wasn't so sure.

Looking back at her date with George by the lake, when Madelyne had started to notice things about him, she had to wonder if her love was really the culprit or his manipulation. Maybe it was both. *He wouldn't do that to me,* a part of her rebelled, except that voice wasn't as strong as before.

Madelyne felt confused. She felt like screaming at the top of her lungs. It wouldn't help solve her dilemmas, but it would, at least for a little bit, silence all the voices inside her head. And she had a lot of those. They were all telling her opposite things, opposite feelings. *Which one of these voices is mine?* she asked in exasperation. Unfortunately, there was no answer.

Regardless of how difficult—or impossible—it looked at the moment, that was precisely what Madelyne had to figure out, and fast, since her actions today had directly resulted in putting her daughter in harm's way.

I'll find real proof that will force you to see the truth, Connie had vowed. *George is rotten to the core,* her daughter had said before leaving the house, and afterward, she'd appeared traumatized on Damon's doorstep. Those two things weren't related, she argued with herself. However, they were closely intertwined. Connie wouldn't have left if they hadn't argued about George.

Although there was no denying something had happened to her, something horrible. Madelyne couldn't even imagine what she would do if Connie hadn't appeared on Damon's doorstep. *Why did she go there and not return here?*

Mom, I haven't felt safe around George from the beginning, her daughter had told her, and Madelyne buried her head in her hands. She couldn't take this anymore. Damon believed someone had tried to take their daughter away. *Who? Why?*

Oh, Lord, she needed to go see her, make sure with her own eyes that Connie was all right. Only then did she realize that was what she had intended to do before losing herself in all the thinking. Checking the time, she discovered she'd wasted too much of it, standing in the hall, impersonating a statue.

Forcing herself to move, she went to her bedroom, and after throwing some clothes on, she rushed out. Adding some shoes, she was ready to finally leave the house. In haste, she reached for the door handle.

"Phone," she reminded herself. After looking about, she felt the thing inside her pocket. She'd had it with her all this time. *Silly woman.*

As she started to leave again, another problem presented itself. She closed the door, but forgot the keys so she could lock it. Madelyne had failed to grab her house or car keys in her absentmindedness. *What is wrong with me?*

Focus, she snapped at herself. Her hands were shaking pretty badly. Was she even in a state to drive at the moment? *I will have to.* It wasn't like she had someone to take her.

George, she remembered. She'd failed to reach him. Madelyne took her phone out and started dialing. *Come on, come on.* He wasn't answering, so she tried again and again. That frustrated her to no end. He was never here when she really needed him.

Since she couldn't wait around for him, she decided to send him a text. As she opened her app to start typing, her phone started ringing. It wasn't George calling her back, it was Damon again. Although she knew Connie was safe and sound with him, her heart started beating a little bit faster.

"Hey, Damon, I was just about to leave the house," she informed him, impatient to end this conversation so she could hit the road. Her daughter needed her.

"Wait," Damon replied simply, which made her frown.

"Did something happen?" she guessed.

"Connie started talking."

That was such a relief to Madelyne. Her daughter was all right. Everything would be all right now. "Oh, good. What did she say? Does she remember what happened to her?"

"She talked only for a little bit," he replied vaguely.

Madelyne didn't like the sound of that one bit. Was her daughter hiding something from them? Or was Damon now trying to hide something from her? Madelyne was about to find out.

"So what happened?"

"I don't know yet."

Madelyne couldn't understand why Damon was so difficult with her all of a sudden. *Why won't he speak with me normally?*

It didn't matter anyway. Madelyne would go to them and learn the truth for herself.

"I'll speak to her, then. I'm on my way," she insisted.

"Wait, Madelyne. There is something Connie was pretty adamant about."

"And what is that?"

"Whatever happened to our daughter, George is somehow involved."

George? Her George? That froze her completely, and she recovered quickly. She couldn't freaking believe it. Damon had really outdone himself this time around. He would stoop to anything, apparently, to make her husband the villain of every story.

"Excuse me?" she demanded.

"Once she started speaking, Connie said his name."

"I can't believe you," she snapped in return. "I cannot believe you would really use a situation like this to trash my husband." Madelyne was beyond herself. "What's he accused of now? Breathing?" she practically shouted. This was outrageous.

What happened to this man? Was he really that blinded by jealousy and hate to use his own daughter? Was this all some kind of ploy from the start? She needed to see and speak with Connie to learn the real truth.

"What? I did no such thing," he said, defending himself like she'd known he would. "I'm only telling you what my daughter told me."

"Sure, sure."

"You don't believe me?"

What gave her away? "Of course I don't believe you because it makes no sense."

Are you sure? You have no idea where Connie went, or where George had his meeting, for that matter. You cannot know for sure that their paths haven't crossed. She shoved those thoughts away.

"This is all very convenient, isn't it, Damon? Connie goes missing again, appears on your doorstep again, only to accuse George, and for what, exactly? You know, it doesn't really matter. Shame on you."

"You know what, Madelyne? I wash my hands of you. I'm done trying to make you see the truth."

Madelyne rolled her eyes. He could be so melodramatic at times. "Oh, I see the truth clearly."

"You see only what George wants you to see," he accused. "He has you completely brainwashed."

Madelyne jerked as though he'd slapped her. She was so done with hearing that. She was her own person, for crying out loud. If she wanted to stand by her husband, that was her right.

"Go to hell, Damon," she snapped, thoroughly pissed off.

He was too quick to accuse George of messing with her, yet here he was doing the same. Damon also wanted her to behave, think, and act the way he wanted.

"Been there, done that. That still doesn't change the fact that our daughter is afraid of your husband. And rightfully so."

"You're lying," she insisted. George had some flaws, but he was not a bad man.

"How can you say that to me, to our daughter? Do you even hear yourself?"

"Damon, stop, you're embarrassing yourself."

"Are you actually choosing George over your own daughter?"

Madelyne really had had enough. "No, Damon, I'm choosing George over you." She thought that was pretty clear since she'd divorced Damon to marry George. Apparently, her ex needed to be reminded, which she happily did.

"Fine."

"Fine?" That got her confused. Was he ready to admit he was lying? Madelyne hoped so.

"I just figured it doesn't really matter what I think or what you think. Connie knows the truth, and I will help her prove it."

"And how do you plan to do that?"

"I'm calling the police. They'll discover the truth."

For some inexplicable reason, Madelyne ran out of air. Still, she forced herself to ask, "Why would you call the police?" She couldn't completely mask how worried she was. "Connie is safe with you."

"Because we still need to know what happened to her. You didn't see her, Madelyne. She was completely traumatized."

Or so he would want me to believe. What if Damon was trying to use all of this to frame George?

Why would he do that? she argued with herself.

Because he is completely unhinged. Jealous beyond reason.

Besides, she couldn't rule out that George and Connie hadn't met someplace. That would certainly look bad. *Why is that man not answering his phone?* She needed to know where her husband was.

"Besides, it was your idea to call them in the first place."

"All right, do what you think is best, but why implicate George? He has nothing to do with it. Let the police investigate without biases," she insisted. She couldn't let Damon tarnish George's good name out of some personal vendetta.

"Madelyne, George has everything to do with this. Connie told me so."

"So you say."

"Then hear it for yourself."

Madelyne strained herself because, as though from afar, she could hear her daughter. "George did it. I swear he did it."

Did what? Madelyne was full of questions, not to mention confused beyond measure. She was quick to accuse Damon of lying, of trying to trick her, but she couldn't do the same to her daughter. She could hear her voice, hear how scared she was.

Madelyne remembered what it had felt like when no one believed her or wanted to hear her story. She'd vowed to never be like that with her own kids.

Did I break that vow?

"Madelyne?" Damon snapped her from her reverie.

"Damon, what did that mean?" Madelyne cried out, feeling like her head was about to explode.

"I don't know, but the sound of George's name was what snapped her from her shock. She then started crying, saying how he... how he did something bad."

Madelyne suspected by the sound of his voice that there was something he wasn't telling her.

Madelyne had been married to that man for far too long to not recognize distinctions. She couldn't bear it, the indecision. *What to do? Who to believe?*

Was it really possible that George was somehow implicated in what had happened to Connie this evening? He had said he would deal with her daughter his way, since Madelyne had failed to keep her under control.

Madelyne was consumed, overwhelmed with panic. *What did I do?*

"Damon," she started, but the front door opened, and her husband walked through it. "I'll call you back," she added in haste, ending the call.

24

MADELYNE

M adelyne was surprised to see her husband, although it was silly to feel like that. This was his house too, after all. From first glance, it was clear that George returned home in a pretty foul mood. He barely acknowledged her, putting the house keys in a ball on the table that stood by the shoe cabinet by the door. Madelyne stood up from the steps she was sitting on to greet him. She couldn't remember sitting there in the first place, but it was safe to assume it had been during her fight with Damon.

Was Damon telling her the truth? she couldn't help wondering.

"Hi, honey," she said, feeling spent. Even if Damon had tried to provoke her tonight, could the same be said for Connie? She continued with her musings.

George looked completely exhausted, sweaty, and there was an unfamiliar smell around him. Not a woman's perfume or anything like that. It was nothing pleasant, either.

Where was he? What was he doing? she couldn't help wondering. Thinking back, he'd told her how he was going to a business meeting. He'd certainly dressed for it as well. That was why his appearance now confounded her so much. He looked more like he had been engaged in some kind of physical labor rather than being at a meeting. That worried her for some reason.

As soon as he took his jacket off, he handed it to her to hang in the closet. She started to put it on the hanger, then noticed how dirty it was. And there was that same smell to it that was downright disgusting. It needed to be washed. She started going toward the laundry room before realizing what she was doing.

She must be in shock because of Connie, because she wasn't thinking straight. The laundry could wait. She had more pressing issues at hand, like discovering where her husband had gone. Had he seen Connie, by chance? *Of course he didn't. Don't let Damon get into your head.* But Connie had said the same thing.

"I need a drink," George grumbled, and Madelyne left the jacket on the balustrade before she followed her husband to the kitchen. He started opening cabinets and visibly became even more agitated, not finding what he was looking for.

"Where is my whiskey?" he demanded.

Madelyne took a moment to reply. "You drank it the other day with your friend." She didn't mean to say it like that, yet it still came out that way, like a reprimand.

He gave her an icy look. "Then why didn't you buy me some more? Do I have to do everything around here?"

"I'm sorry. I'll buy you some tomorrow," she promised.

"You'd better."

Madelyne wanted to tell him about what had happened to Connie, but hesitated. Not only because he was in such a state. Something else was preventing her. Fear.

Besides, what could she say to him, anyway? She didn't want to repeat what Damon had told her. That would only make him madder. Madelyne had to think up something because he would notice that Connie wasn't here. Besides, Madelyne really wanted to go to Damon's place and see her baby girl.

"You look tired," she commented.

He failed to reply, grabbing a couple of beers from the fridge. Upon opening one, he started drinking right from the bottle.

Madelyne had never seen him act like this. This was just one of many anomalies as of late, which made her question how well she knew her husband in the first place.

"Where were you?" she tried again, observing how high-strung he looked. Was there a problem with the restaurant that she wasn't aware of? Maybe one of the deep freezers had broken down, or he'd had to help with unloading something. That would certainly explain his strange look.

"Mind your damn business," he paused long enough to snap at her. He must have been drinking before coming home. She hated it when he was like that.

Besides, what was with all the people in her life who couldn't help yelling at her all the time? She was sick and tired of it.

So why don't you do something about it? She was fed up with herself as well.

"I called you a bunch of times tonight, and you didn't pick up."

She understood that he was a busy man and had some problems, yet she was in the middle of a crisis and couldn't find her husband. That was not acceptable. She really needed him.

It was a blessing that everything had turned out for the better. Connie had found her way to Damon, but what if she hadn't? Could she expect her life to look like this from now on? Always wondering where her husband was, what he was doing? And would he be returning drunk and taking his frustrations out on her?

As though to prove her point, George slammed the empty bottle of beer on the counter before reaching for the other. "I've been busy," he replied with finality and a clear command not to disturb him further.

Madelyne felt like walking away from the kitchen, the house, right then and there, to leave him wondering where she was and if she would be returning home. *See how you'd like that.*

Despite her inner thoughts, Madelyne chose the higher road.

"I've been calling to let you know Connie has been missing most of the night. And I needed your help to look for her. I've been so worried."

"What do you mean she's been missing?" He picked up on that quickly.

"Damon found her, luckily."

George gritted his teeth. "How come she left in the first place? Isn't she grounded?" he boomed.

Madelyne felt nervous while replying, "I allowed her to go for a walk before dinner, and when she didn't return, I started to worry. I called, but her phone was off."

"That brat must have turned it off," he grumbled.

Madelyne ignored that and continued speaking. "I was really worried, panicked, so I called Damon, and he went to look for her. He visited all her friends, trying to see if anyone saw her or spoke with her."

George made a face, clearly not pleased with her narrative. His next words confirmed that. "You called Damon and not me?"

Madelyne folded her arms. "As I said before, I tried reaching you multiple times, and you weren't responding."

Locking his eyes on her, he pulled the phone out of his

pocket. He clearly checked the log before putting the phone away. "Either way, you don't have reasons to call your ex in the middle of the night. And that's final."

"George."

"And so help me God, if I discover you disobeyed me…"

"Connie was missing," she insisted, not caring if he was angry with her. "Of course I called him when you weren't here."

"So did he find her?" he mocked.

She couldn't understand him one bit.

Madelyne nodded.

"See, you worried for nothing."

"Easy for you to say." Things like that showed he was no parent. "She is with Damon now."

He chuckled humorlessly. "I knew it. Just one of her stunts. Your daughter is constantly seeking attention, but I will get her in line."

Madelyne had so many issues with what he said that she didn't know where to start. "You're wrong, George; it's nothing like that. She was in shock. Damon was freaked finding her in that state. He's convinced someone took her against her will. Or maybe she saw something traumatic that made her shut down." Madelyne added one of her own theories to the mix.

She left out how Connie kept saying his name. How he'd done a terrible thing. How did her daughter know that? What terrible thing? Her head was full of questions and so few answers.

"He's about to call the police." If he hadn't already.

George narrowed his eyes, taking a small sip of his drink. "Did she say anything?"

He finally started to believe her. *Good.* "Not much. She's still in shock. I was actually thinking of going over when you came home," Madelyne explained.

Maybe he'll want to come with me. That concerned her, considering Connie had said his name. *What to do?*

George started nodding and then stopped as though something just occurred to him.

Madelyne gulped, not really understanding why.

He pointed with the beer bottle at her. "What time did you say Connie left for her walk?"

That was such a random, unexpected question that Madelyne was taken aback. Also, she couldn't fathom why he looked so upset all of a sudden. What was it to him when she left?

I'll find real proof that will force you to see the truth. George is rotten to the core. Did her daughter do something she shouldn't have? That frightened her even more.

Madelyne shrugged, looking anywhere but at him. "I don't know exactly," she replied vaguely. Considering everything, although she knew nothing for sure, Madelyne was convinced that she had to protect her daughter at all costs. Even from her own husband.

"Remember exactly when she left, then tell me," he demanded.

She jumped a little from the might of his voice. "Connie left before you."

"When?"

"At least an hour," she lied, fidgeting the whole time, fearing he could see right through her.

Madelyne was never a good liar. In the past, she refused to speak when she didn't want to tell the truth, and that technique usually worked. Unfortunately, it didn't look like something like that could work on George. When he demanded to know something, she had to comply.

Now she felt it was imperative to hold her ground and stick to the lie. She wasn't sure why, but it was crucial that

George didn't learn Connie had left mere minutes before him.

Since she hadn't had a chance to speak with her daughter face-to-face, she couldn't say where her daughter had gone or why. There was a possibility that George was involved. It could be the shock speaking as well. Madelyne trusted her daughter, but in a crisis, things could get mixed up. Connie could insist that George had done something bad and could really mean that. And still, that didn't have to be the truth. Her brain could be confused at the moment.

All the same, since Connie had implicated him, Madelyne couldn't tell him the truth for several reasons. First of all, she didn't want to hurt his feelings. If Connie did make a mistake, then all of this would unnecessarily hurt him. They already had a strained relationship. This would mean the end of it, and Madelyne couldn't live like that.

On the other hand, Connie might be speaking the truth. For that reason, it was imperative for Madelyne to keep quiet until she learned what had happened. What role did George play in all of it? Was he the one who tried to take Connie away? That thought filled her with dread. Or did something else entirely happen? Madelyne's head was full of speculations.

The biggest questions were what had happened to Connie, and was George involved?

Madelyne's head was spiraling from all the possibilities. She continued to hope like hell this was all just a big, huge, monumental misunderstanding, that George was innocent, and that Connie would fully recover from her accident.

Accident? Is that what you will call it?

As she had a stare-down with her husband, with her head full of questions, Madelyne had a sinking feeling that she was about to get all of her answers, and was dreading it.

25

DAMON

What the hell?

Damon had sensed something was off with Madelyne in those last few moments of their conversation. The only explanation he could come up with was that it looked like her husband, whose name Damon preferred not to even think since it put him in a state of rage, had returned home. Madelyne really didn't want her husband to know what was going on or that she was speaking with him in the first place.

You're reaching. There was also a chance that she just wanted to fill him in without having Damon as an additional listener. Damon really didn't want to get into the middle of their marital dynamics. Unfortunately, he had to, considering what had happened this evening. Damon was worried about Connie. What she'd seen changed everything, and now he had to find a way to safely resolve these issues for his family's sake. The status quo was no longer an option.

It was hard not to wonder if Madelyne would tell George anything. That would certainly make things harder for Damon and in all kinds of different, possibly dangerous ways.

George getting involved more than he already was could be problematic, and Damon went through all kinds of scenarios in his head, exit strategies, preparing for the worst.

Perhaps he'd made a mistake by calling Madelyne before getting the whole story out of Connie. What could he say? He'd gotten worried and acted before thinking things through.

His daughter had completely shifted his world with her statement. Connie had witnessed a murder, implicated George, and that was enough for him to want to get Madelyne out of that house. She needed to know that she couldn't trust that man. Things did not go as Damon had envisioned in his head. Unfortunately, his best intentions had backfired, and Madelyne had refused to believe him. *At least at first*, he corrected himself. He felt he'd managed to make her doubt, at least in part, at the end. Right before she hung up on him.

He hoped she would be all right, debated if he should call her again, then dismissed it. That would only make matters worse. With all that on his mind, he returned to his daughter's side. Connie looked slightly better than before, yet still pretty scared and haunted. He hated that that man had managed to do something like that to his daughter. George would pay, he vowed, no matter the cost.

"Where's Mom?" Connie asked, in a voice that showed her concern.

"Still home," Damon replied, trying to mask how much that worried him. He didn't want his ex-wife anywhere near George, like he didn't want his daughter to come into contact with him ever again.

"Is she coming?"

He really didn't want to answer that. This whole night had turned to shit, and Damon didn't see a way out. At least not yet. "I don't know."

Connie took that much more calmly than he expected.

At the same time, she was in shock, so maybe she needed time to process the latest information. Much to his relief, she'd stopped crying. Damon felt like, although he hated himself for it, this was the perfect time to get the full story out of her.

"Connie, can you tell me what happened tonight?"

His brave daughter nodded ever so slightly. Since she didn't start talking immediately, Damon decided to give her a little nudge. From Madelyne, he knew how all of this had started.

"I heard you argued with your mother." There was no reprimand in his voice. It was only a statement.

Connie looked sad. "Yes, she came to my room, and I couldn't bear it anymore."

"What?"

"To look at her as she so calmly accepted George's lies. She actually looked happy to share the 'good news' with me. I lost it."

"What good news?" Damon interrupted.

Connie made a face before replying, "Mom spoke with George, and he told her how sorry he was for yelling at me, for threatening me."

Yeah, right, Damon grumbled.

Apparently, his daughter was of the same mind. "Yeah, right, like I could ever believe that shit."

Damon gave her *the look.*

"Sorry," she added.

"And then what happened?"

She shrugged, looking away as some of the heat left her body. "I got so mad at her that I promised I would find proof that would show her George is a bad guy. And I guess I did."

Damon felt like a schizophrenic at the moment. He couldn't believe his daughter had decided to do something like that, and at the same time felt pretty proud. She felt confident about something and decided to act upon it. Connie was his daughter, after all, through and through.

He couldn't say that to her, of course. This kind of reckless behavior couldn't be encouraged. Although done for the right reasons, this story could have ended differently. Damon tried not to think about what could have happened if George had seen her.

"Connie, that was pretty reckless of you."

"It worked, didn't it?"

Damon remained silent, and Connie rolled her eyes, continuing to speak. "When I told Mom I wanted to go for a walk, I had no idea things would turn out like this."

"Where did you go?" Damon asked.

"I didn't go anywhere."

That confused him for a second. "What do you mean?"

"I hid in George's car, waiting for him to go to his meeting. He has a lot of those, especially late at night. I was sure I would catch him with a mistress."

So that had been Connie's original plan. Catch George cheating, snap a few pictures, then show them to Madelyne. That was a solid plan, Damon agreed. There was just one small issue with it. As it turned out, George was keeping secrets that had nothing to do with a sleazy mistress.

"So you hid in the back of his pickup truck, waited for him to appear, then went to his meeting?"

George had one of those new fancy pickup trucks that Damon always considered an odd choice for that man. It didn't suit his character, or status, for that matter.

"No, yes, I don't know," Connie responded with a frown.

She became haunted again, and Damon hated seeing that look on his daughter's face. As a father, he wanted to take all her pain away. And in this case, he didn't know how to achieve that. What she'd seen, what she'd experienced, was something she would have to deal with herself. *But not alone.*

"George drove for a while. And even though I couldn't see where he was going, I knew he wasn't heading to his restaurant."

"The drive was longer?" Damon guessed.

"Much longer." She paused again, as though struggling with her memories, her feelings.

Damon took her hand, showing her with that simple gesture that he was there for her. "What happened then?" Damon prompted.

Connie took a deep breath before continuing with her story. "Eventually, he stopped, and when I heard a door opening and closing, I decided to sneak out. I was so sure I was about to catch him with another woman. I was practically skipping with joy, and then I discovered he'd parked us inside some kind of old boathouse. It reeked of mold and something else, dead fish, maybe." She shook in disgust.

"Boathouse? You sure?" Damon insisted, needing as many details as possible.

Connie nodded. "Yeah, we were at the lake. It's not a part I know of."

Damon had a sinking feeling where this was going. If you wanted privacy for shady business, that was one of the places to do it.

"Staying hidden, I watched George approach another man, who looked startled to see him."

"Did you see what the other man looked like?"

Connie nodded again. "Kind of small and very skinny, with balding black hair. He had a shabby beard, as though he'd stopped shaving."

"What did George do then?" Damon reluctantly asked, knowing the narrative was reaching its gruesome end.

"He tried to give the other man a hug, calling him Dandywood or Dunwoody or something like that, but the other man stepped out of his reach. He wasn't happy to see George."

Who is? "How did George react to that?"

Connie made a face. "He started laughing, and then pretty soon, they started arguing," she explained.

"Could you hear them? What were they saying?"

"Some. But it didn't make any sense. They spoke about the last job and 'rocks' that got lost."

What was that about? Damon couldn't help wondering. And why was that so important that George was prepared to kill for it?

"Did you hear anything else?" he prompted.

Connie did her best to recollect. "George demanded to know where his cut was."

"Cut?"

"Yes, and Dandywood was adamant that he didn't know anything about the money and the jewels."

What money and jewels? That made no sense to Damon. "Are you sure they said that?"

"Pretty sure. And then George lost his patience and started screaming, 'Where are they?' and getting into his face."

Damon really didn't know what to make of it. One thing was for sure. George wasn't the man he pretended to be.

"Eventually, the other man pushed George away," Connie continued, "or at least tried to, insisting that he knew nothing."

Connie clammed up there.

"You okay, Con-Con?"

She nodded but closed her eyes. Damon could see a display of emotions crossing her face. "George swore, calling him a traitor, then pulled out a gun." Connie opened her eyes again to look at him. "He shot him," she added in a much smaller voice. New tears formed in her eyes.

Instinctively, Damon grabbed her into his arms, trying to shield her with his body from the bad memories, but Connie wasn't done.

"After he shot him, I couldn't move. My whole body froze. And George just stood there, looking at the dead man for a bit before spitting at him."

Monster. Damon felt beside himself that his daughter had witnessed something like that.

"Once he stored his gun away and moved to return to the car, I panicked, but managed to get back in the truck."

"Good girl," Damon mumbled, not really knowing what to say.

"He just left him there and drove away," she sobbed. "When he reached the restaurant, I climbed out and came right here. I don't know how," she confessed.

Damon closed his eyes, trying his best not to take his gun and hunt that man down. "It's all going to be okay," he reassured her, purely out of habit.

This situation was serious, and Damon knew it needed to be dealt with and fast. At the same time, his number-one priority had to be Connie, her well-being and safety.

Was she safe with that killer on the loose? He didn't think so. Especially while not knowing if Madelyne had told him anything.

"Dad, I'm scared. I don't want to go back to that house," Connie cried out.

He held her tighter. "Don't worry, Con-Con, you're not going anywhere," he replied with utter conviction. He was not letting his daughter out of his sight. And he pitied the man who would try to break them apart.

26

DAMON

Despite his reassurance, Damon barely managed to calm Connie down. She was afraid he would send her home. As if there were a universe in which he would do something like that. *To send her home to that killer? I don't think so.*

"Do you want me to make you some hot cocoa?" Damon asked, feeling quite ridiculous, but he watched a lot of movies where hot beverages solved all problems, so he decided to give it a go. Connie nodded, so he sprang into action. He'd never made one, wasn't even sure he had cocoa, but he would give it his best. Damon could use a beer himself, but would pass. He needed his mind sharp.

What Connie had told him was mind-blowing. George was a killer. And as far as he was concerned, there was only one way out of this mess. They had to report him. That was the only thing they could do—*legally*, Damon corrected himself—to make sure George couldn't harm anyone else.

It might be a bit cold of him, but Damon couldn't care less why George had decided to kill someone. The fact that he did meant that he was dangerous, dangerous for his daughter, and for that reason, he needed to be put behind bars.

Damon cringed trying to picture Madelyne's reaction. *She will find some way to blame me for everything,* he thought snidely, and instantly felt sorry. Madelyne wasn't a bad person, simply misguided. Yet, not even she could ignore the fact that her husband was a murderer, and that Connie was now in danger because of what she'd seen. *I hope she keeps her mouth shut,* he prayed.

Damon did his best to make hot cocoa. The end result looked good enough. He carried the steaming mug to his daughter. She accepted it but didn't try to drink it. Maybe that was for the best.

"What now, Dad?" she asked, as though reading his mind.

"Now we call the police to report a crime. You need to tell them what you saw."

Damon expected his daughter would become slightly anxious or nervous about having to do something like that. What he did not expect was her experiencing a full-blown panic attack.

"You can't call the police, Dad. You can't," she pleaded, all wide-eyed and flustered.

He frowned, confused. "I have to. A man is dead, and George is responsible. Dangerous men like him need to be apprehended. This is the only way."

Connie started shaking her head even before he finished speaking. "No, I can't. I can't speak to them."

That completely dumbfounded him. "Why?"

"I simply can't," she replied stubbornly.

"There's nothing to be afraid of," he tried to reassure her.

"It's not that, Dad."

"Then what is it?" he pressed.

"I can't. Isn't that enough?"

He couldn't understand his daughter's behavior one bit.

Was she that afraid of George? She didn't look like that. There was something she wasn't telling him. He was sure of that.

"Connie, that is not a viable explanation. This is a serious matter, and you are old enough to understand that." With that said, Damon took his phone to dial the police. In one quick move, Connie grabbed it from his hand. He was getting old.

"Connie," Damon snapped.

He tried to be full of understanding that she might still be in shock from what she'd experienced, but he really needed to report this crime. For all their sakes. God only knew what was happening between Madelyne and George right about now. And he couldn't say that out loud, not wanting to alarm Connie further.

"Dad, please just trust me," she insisted stubbornly. "They won't help."

That confused him even more. "What do you mean? Of course they'll help. It's their job."

Why was she acting like this all of a sudden? Who was she protecting this time? The last time Damon had wanted to call the CPS, Madelyne had pleaded with him, and Connie had stopped him, and now she was doing the same. He found that suspicious.

"Connie, give me my phone back. I have to call them because we need to deal with this," he insisted.

"We can't," she cried out, taking him by surprise. "They won't believe me."

What? "Why would you say something like that? Of course they'll believe you," he insisted. Connie was having such an unreasonable fear that Damon didn't know what more he could say.

"No, Dad, they won't," she insisted, starting to cry all over again.

"Connie, hey, what's the matter?" He tried to reach her.

"I've been lying to you, Dad. Mom and I, we both did," she confessed.

That pretty much stunned him, so it took him a moment to reply. "Lied to me? How?" He wanted to know.

Connie closed her eyes before replying, "I was so mad at you when you left us."

Left them? He wanted to ask, but then realized what she meant. "Connie, it was my job to go and fight. I had to."

She opened her eyes to stare at him, and Damon could see pure fury in them. "You had a choice," she accused, sounding a lot like someone else Damon knew, "and you chose to go and leave us, and right after you promised me you never would again."

Damon knew his daughter was right. He did break his promise, so her anger was completely justifiable. "Circumstances changed." He pleaded with her to understand.

He had been offered a lot of money to re-enlist, so he'd justified his actions by convincing himself that he was doing it for his family, for Connie's future. *Was I lying to myself? Did I want to leave?* He didn't dare answer.

"Whatever. I'm over it now."

Damon wasn't so sure she was. "But?" he prompted.

Connie shrugged. "It was a different story back then. I was really mad at you and wanted to take revenge," she confessed, ashamed.

Damon was very disturbed to hear this. "What did you do?" he forced himself to ask.

"You made me promise I would be a good girl while you were away."

"I remember."

"Since you broke your promise, I decided to break mine."

She paused as all kinds of things passed through his

head. "Connie, what did you do?" he repeated. He couldn't take the silence anymore.

"The usual stuff."

"Meaning?"

"Lied, stole, skipped school. And you know what? It wasn't that hard. The first couple of times I stole something from a store, I didn't even get caught." She sounded almost proud of herself. "And then when I did get caught, Mom took care of it."

Of course she did, Damon grumbled.

"The worst part was that she didn't want to tell you, and that was the whole point. So I continued doing all kinds of stuff."

Damon felt sick to his stomach.

"I started skipping class, forging Mom's signature on absence notes, and eventually, I busted my teacher's car."

"You did what?" he exclaimed.

"He gave me an F. I got angry." She shrugged as though it were no big deal.

Damon thought it was a big deal, huge, monumental.

"Mom smoothed everything over, pleaded with the school to give me another chance, to suspend me for a month, and they did."

"She never told me any of this," Damon replied in shock. How could Madelyne do this to him? He was Connie's father, after all, and deserved to know everything that was happening in his daughter's life. If he'd known she was this unhappy, he would have found a way to return home.

Would you, really? a part of him challenged.

"I know. That got me so mad. I wanted you to know, but she kept pretending everything was all right."

"Connie, how long did this phase of yours last?"

She was reluctant to reply. "About a year."

A year? Damon screamed inside his head. God only knew

what kind of shit she'd done during that period. She was a smart girl, which could cause a lot of damage.

"I have a couple of minor juvenile charges, mostly for shoplifting, truancy, vandalism, and underage drinking. I never did drugs, though," she added, as though that would make him feel better after everything he'd heard.

Damon didn't know what to say to this small revelation. He felt like he didn't know his own daughter. Not really. He especially felt betrayed by Madelyne. She'd kept so much from him.

One thing was clear, though. It was all his fault. His daughter had acted out because she'd felt abandoned by him. While he'd believed he was doing the right thing, fighting the good fight, his family had felt abandoned, alone. That broke his heart. What good did it bring him that he'd gone to fight, to serve his country? For all his troubles, he got a broken family and a broken brain.

To top it all, Madelyne had had to deal with all of that on her own. No wonder she'd started to resent him. He was sure she'd done her best, believing she was doing the right thing keeping all of this a secret. That was probably true. He could have gotten pretty hurt if he had been stressing over Connie rather than worrying about himself and his platoon. Madelyne had probably saved his life. At the same time, she should have told him once he returned.

Since he failed to say anything, processing, Connie continued. "I don't do that anymore, Dad," she reassured him.

And he had to admit there was some small comfort in that.

"I realized how silly of me that was."

Silly wasn't the word he would ever use to describe any of this, but okay.

"And Mom didn't tell you, not wanting to worry you. I realize that now."

"Why didn't you tell me?"

"I was embarrassed, I guess. I didn't want you thinking poorly of me."

"I could never think poorly of you. However, you and your mother should have been honest with me."

"It was all my fault. I begged Mom not to tell you anything either, since she planned on telling you everything upon your return."

"And she agreed?"

"I promised I would be better, and worked hard on fixing all my grades, too."

Damon had always felt lacking, like he was not the husband or father he was supposed to be, and now he had real proof that he'd failed miserably at both.

"Are you mad?" His daughter wanted to know.

To be perfectly honest, Damon had no idea what he was at the moment. He was mad, but he was also sad, confused, and a whole lot of other things, depending on his current thoughts. This was a bitter pill to swallow, and it would require some time to move past it. All the same, this wasn't the time nor place for him to question his whole existence. He wasn't the important one at the moment. Connie was.

He said as much, if not in so many words. "We'll talk about all of this some other time. Now we have to call the police."

Connie looked at him in surprise. "But, Dad."

"No buts. George needs to be stopped, and you are the only one who can do it." He was adamant.

She shook her head. "Don't you understand? After everything I've done, they won't believe me."

That made him pause. Was Connie right? Was there really a chance the police wouldn't consider her to be a credible witness? What could that mean for their future? Damon was worried. *I guess there is only one way to find out.*

27

DAMON

"We have to call the police."

"We can't."

Damon felt torn while he evaluated everything all over again, doubting his daughter and himself. Although he understood why Connie had acted out in the past, it still hurt. It also showed him that he was far from being the parent he wanted to be. This showed him how deeply he'd managed to hurt those he loved, without even realizing it. Sadly, he couldn't dwell on that at the moment. He had more pressing issues.

Damon really tried to figure out if Connie's fear had merit. Was there a possibility the police wouldn't believe his daughter? If she was this reluctant to contact them, there had to be a reason. Was she hiding something else from him, a bigger crime? She swore she'd told him everything.

Should I believe her? Damon didn't want to have doubts about his daughter, yet how could he not? She'd lied to him for a long time. While he was away, he'd believed she was a good girl, going to school, participating in school activities, when in reality, she hadn't gone to school and liked to steal and vandalize cars for fun.

"Connie, how could you keep all of this from me?"

Connie looked at him oddly, probably thinking they were done with this subject.

Damon couldn't let go. Not yet and not now, when they were in a world of problems, deep in piles of shit. Connie had witnessed a murder, and since the killer was someone remarkably close to them, it couldn't be ignored.

She shrugged. "I didn't know how to tell you, and I was angry for so long."

His heart broke all over again. *You did this, asshole.* "Do you still feel like that?" he forced himself to ask.

Connie shrugged.

That hurt. All the same, it didn't change the biggest issues.

"Mostly, I'm embarrassed for behaving like that," she replied eventually, "and I stopped doing all that shit."

How could he trust her? "This is a lot to take in, Connie." He decided to be completely honest with her. If he wanted honesty, then he had to give it in return.

"I know," she replied softly, looking away, but then she looked up again as though something occurred to her. "I'm telling the truth about George. You have to believe me."

And that was his biggest conundrum. "How can I after everything you just told me?" he challenged. He really wanted to, but it was difficult. Damon had had no idea his daughter had a record. He would have to have a serious conversation with Madelyne about her keeping this vital information from him.

Madelyne is with George now, remember? he snapped at himself. So he needed to put his wounded pride aside and deal with this problem. He knew something was wrong with George, he was an abusive person, but was he a killer as well?

Connie insisted that he was, and Damon really wanted to believe that. Was his daughter telling him what he wanted to hear? Damon felt conflicted and then some. His emotions were all over the place as well. On one hand, he was furious that those two had kept so much from him. On the other, he couldn't help blaming himself. He was the catalyst that had started the fire.

He now understood Madelyne's resentment completely. Perhaps the breaking of their family was his fault, at least in part. If he'd kept his promise and chosen to stay and not re-enlist and go fight in a war that wasn't his own, they would be together.

And not worry about homicidal new husbands. He stopped himself there. Those kinds of thoughts were bad for him. He couldn't rewrite the past, only worry about the present. And the present looked pretty glum.

Connie burst into tears again. "Please, Dad, I know I did all kinds of awful things and lied to you about them. You can ground me forever when all of this is over, and I won't say a word, just believe me now. I know what I saw. George killed that other man. He did, I swear to you," she said in a rush, desperate to make him see the truth.

What is the truth, anyway? He felt like slapping himself. Damon came to a realization. Connie was his daughter, and he would stand by her. Always. No matter the past, Damon believed his daughter. She was telling the truth now, and his gut feeling agreed.

"I believe you. Please stop crying."

She hugged him with all her might. "Thank you."

"No need to thank me. You're my daughter, and I love you with all my heart."

"I'm scared," she confessed.

"I got you." Damon wouldn't allow anyone to hurt her.

"I'm scared for Mom too. George is a killer."

Damon was scared for Madelyne as well. "We have to call the police now." They'd wasted enough time as it was.

"They won't believe me."

"I'll make them believe you." Damon was adamant. Even if he had to go and find the body himself, he would make sure George paid for his crime.

"Dad," she started, then paused.

"What is it?"

"Does this mean you won't send me back to that house?"

Damon was aghast, not to mention confused by that question. Why was she so hung up on that? How could she still think he would send her off to her mother after everything he'd learned? Was she really that worried about it? *Apparently, yes.*

"Of course I'm not sending you back. You're not leaving my sight."

She looked visibly relieved by his reassurance. This was one big fucking mess.

"What are we going to do with Mom?" Connie asked next.

To be perfectly honest, Damon had no idea. He couldn't just ring her and ask her to come for some tea. That piece of shit, George, would know something was up. That was assuming Madelyne didn't already tell him everything on her own. Her behavior was pretty strange these days, and Damon couldn't predict her reactions.

When he'd told her about George, her first reaction was to negate everything, to accuse him of lying. Although that did kind of make sense now. She had a history of Connie lying to her, so she was bound to become skeptical.

But she'd started to turn around and was on the fence, right before abruptly hanging up on him. Damon was sure that meant George had come home. That filled him with guilt and fear. Damon felt like he was abandoning her, focusing solely on Connie. It couldn't be helped. She had to be his priority.

Did he put his daughter in danger by sharing vital information with Madelyne? She was Connie's mother and deserved to know the truth, be privy to everything that was going on. Telling her that George was the source of Connie's shock was not a mistake. She needed to know so she could be on guard.

Would she be, though? What if he'd only put her in further danger? What if Madelyne confronted him, and he harmed her?

Damon hadn't been completely honest with his ex. He'd merely told her George did a terrible thing, not *what* he did. He couldn't explain, even to himself, why he'd decided to withhold that information. Was that a dangerous mistake?

No. Damon couldn't think like that and couldn't leave things as is, either. He needed to call her again, to tell her to get the hell out of that house.

"I'm calling her again. She needs to come and be with us." And together, they would plan their next move.

Connie nodded.

Damon dialed. This time, Madelyne didn't answer immediately. He tried not to put much stock into that.

"Damon," she greeted him, as though it had been far too long since they'd last heard from one another. In reality, Damon doubted if fifteen minutes had passed. That was a big tip that something was wrong. Seeing no other way, he greeted her back.

"Hi, Madelyne. Is everything okay?"

"Of course it is. Why wouldn't it be?" she said brightly.

Because you sound weird. Damon almost asked if she'd suffered from head trauma, got amnesia, and stopped himself in time. This could all be an act for George. So he decided to proceed with caution.

"I wanted to speak with you about Connie," he said vaguely, waiting to see what she would say in return.

Besides, as per their agreement, Connie could spend time with him only during the weekends. Or when Madelyne gave permission. Since Damon wanted to keep her now, that was a direct violation of their custody agreement. He was aware of that, but couldn't return her home, not while that killer was there as well. He was sure Madelyne would agree.

She doesn't know all you know, he reminded himself. Madelyne only knew that George had done something that freaked Connie out, nothing else. *That should be enough,* he argued with himself.

It changed nothing. The only way Connie could return to that house was with an armed bodyguard. There was no need to say who would play that part. And if Damon was confronted with that man, he would eliminate that threat without hesitation. So it was better to alert the authorities and, in the meantime, keep Connie as far away from George as possible. Or so Damon believed.

Madelyne was of a different mind, as it turned out. "I'm grateful you managed to find her. Please bring her home now. It's late, and I'm sure she needs a good night's sleep."

What the actual fuck? Good night's sleep? It was freaking dawn.

And did she really think Damon would only return her home after all that had happened? Was that even Madelyne on the phone or some strange body-snatcher alien? Nothing she said made sense.

"Madelyne, are you all right?"

Maybe she'd taken something to calm herself and went overboard with a dosage. That could make her act all loopy.

"Yes, I am, but are you?"

"Why do you say that?"

"Because you keep asking me the same questions. Everything is fine now that Connie is found. George was worried, too. It would be best to bring her home now so we can put this crazy day to rest."

And just like that, it dawned on him. Madelyne was back to her Stepford Wife routine of pretending everything was perfect, which could only mean George was standing beside her. Was he listening in, as well? Damon couldn't rule that out.

Part of him wanted to greet the man, but he resisted the urge. George was one dangerous man, and there was no telling what he could do to Madelyne if he sensed he was threatened in any way. It was imperative to not tip him off and pretend everything was all right. They didn't need a hostage situation on top of everything else.

As for Madelyne, Damon couldn't be one hundred percent sure she was only pretending or believing in what she was saying. With a heavy heart, Damon knew he had to make a choice. Madelyne would do the same if the situation were reversed.

"Connie will stay with me for a little while. I don't want her anywhere near George."

"Oh?" That was all she managed to say before he continued.

"Don't worry, Madelyne. I will keep our daughter safe, no matter what," he delivered before hanging up, praying like hell he'd done the right thing and had not sentenced the mother of his child to death.

28

MADELYNE

George scrutinized her as she hung up. Madelyne was sure Damon realized that George was beside her, and didn't want to speak with her for that reason. She only hoped Connie was better. In all the haste, Madelyne hadn't had a chance to ask if he'd called the police.

What was she to do if the police came knocking on the door? What would George do? How would he react? She didn't dare think about it, yet couldn't stop herself.

"What did he say?" George asked through gritted teeth.

Madelyne forced a smile. "He said Connie dozed off, so it's better to let her sleep at his place and then bring her home later."

Madelyne noted that she would have to call the school in a couple of hours to let them know Connie wasn't coming. After a night like this, it was better for her to stay home and rest.

"What?" George exclaimed, clearly not pleased with such an outcome. "So he refused to bring her now."

"He didn't refuse. This is for the best. When she gets some

sleep, he'll drive her home, and that's that," she tried to reassure him. "This was a tiring day, after all. Maybe we should do the same, have some well-deserved rest." God knew Madelyne needed it.

Her head was full of questions, and she planned on sending Damon a text when George fell asleep. She needed to know what was going on. Madelyne reached for him, offered her hand to go to the bedroom together, but he wouldn't let her.

"Can't you see what is going on?" he boomed, startling her a little.

"What?" Madelyne asked, confused.

"He's deliberately keeping Connie at his house. He is trying to take her away from us."

"He is not," she replied instantly, although deep down, she knew George was right. Something had happened to Connie, and George was somehow involved. Damon was protecting his daughter. Or at least he believed that. Madelyne still couldn't fully believe George would do anything to harm Connie. She would need proof before deciding.

"This is against the agreement," George insisted.

That was true. Damon was breaking the custody agreement by keeping Connie, although Madelyne understood the reasons behind it. He thought George was abusive and dangerous. That wasn't something she could share with her husband. She wasn't stupid. She knew she had to get to the bottom of things, but knew she couldn't achieve anything at the moment.

George had already come home in a terrible mood, and anything else she could say was a cherry on top. She would find out the truth, learn from George if his path had crossed with Connie's during this evening, but not now.

"He has my permission."

Madelyne only prayed that Damon wouldn't do anything foolish in the meantime. Or George, for that matter, since he looked well past enraged, ready to fight some more and not go to sleep, as she wished.

"You have to go and get her," George commanded. "He is violating the agreement and using your good nature to have things his way."

"George, don't be ridiculous," she blurted out before she could stop herself.

George glared at her. "What did you say to me?" he shouted.

"I'm sorry," she instantly apologized. "I just don't think we need to overreact." She tried to downplay it. He was having none of it.

"You really are blind," he spat. "Didn't it occur to you that this whole 'Connie's gone missing' thing was just a lie they served to you so that Damon could keep her?" he challenged. "For all we know, they could be leaving the state right now."

Madelyne wanted to chalk everything up to crazy talk and couldn't. It wouldn't be the first time Connie had lied to her. No one knew better than her how good a liar her daughter truly was. Not even Damon knew that. And Connie did want to live with Damon because she hated George.

Madelyne hoped her daughter had outgrown that rebellious phase, except... what if she hadn't? That horrified Madelyne. *Did I fall for another lie?* Was it possible this was all a stunt? A ploy for Madelyne to let Connie stay with Damon instead of calling the police?

"Oh, my God," she said, eventually putting all the pieces together.

"See what you did?" he chastised.

Madelyne grabbed her phone. "You're right," she allowed, dialing in haste.

"What are you doing?"

"I'm calling the police. What if you're right, and they're already halfway across the state? I need to stop them." She couldn't let Damon take her daughter away from her.

To her surprise, George approached and took the phone away from her. He hung up before the call could get through.

"Why did you do that?" she demanded. Wasn't he on her side, at least?

"Why would Damon want to keep Connie?"

That confused her. Her face must have conveyed that because he continued.

"Why tonight, specifically? Did something happen?"

Madelyne hesitated. She didn't want to tell him anything. Especially not now when she couldn't know for sure what was the truth and what was a lie.

"Madelyne, tell me right now," he boomed, getting into her face.

"It's because of you, okay? He doesn't trust you," Madelyne replied, cowering from his reaction.

George narrowed his eyes. "Why?"

"Because of the way you treated Connie."

He calmed down completely, offering a small reassuring smile. "I explained all that. I was a bit drunk. No need to over-react like this."

Connie and Damon disagreed.

Her thoughts must be clear on her face because he became serious once again. "Did something happen tonight?" he repeated the question.

"You know what happened," she replied, slightly irked. Was it possible he'd already forgotten her daughter was missing?

Was she really?

"I can see you're keeping something from me." His words snapped her from her reverie. "I want you to tell me the whole story." To emphasize his words, he grabbed her by the arm.

"George, let go; you're hurting me," she protested.

"Speak," he practically shouted in her ear.

She didn't know what to say, since she didn't know what the truth was anymore. She had been full of doubts even before George returned home, and now she was totally confused. Sadly, she knew George wouldn't take that as a viable answer. Her arm started to burn from the force he was using.

"Connie saw you doing something," she said—more like screamed—and George loosened his grip ever so slightly. Madelyne felt like biting her own tongue. She shouldn't have done that. She'd ruined everything.

"Explain," he said forcefully.

Unfortunately, by George's expression, she knew she couldn't stop now. *Please forgive me,* she prayed.

"Connie and I had a disagreement today, and—"

"I don't care about that. Tell me what you meant by 'she saw me'. Where? When?" he demanded, ill-tempered.

There was something else in his voice. Why was he alarmed by the fact that Connie had seen him? That notion alarmed her in return. Connie had kept saying he did it. *Did what?* Did George really have a mistress? Was that what Connie was trying to say and didn't know how, knowing how much it would hurt her?

It did make sense, and it didn't at the same time. Damon wouldn't bother to call the police for something like that. It had to be something else, something more sinister. Madelyne worried about all the possibilities. Could her husband really be a bad guy?

"I don't know anything else," she replied in a small voice.

"You're lying."

"I'm not. She went missing. Damon found her in a state of

shock. At first, she wouldn't talk, and once she did, she said you did a terrible thing."

"What terrible thing?"

"I don't know. I swear."

"Were those her exact words?"

Why was he so adamant about it? "Yes," she replied in haste, fearing he was on edge as it was.

"Madelyne." Her name on his lips sounded like a threat.

"I swear to you. That's all I know. Damon didn't want to talk with me over the phone."

"Okay, okay, I believe you," George replied as his smile returned.

Madelyne felt all over the place. She couldn't keep up with his mood swings anymore.

"Let's go."

That confused her even more. "Go where?"

"To Damon's house to retrieve our daughter."

Retrieve? As though she were a missing dog.

"She's asleep now," she argued.

George wasn't swayed. "I need to speak with her, reassure her that it was all a misunderstanding."

"Can't that wait for tomorrow?"

"No. I can't have her going around town saying things about me."

"So did she see you doing something illegal?" she guessed.

"It was all a misunderstanding, I assure you."

Madelyne wasn't assured. He was behaving very strangely, and although Madelyne questioned everything at the moment, one thing became clear to her. She couldn't let George speak with Connie. Not now, when he was this angry. Her daughter needed to be protected.

"A misunderstanding?" she repeated, like a parrot.

"Yes, but I'll straighten her up."

Madelyne didn't like the sound of that, and neither would Damon. She could only imagine how her ex would behave if they came knocking on his door, which only strengthened her resolve to keep those two apart. Damon was right all along. They needed to alert the police and let them sort through this mess.

In a moment of inspiration, she said, "Isn't it better to call the police?"

"Why?"

"For all the reasons you stated. Damon said a bunch of lies in hopes of stealing Connie away from us. We have to stop him. The police need to be informed so they can't leave the country."

This was all a test, of course, to see what George would do next. If he refused to call the police, Madelyne would know for sure what Connie had seen was the truth and that Damon wasn't trying to steal her away. If he refused, Madelyne would know she needed to keep George away from her family.

And what would she do? Could she be with a man who'd hurt her daughter? Of course not. At the moment, she didn't know how to get away. Besides, Connie came first.

"This is a family issue, my love," he replied, breaking her heart, "and we should resolve it as such. No need to call the police. We can handle it. Trust me."

Oh, my God.

George's attitude completely changed anew. He had been angry and aggressive before, but now he was perfectly calm, composed, reassuring. This was the George she knew and loved.

Loved, how that word sounded dirty at the moment. The shift in him, the sudden need to go and get Connie, scared her like nothing else could in this world.

She couldn't allow that. At the same time, not seeing how

she could refuse him anything without tipping him off, Madelyne nodded. "Okay, George, whatever you say."

"Good." His smile grew even bigger. "Now let's go get our daughter back."

Please, God, help us.

29

DAMON

"Dad, what happened?" Connie asked in alarm, since she'd watched his bizarre exchange with Madelyne. "Did George—"

"Everything is fine," he lied, trying to stop her from panicking. By the look she gave him, she wasn't buying it.

Damon turned from his daughter, then stood from the couch altogether. He needed some time to think. *What just happened?* he asked himself. Madelyne had acted weird, even by her own standards.

"Dad?" Connie said, clearly confused by his reaction.

"Everything is fine," he repeated, a bit absentminded.

Needing something to do, he went to the kitchen to pour himself a glass of water. He replayed his entire conversation with Madelyne.

Was she in danger? *Probably.* If she told George what Damon had told her, which wasn't much to begin with, then definitely. If Madelyne had told her murderous husband Connie had seen him tonight, then there was no telling what he would do next. Would he try to hurt her? Torture her to get the full story, or maybe manipulate her into submission?

He couldn't know for sure. *What if he simply kills...* Damon stopped himself there.

No matter how much it pained him, Damon couldn't think of Madelyne right then, because Connie had to come first. Her safety was all he worried about. She'd witnessed a murder, and that put her in an extremely dangerous position. It was logical to assume George would do everything in his power to stop Connie from identifying him as the shooter.

Damon couldn't be sure whether Madelyne had told George about what had happened or not. He could have forced the truth out of her. Considering how she'd just behaved, it was pretty safe to assume she'd told him something, if not all. *Yet.* Damon was sure Madelyne had insisted that he return Connie home because George wanted that. Of course Damon couldn't comply.

George was a dangerous man, and if he discovered that there was a witness to his wrongdoings, Damon could predict his next course of action. As a general rule, murderers didn't want witnesses to their crimes.

Maybe he'll skip town, run instead of trying to silence them, came a sudden thought. Damon dismissed it. George didn't look like the type who would run away. A bully, an abuser like George was used to being a top dog, to having things his way.

Not this time. Damon was prepared to do whatever it took to protect his daughter, period. Damon had no problem killing him. He would gladly go to prison if it meant that his daughter could sleep safe and sound in her own bed, without fear that some man could come and hurt her. Besides, he had a lot of friends, Army buddies who would help him in a flash to dispose of that piece of shit. No one would ever know how he died. If there was no body, there was no crime.

Damon could put a bullet in that man's head and still sleep without a guilty conscience. He hoped it wouldn't come to that, because he didn't want to subject his daughter to any additional stress. Damon hoped the police would deal with this mess so he wouldn't have to.

What if he hurts Madelyne? he worried. He just couldn't help himself. Madelyne was the love of his life, the mother of his child, so of course he couldn't bear knowing what was happening to her.

Who says he didn't already? That was what troubled him the most. Damon would protect Connie, but Madelyne was out of his reach. *Why wouldn't that damn woman listen to me?* he fumed. If she'd believed him from the start, then she would be right here with them now. Of course, the what-ifs were a dangerous place to be, especially at this moment.

Damon would do everything in his power to help Madelyne, but he had to help Connie first. They needed to move, and fast. Presuming Madelyne had told George everything, this was the first place he would come knocking, so Damon had to move Connie someplace else before he was ready to play the hunter's game with George.

Damon was very much aware that he was breaking the law with this stunt, but that was pretty low on his list of concerns right about now.

Connie came to join him. He realized that he was standing in the kitchen in front of the fridge without opening it to get that water. No wonder she came to check up on him. He looked like a basket case.

He pretended to be inspecting something before opening the fridge. The thing was completely empty besides a few condiments. The bottle of water was already on the counter. Talk about an exercise in futility.

"Dad, what are we going to do?" Connie asked, and rightfully so.

He closed the fridge and turned to look at his daughter. In Damon's mind, there was only one thing they could do.

"You will now tell me everything you remember about that boathouse and the exchange George had with that other man before he killed him."

Connie made a face.

"I know it's hard, but it's important," he stressed, "so I can call the police, tip them off, and then we'll be leaving this place."

"And go where?"

"Someplace safe," he replied before realizing he'd said that out loud.

As expected, Connie's eyes grew wide, frightened. "Dad, aren't we safe here?"

He hugged her. "Don't worry, Con-Con, I have everything under control. This is only a precaution."

"Okay, okay."

They returned to the living room, and with a heavy heart, Connie tearfully managed to recount the whole scene to him. Damon hated putting her through all of that again, but it was imperative to see if she'd missed some detail the first time around.

"You were so brave, Connie," he said at the end, realizing he'd failed to tell her that the first time around. After calming her down, Damon dialed 9-1-1.

"9-1-1, what's your emergency?" the operator greeted.

"Hello, I have some information for you."

"What is your name, sir?"

Damon decided to go full disclosure without trying to conceal his identity. He was calling from his landline, so it would be pointless anyway. If they wanted to know who made the call, they could.

"Sergeant Damon Blake."

"What kind of information?"

"A serious crime occurred in one of the abandoned boathouses at the lake."

"Do you know the address?"

"No, I don't."

"What kind of crime?"

"A murder."

"Do you know the victim? Did you see the person who committed the crime?"

"No, but I have a witness with me right here."

Connie grew alarmed, guessing he was talking about her, and Damon took her hand with his free one in reassurance.

"Sir, let me connect you with the detective on duty."

"No time. I have to protect her first." Only when his daughter was safe would Damon think about their next move. Reporting the crime had to be enough for the time being.

"Sir, are you in danger?"

You have no idea.

"We can send a patrol car to your address right now."

"Look for the body of a middle-aged man in one of the boathouses," he insisted before disconnecting.

"Did they believe you?" Connie asked in concern, crushing his hand ever so slightly.

"Yes, they will go to investigate," he reassured her. "Now please go and pack up some of your things from your room in your backpack."

"Okay," Connie replied, and after grabbing her backpack, she disappeared into her room. She had some spare clothes in there, so Damon didn't have to worry about shopping for the time being. He didn't know how long they would have to hide, so he was prepared for the worst, while expecting the best.

Damon was sure that the police would find the body in the next couple of hours. All the same, would they connect it with George? That was the real question. He didn't say his name by design. Damon didn't want to tip that bastard off and send the police to him when they had no proof of his involvement.

With all that on his mind, Damon started packing as well. He used his gym bag, dumping his workout clothes on the floor before replacing them with fresh ones. All the essentials went inside.

He thought they could check into some hotel and lie low until he figured out their next move. He hoped the police would come knocking on George's door and arrest him, but Damon couldn't wait indefinitely for that. He needed a plan B in case the first one failed.

Once he finished, he realized there was one more thing he needed to bring with them. Kneeling inside his bedroom closet, he pulled out a small safe, and after entering the right combination, Madelyne's birthday, he pulled out his licensed pistol, a 19 mm Glock. He was going to protect Connie no matter what. Without even thinking about it, he packed extra ammunition as well. Perhaps he was acting a bit paranoid, taking all possible precautions.

There was a chance that George would skip town, realizing he had police on his tail, but better safe than sorry. Besides, if George went ballistic, there was a possibility he would want to fight his way out of this mess. Damon couldn't know for sure which way the wind would blow, so he decided to prepare for any outcome. He would deal with George on his own, in his own way, if he had to. But first, he had to take Connie someplace safe.

Where are we going to go? he debated. After adding some stashed cash that he had inside the apartment to the bag, he was ready to go. Returning to the living room, he could see his daughter was finished as well and was waiting for him. This was the quickest he'd seen her pack. *I should simulate emergencies more often from now on to avoid constantly waiting on her.*

To his relief, Connie looked completely calm now, as though the knowledge that they were putting a certain plan in motion with him there to protect her gave her the strength to overcome her fear. Damon was immensely proud of his daughter. Connie was a fighter, a soldier like him.

He debated for a few moments whether they should bring their phones with them or leave them behind. Damon had no idea what kind of pull George had at his disposal. They would bring them, he decided. If he noticed something was wrong, they could always dump them and buy new ones, he rationalized.

Checking that the coast was clear, he ushered Connie outside, and after locking everything up, they walked toward his car. It was early morning, and he didn't want to alert the neighbors that something was amiss. They were just a father and daughter preparing for their day, nothing else.

Damon felt much better once they settled in his car. For some reason, he felt too trapped and vulnerable in that apartment. This was much better. This way, they were free to go wherever they pleased.

"Ready?" he asked, looking at his daughter.

She nodded before replying, "Ready."

Damon started the car.

First stop, getting to a safe place for Connie. Then it would be time to deal with that son of a bitch once and for all.

30

MADELYNE

*O*h, my God, oh, my God, oh, my God! Madelyne was freaking out. She was trapped in a nightmare, and just like when she was a child, she couldn't wake up. She didn't know what to do, what to say. George expected her to come with him, to get her daughter from Damon's house, and she knew she couldn't do that.

Madelyne had no idea what was going on, why Damon had insisted that Connie should stay with him, why George was so adamant to bring her back. However, there was this deep urge inside her to stop him.

They were at the front door when Madelyne decided to try again. Maybe she could reason with George.

Yeah, because that worked before.

"George, look at the time. Maybe we shouldn't do this now."

He looked at her like she'd lost her mind. Maybe she had. "When would be the right time for you? When Damon decides to leave town with Connie? Or worse, the state?" he challenged.

Madelyne knew Damon would never do something like

that. There had been a moment of doubt before, and it had passed. She knew better. Damon wasn't like that. He wouldn't try to leave town. Not without a good reason. And she would completely understand if he skipped town while thinking he was protecting their daughter's life. She would act in the same way.

That wasn't the real issue here. George's investment in getting Connie back home was. Why was he so unyielding? What was he trying so hard to hide? She couldn't help wondering.

As she mused, George continued to rant. "Are you really that blind, under your ex's spell, that you can't see what's really going on?"

There was that phrase again. She was sick and tired of people telling her how blind she was. She knew how Damon and Connie kept telling her George was manipulative. Was it possible they were the manipulative ones and George was telling the truth? She had a tough time accepting that.

George had had a lot of outbursts lately that had caused her to doubt him. Even now, he was acting strange and unnerving. It frightened her. Realizing she didn't know him as much as she thought made him completely unpredictable.

Madelyne couldn't fathom why it was so important to him to get to Connie, because there was no doubt in her mind that this was his real agenda.

If Connie was telling the truth, and Madelyne believed so, perhaps George was worried about what she had to say. Damon had said he was about to call the police, and that was something Madelyne had conveyed to George. Was he hoping to prevent that? To reach Damon and Connie before the police got involved? It was a possibility.

Was George really that afraid of Connie speaking with the police? He certainly looked like it. *Why?* Madelyne's head was full of questions.

She couldn't even start guessing why a respectable restaurant owner would be afraid of the police. *Did he fail to pay all his taxes?* She dismissed that instantly, since that was nothing that would frighten Connie. And when Connie had reached Damon's place, she'd been well past traumatized. What had she seen?

It was on the tip of her tongue to confront George and ask him what he had done, but she knew she couldn't. She was afraid. And not only for herself, but for Connie as well. She knew that Damon would never let anyone or anything hurt their daughter, but George was unpredictable and alarmed, and that made him extremely dangerous.

By the way he looked at her, she realized it was her time to say something in return. Madelyne tried to hide how nervous she was while saying, "I don't believe Damon would take Connie away from me. He's worried about you, not me."

She knew this was a risky move, but she had to do something.

"You're so gullible, Madelyne." He almost sounded as though he pitied her. "They're playing with you, but I will show you the truth." He said that with utter conviction. "Let's go," he commanded, and Madelyne knew that there was no room for complaints. She had to comply. Every part of her being rebelled.

"What happened this evening?"

"Nothing. Come on, let's go."

He was lying to her. "Let's just call him. If he answers on his landline, you will see he is not making a great escape."

"To tip him off that we're coming?" he screeched. "Not a chance."

Then he approached her, looking her deep in the eyes, frowning. "What got into you, Madelyne? Why are you defending him so much?" he growled. She couldn't help shuddering in return.

"I guess I have trouble accepting that he would do something like that."

He patted her cheek. "That is why you have me. Let's go."

George turned and reached for the door, and Madelyne followed closely behind.

To her chagrin, he waved her phone. "And no more phone calls," he announced, putting it inside his pocket.

Damn it.

Madelyne moved toward his car, still stressing over what to do next, when George stopped her.

"Let's take your car. Mine is out of gas."

Madelyne turned to return to the house, since she didn't have the keys with her, but George beat her to it and then completely took her by surprise by throwing the keys to her.

Madelyne caught them in midair. *He wants me to drive? That's never happened before.* He liked to be the one driving no matter which car they took. Not commenting on it, Madelyne did as she was told.

Unlocking the door, she settled inside. She had a second to herself where she tried to take a deep breath before George joined her. *Everything will be all right,* she tried to reassure herself. The mantra wasn't working.

As she started the engine, she could see with the corner of her eye how George opened the glove compartment to stash something inside. *Is that a gun?* All kinds of warning bells and alarms started ringing inside her head.

Why does George have a gun? She wasn't opposed to guns in general. Damon had one, and Madelyne never had a problem with it. Quite the contrary. When he'd offered to teach her how to shoot, she had accepted.

The issue was, why did her husband have one, and more importantly, why did he decide to bring it with them? What did he plan on doing with it?

Isn't it obvious?

And just like that, it all came crashing down on her. If Connie had seen something she shouldn't have, then it was obvious that George would do everything in his power to stop her from speaking with the police. That filled her with dread. *What did Connie see?* she asked herself for the hundredth time.

What was so bad that George could do that would make Connie freak out? She didn't dare speculate, but knew she had to. It was clearly something he could go to jail for.

Oh, my God, what did I do? she realized, completely horrified. In fear and confusion, Madelyne had confessed everything to George. Once again, she'd allowed him to confuse her, and now, they were about to go to Damon's house so George could do God knows what.

"Madelyne, drive," he commanded, snapping her from her thoughts.

Madelyne realized they were still in their driveway. She did as she was told, slowly leaving the neighborhood, obeying every sign, every speed limit, basically stalling.

Madelyne was terrified and deeply ashamed of herself that all this time, she'd sided with this stranger over her own family. And why? Because she had been so blinded by all the love and affection he was giving her. She wanted to smack herself in the face. *You are so stupid, Madelyne.*

She was so desperate to have her happily ever after that she'd found herself in harm's way once again. The first time, it wasn't her fault. This time around, she should have known better. How come she'd learned nothing after all this time? Because she didn't have to. She'd had Damon to keep her safe.

Her heart squeezed ever so slightly thinking of her ex. She was afraid of confronting him now. She'd made a terrible mistake, trusted the wrong man, and now she was trapped.

This is all my fault. They were in this mess because of her.

They had been right about her all along. She was gullible and blind. She'd fucked up, and that was precisely why it was on her to fix everything. *But how?*

Think, Madelyne. She didn't know what George was planning to do, but the fact that he'd decided to bring a gun didn't look good. She knew she had to stop him.

Maybe she could cause an accident. Not while driving twenty miles per hour. It was true she'd slowed down, not wanting to reach Damon's apartment. By the way George was looking at her, while she pretended not to see it, he was suspecting she was doing it on purpose. Sadly, he was no idiot.

That would be you in this story, she chastised herself.

"Are you okay, my love? You went quiet on me," George said at some point, startling her a little.

Madelyne forced a smile. "I guess I'm a bit tired, that's all."

He nodded. "Understandable, considering what those two put you through," he lectured. George was back to his usual self, except now, Madelyne could hear pure manipulation behind his words.

Looking back, she couldn't help noticing certain patterns. Right from the start, he had deliberately been trying to create friction between her and her ex, between her and her daughter. She guessed isolating her completely was his end game, but for what purpose? She couldn't say.

He'd even tried to ship Connie to boarding school, for crying out loud, since she saw right through his bullshit. And Madelyne had almost let him. *I should have listened to her.* That was too little, too late. There were a lot of things she should have done differently, and then maybe she wouldn't have ended up in this situation.

There must be something seriously wrong with her when

she thought George was a good husband and stepfather for even a second.

"Madelyne?" George snapped.

Apparently, she'd lost herself in her musing again when he was trying to have a conversation with her. He didn't look pleased that she wasn't paying attention.

"Yes?" she asked, as though nothing were amiss.

"You missed your turn," he snapped, irritated.

That was true, and completely on purpose. Not that she was about to share that. "I thought about going another way. It's a shortcut," she lied.

He was frowning, but Madelyne guessed he bought it. "Hurry up," he grumbled.

Even with her best efforts, they would be reaching Damon's apartment soon. Unfortunately, Madelyne had no way to let Damon know they were on their way. George had taken her phone from her.

Madelyne hoped Damon had taken Connie someplace else, perhaps to the police station. She really didn't want to catch them off guard, especially not when George was armed and on some kind of mission. At the same time, Damon had no reason to leave his place or suspect that George would act like this.

Maybe we'll get lucky and find a police patrol in front of the apartment, Madelyne fantasized. Either way, Madelyne would never allow something to happen to Connie. She would defend her with her life.

She might not be privy to the whole story, but she knew enough. George was dangerous despite his act, and that meant Connie needed to be protected from him no matter the cost. Luckily, Madelyne wouldn't be alone in her efforts. She would have an ally on her side who thought and felt exactly the same. *Damon.*

31

DAMON

Damon and Connie drove in silence for a while, although there was a certain tension present in the car. They were both lost in thought, worried about the future. At least, that was what was on Damon's mind.

You're doing the right thing, he told himself for the hundredth time. Unfortunately, that sounded like a lie. All of this was wrong on so many levels.

He couldn't help feeling like shit. There was another passenger missing in this car; he couldn't ignore that. He'd totally abandoned Madelyne. She was constantly on his mind as he tried to put as many miles between them and George as possible. It went against his nature to leave someone behind.

You're doing the right thing. Although it didn't feel like that.

You had no choice. You had to think of Connie. That rationalization didn't help either. He'd left Madelyne to deal with that killer on her own as he took off. He couldn't bear it.

As soon as I take care of Connie, I'll be returning for Madelyne. But that meant he couldn't just leave his daughter at some motel. He needed to know someone was watching over her so he could concentrate on rescuing Madelyne.

There was one place he could go to in a situation like this one. There was no need to adjust his trajectory. As it turned out, he was already driving toward eastern New York. Damon knew Uncle Joe would help him.

Uncle Joe wasn't his real uncle. Being an orphan, Damon had been constantly passed around foster homes, like a basket of old clothes that nobody really wanted or needed. It didn't help the fact that Damon had been an impossible kid, always starting fights and causing trouble. He had been an angry kid.

It was no wonder he became an angry man as well.

Regardless of his nature, there was one pair, one family he liked the best. Uncle Joe and Aunt Betsy were the ones he loved. He'd stayed with them the longest. Uncle Joe had inspired him to join the Army once he came of age.

He knew that Connie would be safe with them, since Uncle Joe was a retired major. He would protect Connie like she was his own granddaughter, and that would provide Damon with the necessary peace of mind so he could go back and deal with George.

The more he thought about it, the more convinced he was that Madelyne was in grave danger. And it was all his fault. He'd failed to tell her the actual truth. He was resenting her for keeping things from him, but here he was doing the same to her. And his dishonesty could very well cost her life.

Stop! he yelled at himself. He couldn't think like that since it would drive him crazy.

"Dad, are you sure this is wise?" Connie asked at some point, breaking his mental aerobics, if only for a little while.

"What do you mean?" He frowned over at her.

"Won't Mom be angry we left without her?"

Angry wasn't the word he would use, since he was sure Madelyne had more pressing issues at the moment. Not that he said something like that out loud. He didn't want to put additional stress on his daughter. *Madelyne can take care of herself,* he thought, trying to pacify himself.

He'd even taught her how to shoot. None of that helped him calm down. Madelyne was all alone with a killer. There was no telling what was happening at the moment. And he couldn't call her to find out. He had to have faith that he was doing the right thing.

"Your mom will understand," he said eventually. And that wasn't a lie. He meant it.

"You weren't supposed to take me out of state without permission."

"Don't worry about it."

His daughter's concerns were justifiable, although low on his list of worries at the moment. This could technically be characterized as custodial kidnapping, and if George forced Madelyne to call the police on him, they were screwed.

George wouldn't do that, considering he had problems of his own with the law, he rationalized. Damon would rather go to jail than live with the knowledge that Connie got hurt in any way because he'd stopped short of doing everything he could.

Some rules had to be broken for the greater good. That wasn't smart thinking in the Army, but that was what life had taught him. Damon wasn't going to make life easy for George and just surrender. He was going to fight until the end.

"I'm worried about her," Connie said, which only meant she was not as unaware of the situation as he'd hoped. Connie was a smart girl.

Damon was extremely worried himself. *You just left her with that killer without trying to help her.*

"Your mom knows how to take care of herself." Damon didn't know if he said that for Connie's benefit or his own. Probably both.

Connie nodded, but it was clear there was something else on her mind. "Do you think she told George what happened?"

Damon cringed inwardly. *Thanks to me, she doesn't know anything. Not really.* "I don't know, kid."

"Should we call her?"

No matter all else, Damon believed that to be a bad idea. He said as much. "We can't risk tipping George off."

Connie was becoming visibly more and more alarmed. "Maybe we should go back. Go and get her."

Every fiber of Damon's being rebelled. He couldn't allow his daughter to be in harm's way. "We can't, Connie."

"Why not?" she challenged. "We totally abandoned her," she pointed out, tearing up.

Damon knew exactly how she felt, torn inside, because he was feeling the same way. He was about to say some lame line, try to pacify her, yet she beat him to the punch.

"I can feel she's in danger, Dad. And it's all my fault. Me and my stupid plan."

"None of this is your fault, okay?" Damon insisted.

"How can you say that, Dad? It so is."

"Look, I know you're worried, but this is for the best. I'll drop you off at Uncle Joe's, and then I'll return for your mother."

"We're going to Uncle Joe's?" she asked, a bit surprised.

It was true that it had been quite some time since Damon had gone to visit them. Connie had still been a little girl when Damon had taken his family to meet the ones he considered his own. Uncle Joe and Aunt Betsy were the closest things he had to parents in this world.

"Yes."

"Dad, it might be too late by the time you manage to get back," Connie argued.

Damon couldn't say that his daughter was wrong. All the same concerns plagued him as well. However, that didn't mean he would turn the car around and go rescue Madelyne.

Who knew, maybe there was no need for any kind of rescuing if Madelyne kept quiet about what had happened. *Yeah, right.* Damon's gut feeling was telling him that he was right about this. Right to leave.

"Connie, we're not going back," he replied adamantly, but perhaps he could offer an alternative. "Do you want me to call the police again?"

It was clear that confused her. "And say what?" she asked carefully.

It continued to bother him greatly that his daughter had had such experiences with law enforcement. *My daughter, a juvenile delinquent.* The irony. Considering he had been exactly the same at that age, probably worse. That proverb about how the apple doesn't fall far from the tree was spot on. Not that he planned on ever sharing something like that with his daughter. Her rebellious phase ended right now, as far as he was concerned.

"Well, I can implicate George this time," he offered.

At first, he'd believed that wouldn't be advisable. If the police went to him without any real proof other than the anonymous tip, there was a chance he would walk free. Damon hoped the police would find the body, gather evidence, and on their own, find connections between the victim and George. And then Connie could solidify that with her testimony. Unfortunately, as it turned out, they didn't have that kind of time at their disposal.

Connie made a face. "That's even worse. We can't know what he's going to do to Mom if we report him."

"You don't know that. Maybe they'll catch him off guard."

She wasn't buying that. "It has to be you," she insisted. "You have to save her."

Damon planned to as soon as he made sure Connie was safe. He said as much, although it was breaking his heart to see his daughter in such distress. She had a big heart, and she felt like she was betraying her mother with this act, and Damon understood perfectly. He felt the same way.

All the same, no matter how much it pained him, no matter how much his daughter might hate him in the future, Damon couldn't turn around. And then it occurred to him. What if George took Madelyne someplace and Damon couldn't find her? What if Connie and Damon would have to stay hidden in return? Damon wasn't built for a life as a fugitive. He liked to handle problems head-on. And he certainly didn't want that kind of life, one of fear, always looking over his shoulder, worrying if George had managed to find her, for Connie as well.

Stop. Connie's comment made him spiral out of control. Those were all unnecessary speculations, and he had to treat them as such and not like something that was actually happening. Besides, there was still a way to prevent all that if they played their cards exactly right.

"Connie, the police are our best shot," Damon tried to reason. "They are equipped to deal with these situations."

She looked dubiously at him. "I don't want anything to happen to Mom because of me. I could never forgive myself, especially not after—" Her voice hitched a little, and she paused.

"After what?" Damon prompted.

She took a deep breath, staring through the window. "I was so cruel to her the last time we spoke. I don't want her to think I hate her."

Damon was aghast. "She would never think that."

"You were not there, Dad. I was terrible," she said remorsefully.

"She knows you love her as much as she loves you," he insisted. "And you will have the opportunity to tell her that in person."

"You really believe that?" she challenged.

"With all my heart." And that was no lie. No matter what, Damon would find a way to help Madelyne, because he, too, couldn't live with himself with any other outcome.

"Okay, then."

"Okay, what?"

"If you think we should call the police, then that's what we need to do."

"I really do," he insisted.

"I agree, then."

Nodding, Damon looked for the first convenient highway exit so he could park before making the call.

"But, Dad, I've been thinking."

"What, Con-Con?"

"What will happen to you then?"

Damon looked at her questioningly, not understanding what she meant by that. "In what regard?"

Connie made a face. "I'm not an idiot. I know you are not supposed to take me to see Uncle Joe without Mom's permission."

"Not technically," he hedged.

"I don't want something to happen to you."

"I'll be fine." He tried to brush it off.

Connie wouldn't let him. "I don't want you going to jail because of me."

It was really heartbreaking that his daughter, at her age, had to deal with all these issues. "No one is going to jail," he insisted, "except George."

"Promise?"

That wasn't something he could promise, but he nodded.

"I promise, Con-Con. I will take care of everything."

"And save Mom?"

"And save Mom."

32

MADELYNE

Madelyne felt like crying from pure joy. The apartment was empty. Damon and Connie were gone. Damon must have realized somehow that their daughter was in danger, that George would be looking for her, and he'd taken her and left. *Thank God.*

It went without saying that George didn't share her sentiments. Not that she was showing hers on the outside. George couldn't know what was on her mind. She felt that would be the death of her. So she continued to pretend.

"They're not here," she stated the obvious as George continued to bang on the door with his fists.

He looked at her without stopping. "Damon, open the door. I know you're in there," he insisted.

"You'll alert the neighborhood."

"I don't give a fuck."

He should. If one of the neighbors called the police, George would find himself in the exact predicament he was trying to avoid. That was precisely why Madelyne said nothing.

"Damon, open this door right now!" he raged, trying the handle. The door was locked.

Wherever Damon and Connie were, Madelyne hoped they were safe and wouldn't try to contact her. George had her phone, so that could have catastrophic consequences.

"Damon, I'm warning you."

Madelyne would have tried to make a run for her car, but sadly, George had taken the keys from her. She was stuck.

"He's clearly not home," Madelyne said, unable to take this anymore.

"He's hiding," he said, through gritted teeth, "but I'm not an idiot to fall for it."

"His car isn't here," she replied before she could stop herself.

You're an idiot. She felt like smacking herself in the face. It wasn't her place to help George, but to sabotage him in any way possible, play interference while Damon took care of Connie. She hoped that included going to the police, because she couldn't know for how long she could stand to be with this man and pretend everything was all right when it clearly wasn't.

George narrowed his eyes and moved a couple of steps so he could look at the parking lot below. She knew the instant he realized she was right. His jaw clenched.

"Do you have a spare key?" he asked.

"For his car?"

"For the apartment," he snapped in return, clearly irked by her slowness—which was on purpose.

"Of course not."

George shook his head, probably thinking of her complete uselessness, as he returned to stand by the door. She was about to ask what he was doing when with one swift move, he slammed against the door with his shoulder, and with minimal damage or noise, he managed to break in.

"What are you doing?" she demanded, aghast.

"Get inside," he commanded.

Madelyne followed him inside, once again confirming what she already knew. Damon and Connie were long gone. She wasn't even concerned about where they went. As long as Damon was beside Connie, she was all right, and Madelyne would be at ease.

"George, this is not all right."

The chances that someone would call the police on them had now doubled.

Isn't that a good thing?

"We have to find them, don't we?" he asked rhetorically, looking about.

Yeah, you'll find them under the couch. Not that she said that out loud.

It was clear that Connie had been here, since her mug with the saying *Daddy's Little Girl* sat on the coffee table. There was some kind of liquid inside that looked like cocoa. It was untouched.

As she pictured Damon using the stove, which was unimaginable, George was frantically running about the apartment, inspecting every nook and cranny.

"They're gone." It was his turn to state the obvious. "I knew it," he raged. "Didn't I tell you?"

He was right. That wasn't something Madelyne could tell him. She had her character to play.

"Where would they go?" he demanded, returning to her side.

She shrugged. "I don't know." And that was the truth. Madelyne couldn't predict what Damon would do or where he would go since he was the one privy to the whole story, not her. The only thing she was absolutely certain of was that something serious had happened. Where he'd taken Connie was a big mystery to her. Damon had a lot of friends he could ask for favors.

"He hasn't been himself lately," she added for good measure.

"Would they go to the gym?" George asked in all seriousness.

Sure, right after Connie saw something traumatic that involved you, he would take her to work. Of course, she didn't say that out loud. "Maybe," she allowed.

George started biting his lower lip. "No, that's a shitty idea."

Madelyne wasn't going to contradict him.

"Call the gym," he said, taking her by surprise.

What happened to 'that's a shitty idea'? Then something occurred to her. This was an opportunity. This was a chance for her to get her phone back. Although she had to play it cool, without reminding him how she'd lost her phone in the first place.

If she got her phone back, then maybe she could find a way to get in touch with Damon and finally learn what was going on. It would be reassuring to know where they were and what they planned on doing. It was obvious they'd left in haste, but where or why, she couldn't know for sure. Being in the dark was maddening. And she had only herself to blame. If she'd argued less, defended George less, then maybe Damon would feel better about sharing everything with her. However, that was a migraine for some other time.

"Okay," she replied, gesturing for him to give her the phone back.

To her chagrin, George grabbed Damon's landline and handed it to her to make the call.

Should she pretend she didn't know the number by heart? George knew that she did. She cursed while she dialed.

"No one is answering," she said. It went without saying that she would say the same even if Damon did pick up. He didn't. "There's no one there."

Damon had a couple of trainers who came in the morning to hold boxing classes, but he was the only one with the key. If no one was answering, that was because Damon had failed to show up that morning to unlock the gym. Madelyne found that reassuring.

"Try again," George urged.

She did, getting the same results. She shared as much.

"Damn it." George started cursing, walking about the apartment, clearly thinking about their next move, as Madelyne slowly put the phone down. For a second, she wondered if she should call 9-1-1. She couldn't. She was afraid George would discover her.

"Maybe we should return home," she offered.

He turned to glare at her. "Home? Are you crazy!" he shouted, completely losing control, and Madelyne cringed.

Maybe she'd gone overboard with this. But she had to do something. She couldn't stay here, and she hoped if they returned home, she would find some way to escape. Then she'd find Damon and finally get to the bottom of things. Asking George why he was acting like this was out of the question. She feared his reaction and response.

"We can't stay here," she pointed out.

He narrowed his eyes. "Tell me where they went, Madelyne," he insisted.

"I don't know, George," she replied calmly.

He approached and grabbed her by the arms. "You're lying," he accused, shaking her to underscore his words.

"Let go," she complained. He was hurting her. That was what she was afraid would happen when he finally discovered things wouldn't go his way.

"Does he have a vacation home?" He started questioning her.

Madelyne thought about her answer before replying. She decided it wouldn't be prudent to lie. The consequences would be too great. "No, he doesn't. Now let go of me. You're hurting me."

He ignored her pleas. "You don't know what hurt is, and you will if you don't start telling me the truth," he threatened, eyes wild.

Madelyne believed him. "I don't know anything," she insisted.

"Does he have a favorite camping site?"

Damon hated camping.

It reminded him too much of the time when he'd run away from some foster parents and lived in the streets. When Madelyne pointed out that being in the Army was no different, he was quick to say it was completely different. In the Army, he was constantly surrounded by his brothers and sisters.

Madelyne shook her head no.

"Where does his family live?"

"He's an orphan."

George shouted in frustration.

Damon didn't know who his biological parents were and had grown up in foster care. That was technically true, but there was an old couple whom Damon considered his family. Joe and Betsy. If Damon felt threatened in any way, that was where he would go. Damon had gone to Uncle Joe with Connie, Madelyne was suddenly sure of that.

Unfortunately, as she realized that, George could see it on her face.

"You are lying to me, you bitch!" he accused, slapping her hard.

Madelyne was sure she would have fallen down if he hadn't been holding her tightly with his other hand.

"Tell me where he took her, now!"

Madelyne looked him straight in the eyes before replying, "I will not!" She matched his tone perfectly.

His eyes flashed with undiluted hatred. "Is that so?"

Madelyne gulped.

Looking about, he smiled. With one swift move, he grabbed the water bottle that stood on the counter and broke it against the counter's edge. The glass shattered, water spilled everywhere, yet the neck of the bottle with its sharp edges remained in George's hand.

Madelyne screamed as he advanced with it toward her.

"Stop screaming," he commanded, and she clammed up. He pointed with the sharp edges against her face. "If you don't start talking, I will slice you all over and start with your face," he threatened, his voice menacing.

His tone filled her with dread. Madelyne was used to pain, but now felt like she would do everything in her power to avoid it.

"Why are you doing this?" she cried out in return, desperate for all of this to stop. She wanted her life back, her peace, her happily ever after. As it turned out, none of that was real.

"Don't pretend like you don't know," he warned menacingly.

"Know what?" she asked in return, fully knowing her questions would enrage him further. Not that she believed something like that was possible. George looked like he'd already reached his plateau.

"That little whelp of yours saw me off Dunwoody."

Madelyne's eyes widened in shock. What did he say? *Off?* *As in kill?* Madelyne had a feeling it was something serious, but a murder? Connie saw George kill someone? *It can't be, but it fits perfectly.* Madelyne was horrified.

No wonder her daughter had been so shaken up after reaching Damon's place. Anyone would react the same way considering the circumstances. Her poor baby girl. *And I accused them of lying.* She felt like dying then and there out of shame.

George scrutinized her face, then chuckled. "You really didn't know."

Madelyne couldn't fathom why he was so amused by that fact. "You're a monster."

He really smiled then, getting into her face. "You have no idea."

She felt repulsed by him. But there was nowhere to run. He was holding her tightly, threatening with that piece of glass.

"Now tell me where they are before I really lose my patience with you."

"So you can kill us all?"

His returning smile was even bigger.

"Damon will never allow you to harm Connie," she added defiantly.

"He's no match for me."

He looked so sure of himself that Madelyne was decidedly worried. Not for herself, but for her family.

"Speak, my love," he taunted.

"I'll never tell you where they are."

"We'll see about that. However, I welcome the challenge."

With that said, he pushed her against the wall and slammed his whole body against her. Madelyne lost all her breath, and that was not all. He took the shard and pressed it against her cheek. She could feel its sharp edges breaking her skin, but she still said nothing, did nothing.

I've been through much worse and survived, she told herself, trying to find the strength to resist, to resist the urge to scream, cry, beg for her life.

"I will kill you." He emphasized his words by pushing a little deeper.

Madelyne was prepared to sacrifice herself for her daughter. She knew Damon would safeguard her.

George shouted in frustration. "Have it your way," he said.

Madelyne closed her eyes, preparing for the worst.

And then nothing happened.

Madelyne looked at George, only to see he was looking at something beside her. Grabbing her by the hair, he turned her around, so her face was inches away from a framed photograph that hung on the wall.

In the photo was young Damon with Uncle Joe in front of a house. *Oh no.*

"Where is this?" he demanded. He placed the shard against her eye, ready to poke it out. "I will fucking kill you."

Madelyne remained quiet.

"I know how to get the truth out of you," he said mostly to himself. And Madelyne could feel him fumbling around, trying to get rid of her pants. She knew what he was about to do. *No, no, no, no.* Madelyne completely lost it. She couldn't go through that. *Not again.*

"No, please," she cried out. She could feel him pressing against her. "Stop."

"Tell me where he went."

"Long Island," Madelyne said through sobs. The pain stopped.

Once again, he turned her to look at him. "That's a good start. Now tell me everything else that you know about it."

Madelyne felt completely defeated. She broke; she wasn't strong enough. And so help her God, she told him everything.

33

DAMON

D amon found a suitable place to make a stop and call the police. He debated whether he should call one of his Army buddies who worked for the police, but ruled against it. He needed this to be one hundred percent legit, done by the book, as they would say.

In his mind, it was like this. It was better to at least try using legal means to deal with this crazy situation, even if he had to face some consequences for taking Connie out of the city without permission, than deal with it on his own and make matters better and worse at the same time.

He could get rid of George, but what would that do to their family? Damon didn't want Connie to have a tarnished conscience. He didn't want her living with the knowledge that her father had to kill someone for her, and to expect she would cover for him for the rest of her life. That was a lot to ask from a sixteen-year-old.

Connie watched in silence as he dialed. When he got to speak with the operator again, at first, he didn't know what to say. *Your name?*

"My name is Sergeant Damon Blake. Maybe you've been looking for me. My daughter, Connie Blake, and I have been on the run since this morning." Although it felt like a lifetime had passed since Connie had first told him about George and what he'd done.

There was a short pause before she replied, "Sir, we don't have any kind of warrants issued for those names."

If there was no warrant for his arrest, then that could only mean Madelyne hadn't called to report him. That was good and bad news at the same time, because it meant George was trying to deal with this on his own.

"But tell me, are you and your daughter in some kind of danger?" the operator inquired, snapping him from his thoughts.

"Yes, we are. My daughter witnessed a murder, and now I fear the shooter will try to harm her." He explained everything in short terms. "We fled my apartment before I could tell my ex-wife." He stretched the truth a bit. "Could you call her, by any chance? We're worried about her."

"Certainly."

Damon gave Madelyne's full name and phone numbers, home and cell, so the operator could call her in his stead.

"No one is answering," she told him after a short pause.

That didn't sound good. He couldn't help wondering what was happening with her. What did George do?

"Do you want me to send a patrol car to her address?"

"Please, and note that her husband is extremely dangerous. He's the one my daughter saw murder someone."

"Sir, could you tell me what your daughter saw?" she asked in return, clearly trying to play catch-up. It was his fault. In haste, out of concern, he wasn't explaining this as he should.

He would try to do better from now on, to be more

concise. "There was a shooting at one of the old boathouses on the lake. I already reported it."

"At 6:47 this morning."

Damon couldn't say with that precision. "That sounds about right. And as soon as we called the police, we fled my apartment, since I feared for my daughter's safety."

"I understand. Let me connect you with Detective Shane Edwards. He's in charge of that case."

"Thank you."

If there was a case, then it was logical to assume they'd found the body. Since his daughter looked at him intently, he gave her a thumbs-up. So far, everything was going according to plan, but Damon wanted to hear what the detective had to say.

After some waiting around, a man answered.

"Detective Edwards," he answered with the deepest voice Damon had heard in his entire life, and that was no exaggeration.

"Hello, Detective, my name is Damon Blake."

"Just the man I wanted to speak with."

That surprised him. Still, he said, "Glad to be of service, then."

"Are you my witness for the boathouse shooting?"

"No, that would be my daughter, Connie."

"And she is with you, I presume?"

"Yes, I decided it was necessary to leave town."

"Okay, put her on, then. I need to have a little chat with her."

The way Detective Edwards spoke, Damon got the impression the other man couldn't be surprised by anything. Damon couldn't decide if that was a good or a bad thing. *Being jaded can't be good.*

Instead of handing the phone to Connie, he put it on speaker.

"Go on, Detective, ask your questions," Damon said.

"Connie?"

"Yes, sir," she replied a bit shyly.

"Could you describe what you saw this morning?"

Connie looked at Damon as though for confirmation, so he nodded in return. She needed to be completely honest with this man so they could resolve this and return to their normal lives.

"Last night," she corrected.

"My mistake, last night."

Damon thought that was some kind of test to see if Connie was speaking the truth.

"Well, I saw two men speaking in one of the old boathouses. They started arguing about some jewels, and then one killed the other, shot him in the head. I think that man's name was Dunwoody, or something like that."

"Could you identify the shooter?"

Connie hesitated, so Damon took her hand. That helped.

"It was George Elway, my stepfather."

"Your stepfather, you say?"

"Yes, I was following him, wanting to prove to my mother that he was having an affair, when he actually went to meet Dunwoody."

"Thank you for speaking with me, Connie. Mr. Blake?"

"Yes, Detective?"

"I would like to speak with you again." *More privately* was his clear meaning.

Connie got alarmed hearing that, but Damon assured her with a shake of his head. He believed that wasn't a bad thing, simply not for her ears.

Damon turned the speakerphone off and put the phone back against his ear. "I'm listening, Detective."

The detective sighed before speaking. "Well, the good

news, if you could call it that, is that your daughter's story matches what I saw at the crime scene."

Damon agreed: he couldn't see the good in the fact that his daughter had witnessed an actual crime committed by her stepfather. "There was no doubt in my mind that it could be otherwise."

"Kids are prone to act out."

Don't I know it. During the night, Damon had discovered his daughter had a juvenile record, which still confounded him.

"She told the truth." Damon was adamant.

"I know. Which brings me to the bad news. Where are you, Mr. Blake?"

Damon felt no need to lie to the detective. He could sense this man would try to help them no matter what.

"We were about to cross the state line when I decided to call the police again," Damon explained.

"The suspect is related to your daughter?"

God forbid. "No, he is my ex-wife's new husband." Damon always felt like a failure when he had to explain George to others, even before he'd discovered he was nothing more than a killer.

"Is Mr. Elway aware of the situation?"

"I can't say for sure, but I fear my ex, Madelyne, told him what Connie saw."

"Mr. Blake, I understand you're worried about your daughter's safety, but I need you and your daughter to come to the precinct as soon as possible to give a formal statement. That way, I can get a warrant for George Elway's arrest."

That all sounded great, but Damon had his doubts. "I wasn't able to reach Madelyne. I'm worried about her."

"We'll look into that, Mr. Blake. You have my word. But I need you to come to see me," he insisted.

"Besides my daughter, Madelyne is my biggest concern."

"Do you believe she is in danger?"

"Definitely," Damon replied, without a thought. "George is dangerous, and there's no telling what he's capable of doing when threatened."

"Does he have a history of violence?"

Like one murder isn't enough? "He was abusive toward my ex-wife and daughter," Damon clarified.

As far as Damon could see, George had worked really hard to create this false persona of an outstanding citizen, a restaurant owner. He wouldn't be pleased to lose that. George would try to do everything in his power to silence Connie, and everyone else who stood in his way, for that matter. Damon couldn't allow that.

"I just received a message that a patrol car went to the address and found no one at the house."

"Oh no." Damon didn't like that one bit. Where was George? Where was Madelyne? Were they on the run? Or was he looking for them? A million questions passed through his head.

"Don't worry, Mr. Blake. We will find your wife. But you and your daughter need to be here with us as soon as possible."

"Connie isn't safe," Damon insisted, especially knowing that George, and probably Madelyne, was looking for them.

"I will personally arrange for your daughter to get protection from the suspect. Nothing will happen to her on my watch." There was such finality, such confidence in his voice. Damon was inclined to believe him.

There was one more thing Damon had to discuss with the detective before turning the car around. He wanted to be completely honest with the other man. "Detective, there's one more small issue of custodial kidnapping."

The detective understood him perfectly without Damon

having to go into details. "You're not the legal guardian of your daughter?"

"It's technically a joint custody where I have the weekends."

"And I presume you don't have the mother's approval for this little excursion?"

"With George involved, the situation is extra complicated."

"I see. Well, despite the circumstances, I don't have to tell you that you will make matters worse by crossing state lines. The best you can do for yourself and your daughter is to return here," the detective advised.

"There's a killer on the loose," Damon pointed out.

"That is why you will come to see me immediately. And I will help you sort through this mess. After all, you were only trying to protect your daughter."

Exactly. He knew this detective would understand his actions. "Thank you, Detective Edwards. We're on our way."

"Glad to hear that, Mr. Blake."

They disconnected.

"What happened?" Connie asked.

"We're going to the police station for you to give a formal statement," he explained.

"And what about George?"

"He'll get arrested, thanks to your testimony."

"And Mom?"

Damon hesitated there. He didn't want to tell her the police patrol had found an empty house. "Detective Edwards will make sure nothing happens to her either."

Connie nodded, then smiled. That was a sight to behold after such a traumatic event. But then she grew serious anew. "Dad, stop driving like an old woman," she chastised. "Hurry, we have a crime to solve," she commanded, suddenly invigorated, as though her confidence and enthusiasm had returned.

"Yes, ma'am," Damon teased in return, hitting the gas pedal.

Hold on, Madelyne. We're coming for you.

34

MADELYNE

After Madelyne told George everything she knew about Uncle Joe and why she believed Damon would go there, her husband from hell forced her to return to the car. Although she felt quite rattled, he demanded that she start driving all over again. A gun in his hand was a good motivator for her to do just that.

"Where are we going?" she demanded, alarmed. Although she had a sinking feeling she already knew the answer to that question.

"Just drive," he shouted in return, so she did.

Pretty soon, by the way he was guiding her, it became apparent that they were going to Long Island. The New Jersey state line was fast approaching, and she didn't know how to stop any of this from happening. She dreaded reaching their destination. She couldn't allow that.

In her defeat and surrender to George, there was one thing she'd failed to tell him. And that was that Uncle Joe was a soldier like Damon. She forced herself to bite her tongue pretty hard not to share that last, final piece of information. She hoped that Uncle Joe and Damon would have no problems in dealing with this man, no matter how dangerous he really was. She was only stressing about her inability to phone them, to alert them in any way that they were coming.

"What do you plan to do?" Madelyne asked, unable to stand the tense silence anymore.

She needed to know what his end game was. It was a bit uncomfortable to speak with dried-up blood on her face that created some kind of macabre half-mask, but she didn't bother to wipe it off. She wanted George to see what he did, not that he looked particularly bothered. He'd killed a man. She was sure torturing someone, shedding some blood, felt like nothing at all to him.

"That is of no concern to you," he snapped.

Madelyne begged to differ, since they were going to meet Damon and her daughter. "Damon will never let you harm Connie."

"I told you to keep quiet."

Yet Madelyne couldn't comply.

Her phone started ringing during their exchange at the house, but George ignored it. Madelyne stressed about who might be calling her. *It's probably Damon, worried about me,* she thought in concern. If Damon kept calling, then George would certainly find a way to use it to his advantage, and that was something Madelyne had to avoid at any cost.

You can always run the car into some wall and be done with it, a part of her pointed out. Her phone started ringing again. *Damon, please stop,* she begged.

This time around, when her phone started ringing, the caller kept calling over and over again. That persistence was quite troubling. Did something happen to Connie? No, it couldn't have. She was safe with Damon, and Madelyne was with George, she rationalized.

Unfortunately, she wasn't the only one rattled by this turn of events.

"Who keeps calling you? Goddamn it," George growled, losing patience as he fished the phone from his pocket.

He was frowning deeply, looking at the screen. "Who is this?" he demanded, putting the phone into her face.

As it turned out, it was an unknown caller who was trying to reach her with impressive persistence.

"I don't know," she replied honestly. That was definitely a number she wasn't familiar with.

The phone stopped ringing only to start all over again. Someone was really adamant to reach her.

"You will answer it," George said through gritted teeth, "but only to get rid of him. If you say anything, so help me God, I will kill you right this instant." He finished his threat with a shake of his gun.

Madelyne didn't feel the need to point out how killing her would mean a death sentence for him as well. She was curious to hear who was calling her. Knowing her luck, it was probably one of the telemarketers wanting to offer her a time-share or something like that.

Madelyne nodded, and George answered, putting the phone on speaker. Of course he wanted to listen.

"Hello?" Madelyne answered, trying to appear calm. She didn't know if she succeeded, though.

"Mrs. Elway?" a pleasant female voice inquired.

"Yes, this is she."

"My name is Officer Jessica Johnson."

"Officer? Is everything all right?"

"I'm calling to inform you that your ex-husband, Damon Blake, and your daughter, Connie, have been found and are on their way to the police station."

Madelyne could see with the corner of her eyes that George wasn't pleased to hear that. She didn't know what to say to the officer or how to tip her off that George was right beside her.

It appeared that George guessed her thoughts because he pressed the gun to her abdomen.

"Oh, thank God. Thank you for that information. This was one stressful time for me and my family," Madelyne said, glancing at George, who looked anything but happy. *Murderous* came to mind.

Damon's deciding to go to the police rather than to Uncle Joe's really put a damper on his plans. Madelyne almost smiled. Although her joy was probably too premature. She didn't care what happened to her as long as Connie was all right and out of George's reach.

"You're requested to join them there, since there's this legal issue of custody that needs to be resolved."

Madelyne frowned. Why was she speaking of custody and not of murder? Did the police even know about that? Madelyne felt extremely confused. Was all of this some kind of ruse so they could entrap George?

"Of course, my husband and I will be right there," Madelyne said right before George ended the call.

"That whelp of yours is about to rat on me," he raged. "If she didn't already."

Madelyne was glad he'd started to feel the heat. Maybe this was the perfect opportunity for her to try to convince him to turn himself in. This was all pointless, anyway.

"You need to come with me and surrender—" she started, but she didn't get a chance to finish since he smacked her.

"I would rather die than return to prison."

Return? George had been in prison before? She really didn't know the man who sat next to her.

You think?

To her surprise, he didn't tell her to stop the car or change direction. There was no need for them to leave the state anymore, since the person he was after, her daughter, was on her way home.

The hit stung a bit. That didn't discourage her in any way. Madelyne had to find some way to run away from this man, and for that, she couldn't pretend to be driving Miss Daisy anymore.

"Where are we going, then?" She intentionally said we, although she detested having to join them together in any way. Madelyne was horrified with herself. She'd married this man, but that was a brain aneurysm for some other time. Now she had more pressing issues.

George kept quiet.

"There's no need to drive to Long Island anymore. Damon and Connie are in Chicago." She stated the obvious.

"Shut the fuck up already and let me think," he snapped in return, hitting the car door with his fist.

So he was aware of the situation and didn't know about his next move. Madelyne started wondering if she could somehow use that to her advantage.

"George, it's over."

"Excuse me?"

"The police are clearly onto you."

"I'm not afraid."

That wasn't her point. "You no longer have a use for me. You should let me go."

George kept quiet, looking at her intently.

Madelyne kept talking. "You can go wherever you want now."

"Without money? That bastard Dunwoody screwed me up good, refusing to tell me where he stashed the jewels."

Madelyne was dumbfounded. "What jewels?"

"Just drive for now and let me think."

Madelyne tried to plead with him from a different angle. "They will be looking for the two of us," she pointed out. Her meaning was obvious. He had better chances of escaping the law if he was all by himself.

"You want me to leave you?" he countered, raising an eyebrow.

"I want you to let me go, to return home to—" She stopped herself before she added *to my family*. Sadly, she fooled no one.

"Didn't you vow to always be by my side?" he mocked.

"I clearly made a mistake," Madelyne blurted out before she realized what she said. The last thing she needed to be doing at the moment was antagonizing him further.

To her shock, George started laughing. "You wound me, my love."

Madelyne felt sick to her stomach each time he used that endearment. "Don't call me that," she said, raising her chin ever so slightly.

He sighed, like before, when he thought she'd acted ridiculously. That irked her. Madelyne refused to be discouraged. She needed to know what his plan was, especially regarding her.

"George, face it, your life is over. No more Nightingale, no more fancy trips, over. You need to let me go and run away as fast as possible, as far as possible, if you don't want to get caught."

"Is that so?" He sounded almost bored, which troubled her. What was he up to?

"Be reasonable," she pleaded. All she wanted was to return home to her family and forget all of this ever happened.

You ignoring and burying things is the reason this kind of shit keeps happening to you. She ignored that. One problem at a time.

"You're my wife," George said, to her chagrin, "and your place is at my side."

Was this the right time to ask for a divorce? "George."

"Shut the fuck up, Madelyne, or I'll slap you so hard that whelp of yours will feel it."

Madelyne squeezed the wheel so hard, it looked like all the blood vanished from her hands. She didn't care about his threats. She continued as though he'd said nothing at all. "It's okay if you're afraid. You should be."

George looked at her with pure hatred. She'd loved this man with all her heart, and as it turned out, he'd never looked at her the same way. She couldn't fathom why he'd decided to marry her in the first place, but she didn't dare ask.

"Afraid?" he repeated, enraged.

Madelyne shrugged. "You killed someone, and now you're on the run. Your whole life changed with the pull of a trigger. It's only natural to be afraid."

"I'm not afraid," he replied, his strong voice echoing in the small car.

"You should be, because if the police don't find you, Damon will." And she didn't say that to force George to accept his dire predicament. She really believed that. No matter what, Damon would never stop hunting him as long as Madelyne was by his side.

To her surprise, George smiled. "I know that retard is still in love with you."

Madelyne was about to protest but didn't get a chance.

"Why do you think I still keep you around? You're not particularly good company, or even a good lay, for that matter."

Madelyne jerked as though he'd hit her. A slap on the face would hurt less than his words. It was all a lie, like she'd feared. "You're a monster."

"But I'm not stupid. As long as I have you, I'm fucking untouchable."

There was no surprise that Madelyne was nothing more

than a hostage to him. She'd suspected as much as soon as he'd brought that gun to find Connie. However, it was good to get that out in the open so they could stop pretending they were loving husband and wife anymore.

"I won't help you," Madelyne said defiantly.

He chuckled. "You're already helping me," he pointed out. "Now mind your driving. We don't want some traffic cop to stop us for speeding."

Madelyne thought how that wasn't such a bad idea.

It must have been clear what she was thinking of, because he added, "And don't get any ideas, because it would be on you if I have to kill someone else," he threatened.

That bastard had her there. Of course, she wouldn't risk some cop's life even if it meant liberty for her. Still, she said, "And if I refuse?"

George placed the gun against her heart. "I believe you get my point," he said menacingly.

"If I die, you will too," she countered defiantly.

He leaned toward her. "There's a lot I can do to you before deciding to kill you." And to prove his point, he moved the gun down her stomach and between her legs.

Madelyne gulped.

He returned to his seat as she remained quiet. "Glad we're in agreement, then." Saying that, he started laughing. It was the most terrifying sound in her entire life.

Please, God, help me.

35

DAMON

Connie grabbed Damon's hand as they walked into the police station. She hadn't done something like that since she was little, which was proof of how nervous she was that they were there.

"Everything will be all right now," he said to her reassuringly. The station looked chaotic, from all the commotion going on.

The officer who stood behind a massive desk eyed them with interest. Damon approached with Connie in tow. "Hello, my name is Sergeant Damon Blake. We're here to see Detective Edwards," he said politely.

"Does he know you're coming?"

"Yes, he's expecting us."

"Wait there." The officer pointed at a couple of benches in the corner.

Damon and Connie went to stand there as the officer made the call. Neither one of them dared to sit down because of how cold and uninviting the benches looked.

After a couple of minutes, a mountain of a man came to

stand in front of them. He was in his fifties, slightly chubby, with tousled red hair and baggy green eyes.

"Damon and Connie?" he inquired, and Damon thought Detective Edwards's voice sounded deeper in person.

Damon nodded. "Yes."

"Detective Edwards." He offered his hand. First Damon took it, then Connie.

Once the introductions were over, he turned to his left and said, "Please follow me."

Damon felt like they were walking through a tunnel, and then they went upstairs to an interrogation room. Inside a small room was a metal desk and four chairs.

Detective Edwards gestured for them to go inside. Connie looked freaked.

"Is this really necessary?" Damon objected.

"Yes," the detective replied simply.

Once Damon and Connie settled at one end of the table, Detective Edwards excused himself.

Damon wondered if anyone was watching them through the glass mirror. *We are not suspects.*

"Dad, I don't like this," Connie complained.

"Everything is fine; standard protocol. You're here to tell them what you saw and that's it."

"Okay."

Shortly afterward, Detective Edwards returned carrying a big folder, a notebook, and a tape recorder. He settled on the other side. As he made all the necessary preparations, he informed them how they could have a lawyer present. "You're here to give a statement. That is your right."

Damon debated whether he should call Nick, but ruled against it. He wanted this over as soon as possible, and looking at Connie, he could see she was of the same mind.

"No need," Damon replied.

"Do you mind if I record this?"

"No, sir," Connie replied, since the question was meant for her.

Damon was proud of his daughter and how she was conducting herself under stress.

After making the necessary intro for the recording, Detective Edwards gave the floor to Connie, so to speak. Once again, he asked her to tell everything she had seen last night, and in as much detail as possible.

"It all started when I had this fight with Mom. I knew something was off with George from the moment I met him, but she wouldn't listen to me. I decided to follow him, catch him with a mistress, so I could show my mom she'd made a mistake by marrying him."

As Connie launched into her story, Detective Edwards refrained from commenting. He let her retell everything in her own words, and only when she finished did he have some follow-up questions. After he was satisfied, he turned to speak with Damon, getting his point of view of the events. He didn't see the murder, but he was the one who saw his daughter afterward, and who spoke with Madelyne numerous times.

After getting what he wanted, Detective Edwards turned the recorder off. He then wrote the statements, and Connie and Damon signed them.

"Thank you, Connie. You've been an immense help to us and this case," Detective Edwards said approvingly.

"Does that mean you'll arrest him now?" Damon's daughter asked.

"I might not have enough to bust him for his previous crimes, but we'll definitely nail him for this murder."

"Previous crimes?" Damon asked with interest. Although he wasn't that surprised that George was known to law enforcement, he was curious to hear what other crimes he'd committed in the past.

The detective looked at him intently as though deciding how much to share before opening that big folder of his.

"For years now, I've suspected George Elway was a part of this highly trained elite criminal group that masterminded robbing exclusive jewelry shops and auction houses," Detective Edwards explained, taking Damon by surprise.

"Three years ago, they fell apart, each member going into hiding, and I suspected it had something to do with the fact that George Craven—that's his real last name—ended up being shot."

"Shot? As in a robbery gone wrong?"

Detective Edwards shook his head. "My theory was that there was some kind of internal power struggle, since they managed to take 8.3 million from their last heist."

Eight million? Damon's head was spinning.

"And since George was in charge of that merry band of thieves, I believed they'd staged a coup, but the bastard survived." He leaned in his chair. The metal protested ever so slightly. "I could never prove it. The gang became active again about nine months ago."

Damon tried to recollect if he'd heard something about a robbery in that period but came up short.

"The former associates of the group were starting to end up dead all over the county," the detective continued.

"Someone was killing them off?" Damon guessed.

The detective nodded. "I started looking for George. Found him downtown impersonating a restaurant owner and going by the name George Elway. Then I discovered he'd even gotten married."

"You believed he turned over a new leaf?"

The detective shrugged. "Or he was lying low."

"Did you think he was the next target?"

"I believed he was my shooter. If someone was killing off

members, he was the perfect suspect, since those same men tried to kill him."

It did make sense.

"It became clear to me that he lay low like the rest, then, once he learned where they were hiding, he started killing them off and settling scores. And now, thanks to Connie, I have my proof," Detective Edwards concluded.

The detective actually smiled at that, and although Damon was glad that he'd managed to solve a case, he wasn't glad his daughter had to be in the middle of it. At the same time, if Connie hadn't found out the truth about George, then who knew what could have happened? He would have continued to abuse Madelyne and his daughter indefinitely.

And then something else occurred to him. That was probably why George had gotten married in the first place. He needed a front while he was in hiding. It was a good plan, but as it turned out, his true nature was showing despite the fact that he was a restaurant owner and had the chance to actually lead a respectable life with a good woman by his side. A lowlife was always a lowlife.

This story sounded almost surreal to Damon. George was a professional thief and a killer. That plot could be used for a movie. It felt insane to experience it in real life.

Damon had always known, as did his daughter, that something wasn't right with George, and now he had his proof. This was one of those situations he couldn't really feel happy for being right about. All the same, it was better to know than to stay ignorant. Who knew how long George would be walking around killing people if Connie hadn't seen him?

Not in a million years would Damon think that George was some evil gang leader, but life could surprise people like that. Madelyne would say that he was acting surprised because he lacked imagination. They'd see what she would have to say about all of this.

Thinking of Madelyne, Damon was very much aware that she was still MIA.

"I need a district attorney's approval for the warrant," Edwards added, "but don't worry, it's just a formality."

Although Damon understood that, he didn't feel like waiting. He wanted this nightmare to end.

"And what about us?" Damon presumed going home was not an option. Not that he would even if he could. It wasn't safe with George still on the loose.

"Legally, you're on thin ice for fleeing with your daughter."

Connie instantly defended him. "It's not his fault. He was only trying to protect me."

"I know. And since you're cooperating now, I will do my best to help you smooth that over."

That wasn't the ideal outcome he was looking for. He wasn't in handcuffs, so it was better than nothing. He couldn't exactly help Connie if he was behind bars.

"And what about Madelyne?" Damon asked next.

"Yeah, what about Mom? Is there any news?" Connie agreed.

Detective Edwards hesitated, as though not wanting to discuss that in front of Connie. That worried Damon. Did he have bad news for them? Was Madelyne all right or even... He stopped himself right there. He couldn't jump to conclusions.

"Speak freely, Detective," Damon encouraged. Connie had the right to know what was happening.

"One of our officers managed to get in touch with Mrs. Elway."

"Is she all right?" Connie asked.

"She was informed about your whereabouts, but the officer got the impression..."

"Let me guess: Madelyne sounded strange and pretended everything was perfectly fine," Damon finished.

Detective Edwards frowned at that. "Something like that. She also told the officer that she and her husband were on their way to the precinct."

"That was clearly a lie," Damon commented.

Detective Edwards nodded. "That was hours ago, and since then, we haven't been able to reach either one of them, and the house is empty."

"Do you believe they're on the run?" Damon asked.

"I can't rule that out," he replied with a sigh.

Especially not when she sounded perfectly fine. Damon filled in the blanks for himself. *Madelyne, what did you do?*

"I tried reaching her, but she wasn't answering her phone," he went on. "I even sent a patrol car to George Craven's restaurant, but none of the staff has seen him in the last two days."

That all sounded like they'd just picked up and left after learning Connie was at the police station.

Would Madelyne flee with that criminal? It was true that she stood by his side, but Damon had his doubts about such an outcome. She'd sounded really concerned when Damon had told her what had happened with Connie. She'd denied it at first, but Damon believed she'd started to see reason and accept that George was involved.

What if she didn't have a choice? What if George had forced her to go with him? But then he remembered their last conversation. She'd demanded that he bring Connie home as though nothing had happened.

"If she really ran away with him, then you should let her," Connie snapped angrily. Damon understood how Connie would feel betrayed by her mother's behavior. He wished he had some words of comfort. Sadly, he was seriously lacking.

"They're on the wanted list, and every cop in this city is looking for them."

What if they're not in the city anymore?

Damon couldn't shake what his daughter just said. How they should let them go. Of course, something like that wasn't possible. Neither the law nor Damon could allow something like that. Damon needed to find Madelyne no matter what. Even if he had to go to jail afterward, he would bring her home. He owed his daughter that much.

36

MADELYNE

Madelyne strained her brain trying to come up with some plan to escape this nightmare. All the things she came up with looked too childish or unrealistic to her to do.

Despite George's words that he needed her as some form of shield, Madelyne was convinced that there would come a time in the near future when he would realize she was a liability and get rid of her.

It was no surprise that Madelyne wanted to prevent that. She wanted to keep living. She wanted to see her daughter grow up, go to college, meet someone, get married, and have children of her own. She wanted her to have a whole life to live.

Madelyne also wanted a chance to make amends to those she loved, to both Connie and Damon. Madelyne needed a second chance. She couldn't accept that she would die at the hands of this man, this stranger whom she considered her husband.

George turned out to be a complete psychopath, and Madelyne was horrified that she'd fallen for his act, his mask.

She didn't want to give him the satisfaction of seeing how much all of this hurt her. She would fight for her life. There was no other way. Madelyne wasn't going to accept her fate silently and meekly. She hadn't done that in the past, and she wouldn't now.

Perhaps she'd forgotten for a while who she was, what she went through, but it all came crashing back. Madelyne was a fighter, a survivor, so she would survive this crisis as well.

But what to do? She had no idea how to escape. She was still driving while George held her at gunpoint.

Should I cause an accident? She ruled against it. She couldn't put innocent people in danger because she was stupid enough to trust the wrong man. *An extremely dangerous man,* she corrected herself.

Madelyne kept quiet, observing George, trying to decipher what was on his mind and failing miserably, while trying to figure out where he was making her drive to. So far, they were heading toward Maine, and Madelyne could feel that she was running out of time.

George was on the phone a lot, speaking to various people, clearly old friends and associates. Sometimes, he used his phone, but for others he preferred hers. Madelyne would like to get the opportunity to make a call of her own. Not that he would ever let her.

From what she could gather, no one was prepared to help him. That put him in a particular state of agitation.

"Benny, you have to help me."

Madelyne had never heard him beg before.

"You're the only person I trust."

Unfortunately, it looked like his dear friend Benny also gave him the boot. Madelyne was really heartbroken about it. *Not.*

"Fucking bastard," he yelled, hanging up.

Problems, my dear? Madelyne wanted to ask, but she didn't feel like getting hit for that.

George scrolled through his phone, probably looking at his contact list. He was visibly sweating and losing hope. Seeing her looking at him, George grimaced. "What are you looking at?"

Madelyne averted her eyes back to the road without commenting. She was glad he was feeling like this. Maybe he would decide to let her go if no one wanted to take him in and give him refuge.

Or maybe he'll just kill me.

That was also an option she had to be aware of. If George decided she was completely useless to him, then that would be game over for her. She couldn't let that happen. How to make herself useful in the first place?

She didn't want to help him. *Even if your life depends on it?* Even if she did help him, then what? Having in mind how George did everything in his power to stop Connie from speaking with the police, it was safe to assume he didn't like loose ends, and that was precisely what Madelyne was. She was a loose end he would need to get rid of as soon as possible.

Looking at him now, all twitchy and enraged, she couldn't believe she'd never seen how calculated and cold he really was. She only saw what he wanted her to see.

No, I only saw what I wanted to see, she corrected, being completely honest with herself for the first time.

It pained her to admit that her daughter was right. She had been blind. And now, that blindness could very well cost her life. There was a silver lining, though. Madelyne had been conflicted and confused before. She was confused no more. She could tell right from wrong, a good guy from the bad one, and that provided her with a small amount of hope. There was still hope for her. That was what kept her going now. She would fight him every step of the way because her life couldn't end like this. Not after everything she'd managed to overcome in the past.

And besides, Damon would come for her and save her.

Will he? After everything she'd said to him, after the way she'd treated him, she wouldn't be surprised if he thought the worst of her. She'd thought of only herself for so long and had managed to hurt a lot of people. For that reason, she hoped she would get a chance to make amends.

In all this madness, there was one thing she couldn't fathom. There was one thing that didn't fit. Why had George married her in the first place? What had he accomplished by that? It was more than obvious that he didn't love her, probably never did, so why had he pursued her? Why had he acted like she was the love of his life?

"George, was everything an act from the start?" she asked before she could stop herself. She needed to know, although there was a possibility the truth would hurt her even more.

George put the phone down so he could look at her, and then he started laughing uncontrollably.

If she had any kind of weapon at her disposal in those moments, she would definitely use it, because this kind of behavior infuriated her. She was talking about serious matters, and he was laughing in her face. He was a monster.

"It took you a while to figure that out," he managed to say through his cackles. "But you were always gullible like that."

Madelyne gritted her teeth. She didn't care that he'd basically just called her stupid. She needed her answers. "Is that why you chose me?"

"Of course," he replied without a thought. "I needed a front while lying low."

"A front?" she repeated incredulously.

"I ran into some trouble, some people wanted me dead, so I needed to disappear."

"You didn't disappear," she pointed out.

He looked at her like he expected more from her. Sighing, he said, "You, like my business, were just a prop that I used to sell my act of being a quiet, law-abiding man, in other words, boring, and not a jewel thief who was, in his spare time, hunting previous associates and killing them off one by one for double-crossing me."

Madelyne's whole face turned bright red. He'd used her so he could kill people without detection. She was horrified. "Was Dunwoody a part of your crew?"

"Yes, and the bastard managed to screw me in the end as well. He died without telling me where my money is," he spat in disgust.

Madelyne was very much aware that it didn't look good for her that he was sharing all this personal information with her. If he was this honest, that could only mean he was confident she wouldn't talk. The only way to achieve that was to silence her forever.

Don't think like that. She couldn't allow herself to feel discouraged. There had to be a way out of this mess.

"Thank you for being honest with me." *For the first time in your life.*

He chuckled. "You are completely insane, not to mention ridiculous," he commented, returning to his previous tack of finding an ally.

Madelyne vowed to have the last laugh.

Finding someone willing to help him was clearly challenging, since he was prone to kill people he worked with. As a rule, people didn't like that.

"I'm glad I don't have to pretend to like you anymore," he added as an afterthought.

"Likewise," Madelyne snapped.

The George that she'd married had clearly never existed, so the love she'd felt wasn't for this man sitting next to her.

He'd never existed. It was easier for her to think in those terms.

George took her phone and started dialing again. In the next instant, he was furiously speaking with someone in a language she didn't understand. *Which language is that?* she wondered. He never told her he could speak different languages.

He never told you he was a thief either. Or that he liked to kill people who wronged him.

Although she couldn't understand a single word, the tone was pretty universal. George got so furious at some point, he abruptly ended the call and started hitting the phone against the dashboard. Madelyne winced with each hit, mourning her phone and her last chance to contact the outside world.

By all the rules, it should have broken, but it didn't. He threw it away, and her phone slid to the floor. George made no move to pick it up, stewing in his fury, preoccupied with his next move. And for Madelyne, that presented a chance. She had to get her phone back. That was her shot.

"We're running out of gas," Madelyne said, knowing this chance wouldn't present itself twice. It was now or never, so she had to act now if she wanted to escape this lunatic.

"Then fill it up," he grumbled in return.

That was all the confirmation she needed. Madelyne turned into the first available gas station. When she made a move to get out, George grabbed her, returning her inside.

"What do you think you're doing?" he demanded.

"You told me to fill it up," she replied innocently.

"I will go, and you will stay inside." George hid the gun at the small of his back. He then used a plastic cable tie to fasten her hand to the wheel. "If you try anything, I'll shoot you," he threatened, taking the keys and going outside like she wanted him to.

As he took care of the gas and went to pay for it, Madelyne used her right leg to reach her phone and push it her way. She felt like weeping from joy when she had it in her hand again. The screen was slightly cracked, but it worked perfectly.

Seeing how George was on his way back, Madelyne knew she didn't have time to call for help. In a stroke of inspiration, she did the next best thing. Madelyne started pinging Damon on her phone with her location whenever she had a chance to do it behind George's back. Which wasn't easy, since he was right there with her in the small car. She did her best, though, praying like hell that Damon would pay attention.

This will work, she encouraged herself. It had to because it was her only chance of surviving. *Please, Damon, help me; find me.*

37

DAMON

Damon and Connie sat in the captain's office while Detective Edwards had a heated argument with Mrs. Conners in front of it. All could be seen through the massive windows. She gesticulated a lot.

Martha Conners, a middle-aged woman in a tight deep blue suit, was a social worker. And Damon couldn't explain why, but she really looked like one as well. Her black hair was pulled up in a bun, and her glasses were big and sturdy. Everything about her screamed rigid. Damon was dead sure she always followed the letter of the law no matter what, and without exceptions. *Just my luck,* he thought in exasperation.

CPS had learned what had happened, and now Mrs. Conners wanted to take Connie away. Damon felt like arguing himself, but Detective Edwards had warned him to let him handle it. At first, he believed that would entail that he would be having a civilized discussion with the woman. He didn't. It was the screaming match that Damon himself had envisioned having with that social worker.

"Dad, this is bad," Connie stated, clearly concerned.

Damon shook his head. "Everything will be all right. He

knows what he's doing." Or so Damon hoped.

Truth be told, Mrs. Conners had every right to take Connie, since they were all unable to find Madelyne, and arrest Damon for kidnapping. All the rest were details that the social worker clearly wasn't interested in. She even had an officer with her, but Detective Edwards was defending Damon like a gladiator.

The office had such poor insulation that Damon could hear them perfectly.

"Mr. Blake broke the law," Mrs. Conners insisted.

There was no denying that. Damon did break it. And he would gladly do it again.

"He was fearing for his daughter's life," Detective Edwards countered.

Mrs. Conners made a face. "He should have come to the police immediately."

Mrs. Conners had already expressed her skepticism, thought this was all a ploy, since Damon wanted custody. Only speaking with Madelyne would sway her. Damon would like to speak with his ex as well. Unfortunately, she'd vanished into thin air with that killer.

Would she truly leave with that man, abandoning her own daughter? Damon had a disturbing thought. He didn't dare answer.

"He did." The detective gestured toward them as though that woman failed to see them.

"Eventually," Mrs. Conners countered. "Look, Detective, this kind of behavior can't be tolerated. Connie Blake is coming with me, and Officer Jacobs will arrest Damon Blake."

"Dad, I won't go with that woman." Connie was adamant. "I'll run away."

"Stay calm. You're not going anywhere."

"If you like rules so much," Detective Edwards boomed,

"here are mine." Saying that, he snatched the warrant for Damon's arrest from the young officer. He tore it to pieces to Connie's amusement and Mrs. Conners's horror. "Connie and Damon Blake stay here with me, period."

"Detective Edwards, this is highly unreasonable of you."

"This is my active investigation, and what I say is the law."

"I will bring you the judge's order."

"No judge in his right mind would rule in your favor. You're actually trying to separate father and daughter while we're all searching for the mother. Don't you have a heart?"

Something Detective Edwards said must have gotten through because she wavered. Damon was wrong.

"Detective Edwards, you crossed the line. I'm here because someone needs to act in the best interests of that child," she countered, raising her chin ever so slightly.

"As I said, this is an ongoing investigation, and Connie Blake is my key witness. Until she can identify the killer, she is staying in protective custody." The detective stood his ground.

"Then I'm staying here as well."

"I don't care what you do, madam, as long as you stay out of my way and stop bothering my witness. Now excuse me; I have a case to solve," Detective Edwards said in a dismissive tone.

"There's still the issue of Damon Blake," she persisted.

"The warrant for his arrest is invalid." Only because the detective tore it up. "Besides, I need him here as well while we search for his ex-wife. He can provide insight that no one else can."

"Fine," Mrs. Conners snapped, realizing she was outmatched. "But I will speak with your supervisor."

"Say hi for me," Detective Edwards replied, unconcerned.

As the pair continued to exchange verbal punches, Damon decided to check his phone. Now that it was obvious that he wouldn't be going to jail, he wanted to try reaching Madelyne. Maybe she would answer if she saw his number on the display. He hoped the temptation of speaking with Connie would be too great for her, even while on the run.

Damon felt like he'd been sitting in that office, doing nothing, for hours. All the red tape around them was maddening.

"Are you hungry?" he asked his daughter, but she shook her head no. He was too nervous to eat as well.

Damon saw that he'd gotten pings from Madelyne—her previous locations. *Did she do that by accident?* There was more than one, which led him to believe it was on purpose. She wanted him to know where she was. Madelyne was trying to communicate with him. As he realized that, another location jumped to his screen. One of the rest stops along the highway.

That smart woman had found a way to tell them she hadn't left voluntarily. As it turned out, Damon had judged her too harshly. She had been forced to run away with George, and this was Damon's proof. There was no other explanation as to why she would deliberately broadcast her location. In excitement, Damon jumped from his seat.

"Dad, what is it?"

He marched toward the glass window. It was time to break up that party in front of the office. Damon started banging against the glass, trying to get their attention. Of course, everyone turned to look at him.

"Madelyne's pinging me," he yelled, gesturing for Detective Edwards to join him inside.

He moved to do just that, but Mrs. Conners got in his way. "This is not over, Detective."

"Yes, it is," he replied calmly, entering the office.

Damon was grateful to this man and hoped he wouldn't suffer consequences for defending them.

"What is it, Mr. Blake?" Detective Edwards inquired calmly, as though he hadn't just shouted at the social worker.

"I believe Madelyne's trying to make contact," he replied in haste. "Look." Damon showed him his phone.

Detective Edwards frowned.

"Madelyne is sending me pings with her locations," Damon explained.

"Can it be that George is sending them and not her?"

Damon didn't think of that. Still...

"It's Madelyne," Damon insisted. "She's sending me breadcrumbs."

And Damon was going to follow them. Even if it meant going straight to hell, he would get her back. He was convinced that George had taken her against her will, and this was her way of rebelling. Damon said as much. "That's the only explanation."

Now it made sense why she wasn't home, wasn't answering her phone. George had taken her with him. Except she'd found a way to alert Damon of her location. That was pretty smart of her.

"I see. Let's go," the detective announced.

Damon felt like cheering. Finally, something was happening. *Hold on, Madelyne, we're coming,* he prayed.

"I'm coming too," Connie said, which stopped the two men in their tracks.

"No," they said at the same time.

"It could be dangerous," Damon added, to soften the blow. He understood Connie was worried about her mother, but Damon needed her safe. And this was the safest place on the planet.

Connie folded her arms. "I'm not staying here with that woman," she said stubbornly. She had a good point. If Damon wasn't here, then that was a chance for Mrs. Conners to take her away.

Maybe she should come with me after all.

Apparently, Detective Edwards came to the same conclusion and gave a small nod.

"Okay," Damon allowed. Connie's joy was short-lived.

Mrs. Conners blocked their path. "And where do you think you're going?" she demanded.

Damon hesitated, not knowing what to say. Luckily, Detective Edwards came to his defense. "Police business," he rumbled in his deep voice. "Move out of our way."

And she did, clearly not wanting to be steamrolled.

Damon and Connie followed behind him.

"Are you sure this won't cause problems for you?" Damon had to ask.

Detective Edwards waved dismissively. "I'm used to working with her. She's a stubborn woman, but her bark is worse than her bite."

Getting to the street, the detective turned to face him. "You take your car, and I'll follow you in mine," he commanded.

"Sounds good," Damon replied.

Reaching his car, Damon and Connie settled inside, and when he could spot the detective on the move, he did the same. He was in the lead, because Madelyne was sending the locations to him. Damon felt charged, energized with the knowledge that Madelyne hadn't succumbed to that man's brainwashing. At least not completely.

She found her way back to us. He forwarded the last location to the detective so the other man would know where they were heading. Madelyne showed him the way, and now it was on him to save her. As it turned out, God, fate, or whoever wanted him to end this once and for all, to save Madelyne from that dangerous man, and Damon was up to the task.

Hold on, Madelyne, we're coming, he sent to the ether,

hoping she would stay as brave as she had this entire time. The guilt he felt for believing that she would choose George over them was pushed aside. Now he had to focus on finding her, saving her. There would be plenty of time for making amends later.

"Dad, do you think she's all right?"

"Yes, I believe so, and I'll make sure she stays that way," he promised.

"I believe you."

"But I need you to promise me you will do exactly what I say," he insisted. He couldn't do his job if he was worried about Connie.

"I promise."

He looked at her, making sure she was speaking the truth. Satisfied with what he saw, he continued, "If I tell you to hide or run, you will comply, without argument."

She hesitated.

"This is war, Connie. And in war, soldiers have to obey orders even if they don't like them."

She thought about that before nodding. "Okay, Dad. I will do whatever you say, run, hide, even steal a car."

He gave her a look.

"Just kidding."

Somehow, he wasn't amused. Overall, he was relieved that his daughter recognized the gravity of the situation and would take care of herself, do as she was told. That gave him the peace of mind needed to focus on Madelyne.

Looking at the rearview mirror, he could see Detective Edwards following them at a safe distance. That was also reassuring.

All together, they were on a journey to save Damon's ex, which meant George's hours were numbered. The thought made Damon smile.

38

MADELYNE

It was getting dark, and Madelyne was still trapped in the car with George. He'd let her go to the bathroom once, so she'd managed to let Damon know where they were. Sadly, George watched her like a hawk otherwise; it was impossible to get away. It was problematic leaving a speeding car that she was driving. Technically, she could do it, but she wasn't confident about her survival chances considering they were on a freaking highway.

And rest stops presented different problems altogether. They were usually in the middle of nowhere. Besides, she was sure he would have no problem shooting her in the back if she tried to make a run for it. Her only hope was Damon, as it turned out. She kept sending him her location whenever she could. Unfortunately, she couldn't know for sure if he saw the pings. It would be of help if he would just send her a text letting her know he was on his way. That would help her immensely to soldier on. The not knowing was pressing heavily on her.

There was a chance that Damon feared to send anything to her, not wanting to tip George off, which was smart. Sadly, all of this was speculation, and Madelyne needed concrete actions. *What to do?* She couldn't wait around for Damon to rescue her. *What if he doesn't come?* she asked in her moment of doubt. Would he even care about what was happening to her?

Of course he cares. He would help, but first, Madelyne had to help herself.

"I'm hungry. Pull over," George announced, like a despot in his small domain, and Madelyne complied after finding a fast-food restaurant. He got himself a hamburger and a Coke, failing to ask if she wanted something.

Madelyne was starving, since she hadn't eaten anything since last night, and was thirsty and tired, but she proudly refused to beg him to give her anything. The adrenaline she was working on was starting to wear off as well, and Madelyne was sure she would crash soon. Before that, she needed to get away.

She couldn't keep driving around, because the longer she stayed with this man, the harder it would be to escape.

"I'm tired. I can't drive anymore," she said after a long silence. And that wasn't a lie. Madelyne wasn't used to driving for such long periods of time. Her back was killing her, and her legs were cramping.

"I don't care," he replied coldly.

"You should," she snapped. Her meaning was clear. It was on him if they ended up in an accident.

George looked at her long and hard before replying, "Fine, we'll stop at some motel."

Madelyne hadn't thought things through. She didn't want to spend the night at some motel, alone with George.

"Do you have any cash on you?" he asked, snapping her from her reverie.

She shook her head. "I left my wallet at home," she explained.

In that initial madness, it was a miracle she had some clothes on, let alone anything else.

"You really are completely useless," he countered with a sigh, checking his pockets to see how much cash he had left.

Madelyne ignored his words. His insults had no power over her anymore. She was bulletproof.

As George looked for a suitable motel in their price range in the vicinity, Madelyne continued to think about her options. Maybe it was a good thing that they were stopping someplace for the night. That way, Damon could catch up with them that much faster. *If he's coming.*

Stop that, she snapped at herself. She had to remain positive.

Eventually, George chose a motel, and Madelyne turned on the nearest highway exit as he guided her to it. Reaching the parking lot, she could see why he'd chosen that specific motel in the first place. Elegance Motel was a complete dump.

Parking, George decided to do his usual song and dance routine, threatening her, yet Madelyne had no patience for it.

"I know, I know, you will kill me if I try anything," she said, instead of him.

He narrowed his eyes. "And beat you to a pulp if you speak to me that way again."

Madelyne remained quiet at that. He started to leave the car, but then something occurred to him. Madelyne groaned inwardly. She really needed a moment for herself.

"Make yourself presentable. You look like shit," he snapped.

Over time, Madelyne had completely forgotten about the state of her face. She remembered how she had some wet wipes in the glove compartment, so she took them out. Looking at the rearview mirror, she managed to wipe the dried blood off her face with some effort. The gash George had created was still an angry red, but there was nothing she could do about it.

"Cover that with your hair," he commanded.

As George left the car, she managed to send another ping to Damon. *Please, God, let him get this,* she prayed, exiting the car herself.

The guy who worked at the reception barely looked at them as he stated the prices for the night or even for an hour. Madelyne cringed inwardly, realizing what was going on at this place. George paid in cash, giving a little extra so they wouldn't have to present him with their IDs. The receptionist booked them as Mr. and Mrs. Smith. *How very original.*

The room was small, and Madelyne was confronted with the fact that the walls stank of tobacco and the carpet of something even more potent and horrifying that she didn't want to identify.

There was only one king-sized bed in the middle of it, a couple of chairs and a small table in the corner. She didn't dare go to the bathroom. Overall, nothing mattered to her since she didn't plan on sleeping. Unfortunately, George wasn't planning on sleeping either. He had other things on his mind. He was on her the minute he locked the door.

"What are you doing?" she objected, trying to push him away as he tried to suck her neck.

"It's time for you to fulfill your conjugal duties."

"The hell I will," she shouted, outraged.

George had managed to push her into submission once, but not this time. This time, he would actually have to kill her, because there was no universe in which she would accept having sex with him ever again.

"I can always make you," he growled.

Madelyne was disgusted to see he was actually turned on by her resistance.

"I said no. You can keep me with you, use me as leverage, but you will not have me."

He grabbed her by the arms, and as he pushed her on the bed, her phone dropped from her pocket onto the floor.

Oh, no. No, no, no.

He stopped with his advances to look at it. It didn't take him long to put two and two together. "What did you do?" he demanded, outraged, picking her phone up from the floor.

Madelyne cowered on the bed, retreating to the furthest corner away from him. She knew that look on his face.

"Answer me!"

"Nothing," she stammered.

"Liar." George started sifting through her phone.

There was no escaping his wrath now. She was doomed. *Stupid, stupid.* How could she be so stupid as to keep her phone in that shallow pocket? Of course it fell out.

"You're a dead woman," he roared.

Madelyne didn't have to be a genius or a mind reader to know this comment meant he'd discovered what she had been doing. There was no point denying it, either. "I'm not afraid of you," she countered defiantly.

She was proud of how her voice remained strong, although she was scared shitless. She felt like her heart was about to burst out of her chest any second now. If this was her moment, then there was no way she was going down without a fight.

Shouting again in fury, George threw her phone against the wall. This time, it actually broke into several pieces.

Madelyne screamed as he advanced toward her. She knew better than to expect someone would call the police in an establishment like this one. She was sure that even the receptionist could hear her, but sadly, in this place, nobody cared. Madelyne had to defend herself if she wanted to survive.

When George reached her, Madelyne jumped to the other side of the bed, nearly missing him, and tried to grab a lamp that stood on the night table to throw at him. He couldn't harm her if he was unconscious. To her horror, the thing was bolted to the wood.

It was clearly a precaution, since this place did look like it was frequented by people who liked to fight and throw things. Having to buy new furniture couldn't be cheap. Madelyne stopped her crazy train of thoughts, frantically looking about in hopes of spotting something, anything, that could be used as a weapon.

The chair. Unfortunately, it was too far away from her. With her luck, the thing would be bolted as well.

George grabbed her by the leg and started pulling her toward him. Madelyne thrashed about, trying to kick him, yet it was all in vain.

"You bitch, I will show you not to mess with me," he said, and grabbing her by the hair, he threw her on the floor.

She didn't get a chance to pick herself up and get away because he kicked her. She lost her breath, and the force of it definitely broke something inside her. Instinctively, she balled up, protecting her vitals. Madelyne had to find a way to stop him, or this madman would beat her to death, here and now.

Please, God, no.

"I am so done with you, bitch," George spat, kicking her again.

"Go to hell, George!" she screamed as tears blurred her vision. She refused to cry, but couldn't stop the tears from falling anyway. For that, he hit her again, and this time, she was sure he'd managed to break a rib. After that, as she tried to catch her breath, he picked her up like she weighed nothing and slapped her across the face in anger.

"How dare you speak back to me!" he raged.

Madelyne could taste blood in her mouth. It was good that she hadn't eaten since yesterday, because the blood was making her nauseated.

She looked him straight in the eyes defiantly. "Is that the best you can do?" she taunted. Madelyne had obviously lost her mind, but she was done submitting, done letting men govern her life and do with her as they pleased.

George's jaw clenched, clearly not pleased that he wasn't making the impression he desired. Madelyne smiled at that, which only pushed him further over the edge.

He made a fist and was about to strike her when she heard the best sound in the entire world. The sound of a car engine roaring. It was so distinct that she could recognize it anywhere, anytime.

He's here. I'm saved! She practically sagged with relief.

George instantly noticed a change in her.

Madelyne started laughing.

"Are you insane?" he raged. "Why are you laughing?"

"Because you're a dead man," Madelyne managed to say between snickers.

With renewed strength, she started to struggle and used that distraction, George's confusion, to break free and run away. Someone honked. Unlocking the door, she started running as fast as she possibly could.

"Damon!" she screamed at the top of her lungs.

39

DAMON

Damon was sure Madelyne and George made a stop at the Elegance Motel because her last sent location told him so. He hoped he and the detective weren't arriving too late. Getting to the parking lot, he could hear shouts through his open window, as though someone was arguing really loudly in one of the rooms.

"Dad, is that them?" Connie asked, alarmed.

It definitely sounded like them. "I don't know," he lied, not really sure why he said that. Damon expected to encounter something bad, but these screams sounded even worse.

He hit the horn a couple of times to get their attention, letting Madelyne know he was there. She always said how she could recognize his car anywhere, and he prayed she would this time as well.

Seconds later, one of the doors opened, and Madelyne came running from the room. "Damon!" she screamed.

He scanned her really quickly, noting she was injured, but at least it didn't seem to be too bad. "Madelyne, over here!" he shouted, getting out of the car.

"Mom," Connie said as well, wanting to get out of the car herself, but Damon stopped her.

"You stay in the car and hide."

She did as she was told.

Damon had had enough presence of mind to arm himself before reaching this place because, as it turned out, he would need his gun.

Right behind Madelyne appeared George, gun in hand, and he looked enraged. "Stop, you bitch!" he shouted from the door.

Damon saw red. *How dare he treat Madelyne in such a way!*

Suddenly, Damon saw all the pieces of shit from Madelyne's life who'd treated her poorly—her dad, therapist, teachers. This time, Damon would stop the monster and save her. *George is so dead.*

Speaking of that son of a bitch, he saw Damon and actually smiled as he fired his gun. Madelyne screamed.

"Move out of the way," Damon commanded, returning fire.

George jumped out of the room, hiding behind one of the cars.

Madelyne managed to reach him, but there was no time for sentiments. "Hide!" he said simply, steering her away from him, knowing George was about to fire again.

She nodded, disappearing from sight. At close range, she looked banged up, but okay. It was time to deal with this once and for all. Damon slowly advanced. He knew the other man had ducked, but by now he could be anywhere.

"A knight in shining armor comes to the rescue," George taunted from his hiding place.

Damon adjusted his trajectory. *Yeah, keep talking, asshole.*

"I always knew you were nothing more than a pussy," he continued.

Damon advanced, trying to approach the car, making

sure he stayed out of sight. "And who will come to the rescue of a piece of shit like you? Nobody," Damon said.

George fired, like Damon wanted him to, and he in return swiftly moved to a different spot.

"I will enjoy killing you," George said, firing another round, but his aim was off. Damon wasn't at that spot anymore.

I should help the poor guy out. "With an aim like that, we'll be here for hours." A bullet grazed beside his head, shattering a window. *That's more like it.*

At that moment, Detective Edwards decided to join the party. Damon wondered what took him so long. The emergency vehicle lighting was on as he theatrically screeched into the parking lot. The car abruptly stopped, and the shooting ceased, as though they were all waiting to see what would happen next. As the detective exited the car, taking in the scene, Damon could hear him calling for backup. He was sure George could hear him as well.

"Damon?" Detective Edwards called out, pulling out his police-issued weapon.

"All good," Damon replied.

"Not for long," George felt the urge to say. The man was a walking storehouse of ridiculous punchlines.

"Mrs. Elway, over here," Detective Edwards called out.

Damon would feel better knowing Madelyne was safe with Detective Edwards, out of George's reach. That would allow him to fully concentrate on the threat in front of him.

"Make a move, bitch, and I'll kill you," George warned.

Damon gritted his teeth, refocusing on George. *Did that lunatic still believe he could win this?* Apparently, he did. "Say something else like that, you asshole, and I'll rip out your tongue and shove it up your ass."

George whistled in return. "Didn't know you had it in you, cowboy."

That was because George didn't know him. "Keep talking, and you'll discover plenty more."

"I would rather kill you, then that bitch, instead of listening to you drone."

Silently, swiftly, Damon jumped behind a different car. Since no one fired at him, he guessed George was too busy looking at the detective, looking for Madelyne, to notice. *Amateur.* This needed to end, and now.

Evidently, Detective Edwards was of the same mind. "George Craven, you are under arrest. Lower your weapon and come out with your hands raised above your head," he shouted.

For his effort, George prepared a couple of insults. "You first, chubby," he shouted, punctuating his words with a few more shots. George hit the detective's car, but not the detective himself.

So it was safe to assume George had no intention of surrendering. No surprise there. Damon figured as much the instant that bastard had fired on Madelyne. Damon started shooting as well. Maybe they could overwhelm him, make him use all his ammunition. How many shots had he fired so far, anyway? Damon tried to recollect.

As he did that, Detective Edwards advanced toward him. George fired, and Detective Edwards jumped behind another vehicle. Damon was impressed that a man of his age and constitution could move in such a manner.

"Son of a bitch," Detective Edwards cursed, slamming against the back of the car.

"You okay?" Damon inquired.

"Yeah, I just realized I'm too old to be playing chicken with this asshole."

Damon chuckled. "Who isn't?" he asked rhetorically as he moved to where Detective Edwards was taking cover.

This right here showed him that he really didn't miss war

one bit. There were soldiers, former colleagues who liked being in the middle of the conflict, who lived for that rush. Damon never judged them. They all had the right to live their lives as they chose. However, if he never fired a gun after this night, he would be a happy man.

"Cover me while I try to flank him," Damon whispered.

The detective nodded, raising his weapon. Jumping to his feet, he started shooting, and Damon used the opportunity to move forward. His goal was to reach George from the side and incapacitate him.

Son of a bitch. Too late, he realized he'd miscalculated. To prove his point, George fired at him, and the bullet missed him by a sliver of a hair, so Damon flattened himself on the ground, crawling for the nearest available shelter, a red pickup truck that looked ancient with its chipped paint and rusty parts.

George fired at the detective. He hit him squarely in the chest. That was Damon's fault. He'd fucked up.

"Motherfucker," the detective yelled, falling down.

"Detective?" Damon shouted in concern.

He was prepared to retreat when he heard his reply. "All good! The bastard knocked the breath out of me."

Damon then realized that the detective had a bulletproof vest on. That was smart, and something Damon should have thought about before running into this, and not behaving like some kind of Lone Ranger. Too late for that, though. *I will just have to be extra careful.* His daughter was in this parking lot, and Madelyne, so getting killed wasn't an option. *Did you hear that, God?*

They exchanged fire a couple more times. *He must be running out of bullets.* Damon was. Luckily, he'd brought extras with him. To him, it felt like they'd reached a stale-mate, yet that wouldn't last long. One of them would lose patience, and then all hell would break loose. Damon wanted it to be George.

"Cover me," he told the detective anew.

The detective aimed and fired while Damon tried to make a run for it. Halfway there, he could feel a bullet biting his left arm. It barely grazed him. He hid. Now Damon was only one car away from George.

"Are you dead yet?" the bastard asked.

"With your shitty aim? I would have to stand still two feet from you so you could maybe hit me."

Detective Edwards decided to chip in: "He likes his victims in close range, that's true."

Damon covered the detective as the other man changed his position this time around. They were closing in on him. His left arm was hurting like a motherfucker, but he ignored it.

"How's the arm?" the detective asked.

Damon had to admit that the bloodstain was getting bigger. "I'll live."

"Good."

"Is that the best you can do?" George gloated. "A basket case ex-soldier and an old man are no match for me."

"This old man is going to enjoy kicking your ass," Detective Edwards yelled in return.

"You're just a bunch of—" George's words were cut off by a loud crash.

Damon's car plowed into the vehicle George was hiding behind, knocking him down hard to the ground. Madelyne, he thought, and he cheered. Without wasting any time, still with his gun raised, Damon ran toward George. The other man was not moving.

Detective Edwards was a few seconds behind him. "Don't move!" he yelled, but he shouldn't have bothered.

They didn't have to check for a pulse to know George was

as dead as a doornail, his head smashed against the pavement. It was pretty unreal to see him like that and realize it was finally over.

She really got him good. Madelyne had thought fast on her feet. Although Damon was heartbroken to see his car in such a state, he was overjoyed to see the end of George. He would torment them no more.

Damon turned to thank his ex-wife for saving all their asses, only to see his sixteen-year-old daughter, all big-eyed and terrified, sitting behind the wheel.

Oh no.

40

CONNIE

Three months later

Connie was grateful she hadn't ended up in jail for what she did. Not that she felt guilty for it. She'd managed to save Mom and Dad. She was glad that asshole was dead.

Does that make me a terrible person? she wondered. Dad would say no. He was like that, always trying to make her feel better. She knew he felt guilty for leaving in the past and was trying to make up for it. Connie let him because it felt nice having him around.

After that whole mess, an even bigger one started with the police and CPS, and considering her previous record, she was really worried that she would be taken away from her parents. Both Dad and Mom fought like hell for her, and that old detective as well. So eventually, everything was sorted out.

She had to go to therapy, though, which she accepted. She told no one, but she had nightmares about George, where he would chase her around, and no matter how fast she tried to run from him, he always caught up with her in the end. After which she would wake up covered in sweat, and sometimes tears. She didn't tell her parents about it, not wanting to worry them. Dad would try to help, but he couldn't, not with this. Besides, she wasn't a little girl anymore. She was a soldier like him, a fighter, a survivor like Mom, and that meant she would be fine... eventually.

Finding Mom that day all covered in blood and bruised, Connie felt a fury like never before. She'd wanted George dead. And she got her wish. When she started the car, her intention wasn't to run him over, just to stop him, but things didn't go that way.

They learned a lot about George Craven in the days that followed. He had been a really bad guy, not only a jewelry thief, but a murderer as well. He had been going around killing off his former associates while playing house with Mom. *A complete psycho.*

The last of his known associates who was still alive was Benny Hamilton. Connie recognized him as the guy who was at her house that one time when George had threatened to beat the shit out of her. He'd been drinking with George. He'd introduced him as his dear friend. *If he only knew...*

From what the detective was able to discover, after their last big score, the crew members were not satisfied with the distribution of wealth. George was the leader, and he declared that he should get the biggest piece of the cake. The rest disagreed and decided to kill him. At the last minute, Benny decided to double-cross his colleagues, probably thinking he would get more money if it was shared with only one person, and he took the bullet meant for George. George had been injured as well, but he'd survived. Afterward, he decided to take revenge and kill them all, sparing Benny for his loyalty.

Connie had found the whole situation ridiculous, because it showed how men were stupid when blinded by greed. Either way, it was all over now, so there was no point in thinking about it.

On the bright side, Dad had completely healed up from his bullet wound. Although he kept reassuring them it was just a superficial wound, the doctors in the emergency room disagreed. It was way more serious than that. He had to go through surgery, and the doctors barely managed to save the functionality of his arm, since the bullet tore some nerves. He hated going to physical therapy, but Connie made him. She made sure he never missed an appointment. Parents were sometimes worse than kids.

It was really cool driving him around, though. After her failed attempt at driving that night, Dad and Mom agreed she needed to properly learn how to drive. They even considered buying her a car. Sadly, it wasn't all fun and games. Overcoming the initial fear was hard.

Whenever Connie sat in a car, let alone in the driver's seat, she had that scene in front of her eyes. Although Dad had told her to hide, she had seen everything. Dad had been on the ground, bleeding, holding his arm tightly, Mom had been hiding someplace, and George had been shooting at everybody. Connie was terrified and knew she had to do something. Slamming her dad's car against the car George was hiding behind had seemed the perfect solution. In the months that followed, everyone tried to tell her that it wasn't, that it had been reckless and stupid, and she could have been hurt or killed, but she still knew she'd done the right thing.

Therapy was helping her put it all behind her, not that she would ever admit it. She hated being forced to do something she didn't want to.

Would you prefer living in a foster home? That was why she endured, because Mrs. Conners had threatened to take her away if she didn't, but it wasn't that bad. Dad's therapist had recommended a really good counselor who worked with kids. Sarah was cool and never judged or pretended to know best, and Connie didn't hate talking with her.

It was really funny and weird that Connie wasn't the only one going to therapy. They all were. Even Mom had finally admitted that she needed professional help, to everyone's shock—especially Dad's, for some reason. So Mom started going to therapy two times a week. At first, Connie believed she only sought help so she could deal with everything that had happened with George—the abuse, the kidnapping—but a few days ago, she'd learned the real truth.

Her mom had suffered a lot in her youth. Mom had completely opened up to her and shared some horrific details from her childhood. Connie was in awe of her mother. She was braver and stronger than she'd ever given her credit for.

Connie often wondered why Mom never spoke of her parents. She knew Dad was a foster child, but Mom had a family. Her father was still alive. With her revelation, Connie now understood the reasons behind her silence. Mom's father, Josef O'Toole, was a monster. Connie felt repulsed that she was related to such a person.

She was so enraged about what she'd learned, what her mother had been forced to endure at the hands of that man, that she wanted to tell everyone. Then she realized that wasn't her story to tell. Connie would stand by her mother when and if she decided to speak of it.

They cried a lot during that day, and despite everything, Connie was grateful, almost glad, that her mother had decided to share her pain with her. In a way, it made them closer. It certainly helped Connie understand her mother better.

Connie was also grateful to have such loving parents in the first place, when, as it turned out, many people should have never been blessed with the title 'parent' in the first place.

Despite all the shit that had gone down, Connie realized, thanks to her therapist, how she'd become less angry. She didn't feel like it was her against the world anymore. That made her feel lighter, happier. She definitely bickered less with Mom and enjoyed her moments with Dad more.

Mom and Dad worked better as co-parents after George's death as well, as though that was the moment that helped them realize that they were wasting too much time on anger and waging wars. Connie hadn't heard them screaming at one another in so long that it felt like an ugly dream, something she'd imagined or made up. It was a shame it had taken a tragedy like this to bring them all closer together. But Connie wouldn't complain, since they got to that place of peace.

Looking at both of her parents, Connie knew that they all changed, and for the better. Dad definitely looked better, as though he was finally more at peace with himself. Connie was no idiot. Although they tried to shield her from the truth, she knew that Dad had returned changed from the war. But now, he was more like himself, like he had been before he had re-enlisted. He was less angry with Mom, which was a good thing, because that anger was making him miserable as well.

The same could be said for Mom. Thanks to sessions with her therapist, she'd managed to accept and overcome certain things as well. She finally made peace with what had happened to her in her childhood, and stopped resenting Dad for not being here with them, and for re-enlisting and going off to war. She was also working hard on overcoming George, their marriage, and his brand of torture.

Connie knew her mom still felt pretty torn up and guilty for bringing that man into their lives. It wasn't her fault.

Connie wasn't angry at her for that. Mom had trusted the wrong man. It could have happened to anyone. Now, she needed time to forgive herself.

"Connie, we need to go," her mother called out to her, snapping her from her reverie.

"I'm not dressed yet," she countered, shouting through the door.

"We're going to be late."

Connie threw on the first T-shirt she saw and paired it with the only clean jeans she had at the moment. The entire process lasted sixty seconds, tops. She walked to open the door. She spotted her mother at the base of the steps, looking up at her.

"You mean *you'll* be late," Connie replied with a smile. "I don't have an appointment today."

"Smarty-pants," Mom replied with the same smile. "However, you're my driver, and if you've changed your mind..." She left the sentence unfinished.

Her mom was baiting her, and despite knowing that, she said, "Of course not. I'll be down in a minute."

She just had to find her sneakers.

Mom had agreed to let her practice driving with her as well, so she played chauffeur whenever she could, after school and on weekends.

"I'll wait for you in the car," Mom yelled.

"Okay."

Seconds later, she heard the front door closing. They had finally moved out of the house George had bought to this one. It was taking her some time to get used to everything, but she liked it. It resembled her childhood home, where she'd lived with Mom and Dad.

Where's the other shoe? Connie found one in the closet, but the other was playing hide-and-seek with her. This was a moment where her mother would chastise her for not cleaning her room. *Eureka.* Of course, the other one was under the bed.

Grabbing her jacket, she was on her way out. A few minutes later, they were driving toward Dr. Weldon's office.

"Turn right here." Mom pointed.

"I know, Mom." Connie suppressed the urge to roll her eyes. No matter how many times she drove this way, her mom always felt the need to help her, as though she could forget where she was going, or how to get there.

About fifteen minutes and a couple more naggings later, they reached their destination.

"Look, there's Dad." Connie pointed.

"Hands on the wheel, please," Mom said.

Connie concentrated on parking the car. She did it perfectly, if she might say so herself. Dad would be impressed. She and Mom left the car to greet him.

"Hey, Con-Con." He smiled, opening his arms, and she went to hug him.

She felt a bit self-conscious hugging her father in the middle of the street, but that gesture made him so happy.

"Hi, Dad."

"Nice job parking," he complimented.

She smiled. "Thanks."

Her parents greeted each other as well. For the last two months or so, they were going to therapy together once a week.

"Ready?" he asked Mom, and she nodded in return.

"What are you going to do in the meantime, Connie?" Dad asked her next.

"I don't know, drive around town, go to the lake." She stopped herself there, because two pairs of eyes looked wryly at her.

Connie tried again. "I'll go to that coffee shop and wait for you." She nodded with her chin.

"Okay, honey. Need some money?" Mom asked.

Always. "Sure."

"Are we going to lunch later?" Dad asked them.

Connie nodded, and Mom said, "That sounds good."

As of late, they'd had a lot of these spontaneous family events, lunches, and dinners, not that Connie minded. It was every child's dream for her parents to get back together. She wasn't thinking about it, though. It was good seeing them acting like before, like when she was little, laughing and enjoying each other's company.

Dad checked the time. "If we keep chatting like this, we'll be late for our appointment," he observed.

"Isn't it weird that you're going to couple's therapy without actually being a couple?" Connie pointed out.

She couldn't help teasing them a little. In reality, she was glad they were doing this because it made their relationship better, more peaceful.

"Nothing is set in stone, Con-Con," Dad replied with a wink, and Mom laughed.

"Go, you don't want Dr. Weldon waiting on you," Connie countered with a smile.

"Bye," they said, almost at the same time.

Connie crossed the street and sat in a coffee shop. Was there a chance her parents would be getting back together? Looking back at them and how they behaved and looked at one another, she realized there was a good chance. *We'll be a real family again.*

Connie liked that thought very much.

THANK YOU FOR READING

Did you enjoy reading *The Stepfather*? Please consider leaving a review on Amazon. Your review will help other readers to discover the novel.

ABOUT THE AUTHOR

Theo Baxter has followed in the footsteps of his brother, bestselling suspense author Cole Baxter. He enjoys the twists and turns that readers encounter in his stories.

ALSO BY THEO BAXTER

Titles by Theo Baxter:

The Widow's Secret

The Stepfather

If you liked The Widow's Secret by Theo Baxter, you'll enjoy these titles by Cole Baxter.

The Perfect Suitor

The Betrayal

I Won't Let You Go

The Night Nurse

Printed in Great Britain
by Amazon

36066881R00191